THE
SUICIDE SKULL

THE
SUICIDE SKULL

A MEDIEVAL MYSTERY

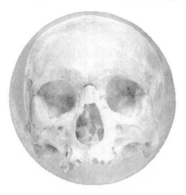

SUSAN McDUFFIE

LIAFINN PRESS

Cover Design, Interior Design, and Formatting by

www.e.m.tippettsbookdesigns.com

Published by Liafinn Press
ISBN Trade Paperback: 978-0-9997682-6-6
Epub Edition: 978-0-9997682-7-3

This has to be for you, Dad, with all my love

CAST OF CHARACTERS

THE
SUICIDE SKULL

On Jura:

Euphemia MacPhee, a recluse

Griogair MacRuairi, Murchard's man, along with

Bricius

Calum

Conall

Tormod

On Barra:

Murchard MacNeil, chief of the MacNeils and holder of Kisimul Castle

Amie, his wife

Angus MacRuairi, Amie's cousin

Clara and Elen, who work in the kitchens at Kisimul

Eugenius MacPhee, Euphemia's son, fostered on Barra

Fingon MacKinnon, the Green Abbot of Iona

Finn: A tabby cat

Morainn, the abbot's daughter

Morag, Amie's housekeeper

Murdina, an herbalist and wise woman

Brona, her young niece, who works at the Castle

Numerous deerhounds, including Mairead and Cuilean

Dubh, Dorchadus, and MhicDubh: Neighborly ravens

Uisdean, who minds the kennels

Una, an elderly woman near Saltinish

Raghnall, her husband, who may be hard of hearing

Sorcha, who glowers

Kenna, Sorcha's daughter-in-law

Tam, Sorcha's young son, who enjoys wrestling

Father Isidor, priest at Cille Bharra

On Uist:

Cristina

Fiona, Cristina's servant

Fearglas, Fiona's son

Padraig Dubh

Annag, his wife

Father Benneit, the priest at Cille Bhrighde

A Few Others:

Donald MacDonald, Lord of the Isles

Muirteach MacPhee, the keeper of His Lordship's records

Seamus, Muirteach's neighbor on Colonsay

Iain Mór, Donald's younger brother

GLOSSARY

A Dhia: (Gaelic) Oh God!

Amadan: (Gaelic) A fool

Birlinn: (Gaelic *bìrlinn*) A Highland galley

Brat: (Gaelic) A mantle

Brehon: A judge

Brisgean: (Gaelic) A nutritious wild plant, known as silverweed in English

Cearban: (Gaelic) A basking shark

Cotun: A leather garment, quilted into tubes and stuffed with wool, cotton, or other material, worn as armor.

Curragh: (Gaelic *currach*) A smaller boat, made of hide stretched on a frame. Similar to a coracle, although not necessarily round

Dhia dhuit: (Gaelic) Good day, literally "God today"

Dreich: (Scots) dull or gloomy

Iorram: (Gaelic) A rowing song

Kertch: A woman's headscarf

Leine: (Gaelic) a linen shirt, often saffron colored

Lymphad: (Anglicized Gaelic) literally a "long ship". The largest of the galleys

Luchd-tighe: (Gaelic) A chief's "tail" of retainers

Machair: A low lying plain

Mo chridhe: (Gaelic) My heart, an endearment

Naibheag: (Gaelic) A small boat (also nyvaig)

Nathrach: (Gaelic) A serpent

Sidhe: (Gaelic) The fairy folk

Uisge beatha: (Gaelic) Whisky, literally "water of life"

Yett: a gate or grill of iron bars, used for defense in castles

CHAPTER 1

My mother did not have the Second Sight. I got it from my father. The Sight, however, will not be bidden like a servant; it comes and goes as it pleases. We who have the Sight must serve it; it does not serve us.

The Sight showed me nothing of what was to befall on the day that Griogair arrived.

I had slept restlessly, disturbed by unsettling dreams I could not quite recall upon waking. Dreams of my sweet son so often troubled my sleep, or dreams of the nunnery, back on Iona. I had learned to sleep poorly.

It was a fine, fair day, that day in May, the sky a rare blue over the Sound, the sun shining, and a brisk wind sending clouds scudding overhead, like little lambs playing on the *machair*. I looked out the doorway of the cave I now called my home and almost smiled at my fancies.

My father had found me this place, after I left Iona and realized life at Finlaggan, or even the more isolated Ballinaby, would suit me no longer. The cave had been long abandoned. It was said a witch had lived there long ago, but no one had dwelled there for years and so no one complained when I settled in. A spring further up the hill provided fresh water. As I had entered the dank and dark cavern I saw the skull, grinning at me through some cobwebs and spider's webbing. It sat on an alcove carved from the living rock. When I asked, later, the local folk swore it was the skull of a suicide, and that water drunk from that grisly cup would cure the falling sickness.

I'd not learned that remedy from my mother, or my grandfather, but I'd dusted off the skull, and the shelf, and set it back to keep watch over my new domain. And it had remained there, as my guardian, for…how long now? Three years.

No one disturbed my quiet this day. No local folk climbed the steep path up the hill to me in search of cures. I had no doubt most folks thought me another witch, like the one that had lived here so many years ago. For others, the reality of my life was worse than witchcraft. A nun who had violated her vows and fled the convent. Still, people came sometimes, for babies will teethe and joints will ache, and was I not one of the healing folk, the Beatons, on my mother's side? Despite my own sad history.

So I mused on this while I sat on a bench outside, drowsing but spinning an uneven yarn, watching the Sound with idle eyes. It crossed my mind to pray, as I watched the sun climb in the sky. It grew close to sext, but my prayers had deserted me long ago. Or I had deserted them.

Across the Sound I saw the dark bulk of Colonsay, my father's home. But closer something caught my eye, a craft amidst the waves. A small *birlinn*, carrying six men. The sail had been raised to catch the breeze and I saw no one rowing; no need for that with such a favorable wind. I watched for a time, thinking they would head towards Colonsay, but the boat began tacking against the wind, making for my own cove and the small shingle beach that edged it.

Visitors, then. No one I recognized. Not my father's men from Islay, bringing supplies and news of home.

I set down the spindle on the bench and wiped my hands, greasy from the wool, on my skirt while my heart began to pound like some wild thing. I stood to see. The boat still approached and would be landing soon. I patted my hair a bit to smooth it. How long it had grown, how neglected. I tried to hide its unruliness by tucking it under my sadly threadbare and wrinkled coif. Then I adjusted my habit, the black dye faded now to a nondescript brown, sat down again on the bench, picked up my spinning, and waited, my heart still hammering and my throat dry.

I heard the sounds as the men beached the boat, their voices as they stowed the sail. I could not catch the words.

Then I heard crunching steps on the shingle as one of the men left the boat and began to climb the steep path up the hill.

I kept on with my spinning, fighting the urge to set it down and flee, disappearing into the hills like some wild doe where no one could find me. The thread snapped, and I started my work again.

When the man finally emerged at the top of the trail, I did not recognize him. He was large, broad-shouldered, with chestnut hair and a beard slightly redder, his face sea-burned, with laugh lines about the eyes. He wore the linen shirt and woolen mantle of an isles-man. The stranger gained the top of the trail and stood a moment to catch his breath, looking at me where I sat spinning on the wooden bench in the sunshine.

"Are you Mistress Euphemia?" he asked. "Or," he glanced warily at my habit and once white coif, "Sister Beathag?"

I met his gaze but did not stand. "Yes. And you?"

"I am Griogair MacRuairi. The MacNeil sent me. From Barra."

I put the spindle down. "And how am I to be certain of that?" I watched him through narrowed eyes.

He smiled a half smile. "The MacNeil himself thought you might be wanting proof." He reached inside his mantle, took out a letter, and handed it to me. "Here. Stamped with his own seal, it is. I watched him do it."

"You are the MacNeil's man?" I asked. He nodded. I did not bid him sit down but rudely let him stand while I glanced at the message. Folded parchment, and indeed sealed with the mark of the MacNeil of Barra. I had seen the mark before, on the contract for Eugenius's fostering. I broke the seal, unfolded the paper and scanned the lines. The parchment dropped to my lap and I felt an icy hand squeeze my heart.

"Eugenius."

"My lady," the man replied. He looked distressed himself; I could see concern behind his hazel eyes. "He is ill." He paused and swallowed before continuing. "I am sorry indeed to be telling you of this. The MacNeil himself sent me here to fetch you. Will you come to Barra?"

My son, my own little heart of my heart—my tongue felt leaden and I could barely form my words. "What ails my son?" The letter had not given details. Just a few lines. *Your son is ill. Come to Kisimul.*

"A fever, when I left. They had thought it nothing of consequence, but he grew worse. So they sent me here to fetch you."

"Because I am a healer, or because I am his mother?"

The man flushed. "Both, I am thinking. Although there are healers on Barra, and others at Howmore on Uist, there are no Beatons there."

"Yes." I fought to keep my voice calm. I must think, remember which herbs to pack. I could not panic, not with my son's health at stake. "I will get my things," I told him. "I shall not take long. But you will be hungry and thirsty," I added, belatedly, "and what of the men with you?"

"They've food and *uisge beatha*, and I think are more eager to nap than climb up here and back down again."

I rose, my throat dry as rough stone. "Come away in, then. You can eat while I gather my things."

He followed me inside, glancing around the dark cavern that I called my home. I'd not whitewashed the walls when I'd come to stay here. It must seem a dreary place.

"I've only water. But here is a bannock, and some cheese." I struggled to keep my voice from trembling. "Eat. I'll be but a moment."

His green eyes flicked around the cave and I saw him raise his hand as if to cross himself, then stop. "What is that?"

I followed his glance. "The skull of a suicide." Despite the rapid thudding of my heart, I almost smiled to see his quickly repressed shudder. "Water drunk from it cures the falling sickness."

"I do not suffer from that," he said, a little stiffly. "God be praised."

I left him to eat my stale bannocks and a scrap of dried-out cheese, and started gathering a few things together. My warmest mantle, my other shift, and the little jacket I'd been sewing, thinking to send it to Eugenius at some time. Now I could take it to him myself, and pray to God he'd live to wear it. Some remedies for fever I must take, whatever herbs might be of use. Willow bark, cress, and wood sorrel. Cuckoo's flower. What else?

"Did he have a rash?"

"I'm not knowing."

"By the Virgin's teeth," I cursed, "did they tell you nothing? How am I to know what is needed?"

"'Tis you who are said to have the Sight," he responded evenly, setting down his bannock for a moment.

"Well, it told me nothing of this." I bit my lip to stop the trembling and took a bundle of dried cuckoo's flower, feeling the leaves crumble a bit against my fingers, smelling the sweet scent of it, as I wrapped it in a linen cloth and tried to calm down, to breathe, to think of what else to pack.

"When did you last see your son?"

"Three years ago, when he was first fostered," I replied, giving my bundle a final tug, making sure the knots were tight. "He had just been weaned."

"You've not seen him since?"

I shook my head. "He went to be fostered with the MacNeil and his wife. It's common enough," I added as I saw his expression. He inclined his head in agreement.

"Aye, I was fostered myself."

"My father has seen him, though, and sends word often. Are they kind to him?" I asked, the words falling from my lips before I could stop them.

He smiled. "They fair dote on him. You know the MacNeil's wife lost a baby."

I had not known. "And when was that?"

The man shrugged his broad shoulders. "About two years gone? Yes, that would be it. For I was off in Donegal, fighting for the Suibhnes. When I left, she was carrying, and when I returned there was no babe."

"I see few folk here," I said shortly. "I did not know."

"Shall we go?" He scanned the table and reached for my bundle. "Have you any more bannocks? Fresh ones?" He almost grinned when I shook my head no. "It's a long sail to Barra."

We took two days to reach Barra. We spent one night on the far side of Mull, uncomfortably camped on a rocky beach, and late on the next day arrived in Castlebay.

I had never seen Kisimul Castle before, or Barra at all for that matter. My father had told me of the place after settling my son there but I had never visited. Nor had I seen my son in over three years. When I'd last glimpsed him, he'd been but a babe, and now he would be four years old, I realized with a little ripple of shock. If the lad yet lived. My stomach, which had rebelled during the two days' sailing, roiled again at that thought. Or mayhap it was just a rough wave, the rocking of the boat, that lurch I'd felt.

The castle, built long ago atop a rocky islet in the bay, seemed to grow out of the sea, floating on the waters. Waves lapped at tall grey stone curtain walls that starkly faced our birlinn as the weary crew rowed into the harbor, for the fine winds of the previous day had abandoned us this afternoon. Most were Barra men, and happy indeed to reach home.

They maneuvered the boat around the great watchtower on the northeast side of the castle. Beyond it and the slipway outside the walls, loomed the main entrance gate to Kisimul. A heavy wooden door and iron portcullis had been opened in readiness for our arrival after the watch spied our approach. The men tied up the boat and we disembarked. Griogair first, then myself. The rest of the crew clambered off the boat, joking with the men at arms, at ease and eager to see their homes and families. I shuddered, and thought I glimpsed a red-haired woman clad in her winding sheet loitering near the gate as I passed by. When I looked again she had vanished, but not the disquiet the sight brought me. At least it was a grown woman I'd seen, not a four-year-old boy. Not my son.

Once inside I looked curiously around the inner courtyard, hefting my damp salt-stained bundle from one hand to another, feeling nervous and awkward, anxious to see my child. The smell of peat fires and roasting meat wafted across the courtyard, and the scents mingled with the moist, salty air of the bay. I fought down the urge to retch.

A woman entered the courtyard from a building in the far quarter. I judged it to be the chief's quarters from the look of it. A second woman, older, followed close behind.

"Griogair!" The first woman had a friendly face, with an upturned nose splashed with freckles like the smattering of shadows from little clouds on a summer's day. Luminous green eyes tilted upwards, like a cat's eyes, I thought. I saw shadows beneath them, and a weary look, and guessed she had not slept much of late. She was also, I noted with an unexpected pang, several months pregnant. "You made good enough time. Well done," she added, addressing this to both Griogair and the crew. "Morag," she said, turning to the older woman, "see about something to be quenching their thirst." Morag complied, and the crew followed her towards a building that I assumed housed the Great Hall.

The lady turned to give me a smile, disarmingly friendly. "And you will be Euphemia. Welcome, indeed. I am Amie MacRuairi, wife to the MacNeil." She looked as though she'd have laughed a bit at the expression on my face when I heard her name, were it not for the worry crowding out the good humor in her eyes. "Yes, I was named for that troublesome aunt of mine. And you were named for the queen, were you not?"

I inclined my head, impatient. The queen had been my godmother. "How does my son, lady?"

"About the same, I fear. The fever has not broken. I prayed you would come, from so far away. It was good of you."

"He is my son. How could I not come? But it was kind of you to send for me. Let me see him," I said, not wanting to spend time on pleasantries when the urge to see my son swept over me like the rising tide.

She led the way back into the chief's quarters, and then into a bedchamber. There sat the grand bed, with curtained hangings, belonging to the MacNeil himself and his lady, and nearby a smaller trundle bed on which lay a pale figure, my son.

I gazed at him like a thirsting man when he sees a fresh running burn of clear water, wanting to drink all of him in through every pore of my own skin.

He was a slightly built child. His face was flushed, his breath shallow, his heartbeat rapid. Even while I checked his pulse and tried to think of what herbs might be needful, I could not help but marvel at him: his face, like my own, or my father's, but with echoes of his own father's face in the broadness of the brow and the chestnut coloring of his hair.

"So," I said, as I felt the hotness of his forehead and tried to think, "an infusion of blackthorn berry, wood sorrel, willow, and cuckoo's flower, that should bring down the fever. And perhaps a poultice also, to draw the fire out of him."

Some peats smoldered on the hearth and I asked for hot water. The MacNeil's wife rushed to prepare it as soon as I'd uttered the words. "Make an infusion of these," I said, handing her some of the herbs, "and soak some cloths in it as well to use as poultices. We must cool him."

I saw her bite her lip. "The herb-wife from the island sent a remedy. And we thought of sending to Howmore, or even up to Trinity, to the college. There are physicians there. But you yourself are a Beaton, and the lad's own mother. I hope we did not wait too long."

I looked at her and saw the worry in her eyes. "If we can bring his fever down he'll do well enough, I pray."

"Such a thirst he had on him, and so confused. Delirious. And vomiting; he'd keep nothing down." She gnawed at her lip. "I'm sorry. I did what I knew to do until you arrived."

"Was there any rash?"

Amie shook her head no. "Look for yourself." She raised my son's shirt and I saw the pale skin of his chest rise and fall with his labored breathing but, thankfully, no rash.

"Have you had visitors here?"

Amie nodded. "Churchmen from Iona. And of course Eugenius wanted to go along when my lord took them up across the island, to Cille Bharra. They wished to see the well that is there, the one said to run with blood at times."

"Blood?"

"Aye. Before fighting, it is said that well runs red. But we've peace now and the water is clear enough. Eugenius insisted on going, and Murchard humored the lad. I should never have allowed it. The lad returned that night with the chills on him, and nothing could be stopping them."

"And when was that?"

"The chills came on him that night, then Murdina sent the remedy. But after that, he grew worse, not better. We sent for you four days ago." Amie paused. "It would have been a week ago that the sickness first came on him."

"What of other children? Is anyone else ill? In the village or here at Kisimul?"

My hostess shook her head.

"And what of the folk from Iona?" I asked, wondering who they might be, and if I knew them.

"They are not ill. No one else here is ill at all. Just Eugenius. I was a fool to let him go with Murchard and the others that day."

"I am thinking it is but some fever," I said, in answer to her worried look. "But if there are other babes here it might be best to keep them apart until he recovers."

Amie looked relieved. "The water is hot now," she said, and brought a pottery basin, filled with hot water, to the table. I poured some of it into a beaker, and then took good amounts of willow bark, cuckoo's flower, wood sorrel, and blackthorn berries and sprinkled them into the water. I voiced an incantation, invoking Saint Brigit and the Blessed Mother, and stirred the mixture sunwise, three times, while the herbs settled slowly into the steaming liquid. Amie added the ingredients for the poultice to the water remaining in the bowl, and put the cloths in to soak. Fragrance filled the room. The air smelled of spring, of green, cool growth, with the darker scent of the blackthorn adding strength. Of healing.

"He looks like you," Amie said suddenly, while we waited for the herbs to steep.

"He does?" My heart did an odd little glad leap at the thought of it.

"You have the same eyes, grey like the sea on an unquiet day. We fair dote on him."

"And you are expecting as well?"

Her cheeks rounded and her lips curved up for a moment. "Just a few more months it will be, if all goes well. I had another, but lost it," she added, a shadow flitting over her face, and I remembered Griogair speaking of it. I had a sudden glimpse of another shadow-like Amie rocking a cradle, humming a lullaby in a corner of the great room. But I thought I saw the death shroud hanging over the cradle. I turned my head to look and the seeing vanished.

"All will go well with this one, I am sure of it," I said, hoping that I spoke truth. The woman gave me a grateful glance.

"And you have the Sight, do you not?" Amie smiled. "So that is a fine thing to hear, indeed. For it was close to the end of my term that I lost the first one. A little boy. Murchard will rest more easily once this child is born." I fancied I saw another shadow pass, but thought it normal, if the poor woman had lost her first bairn. "He will be hoping for a son this time as well, for then his claim here will be strong and he won't be thinking any of my MacRuairi cousins can take the castle away from him.

I judged the mixture had steeped long enough and began to wring out the cloths, putting them on my son's chest. He moaned a bit, a weak little cry, and tried to move away from the warm, wet wrapping.

"Wheesht now, my little one. Do not cry," Amie said, patting Eugenius's forehead.

I tried to remember what lullabies had soothed him as a babe, and felt embarrassed I could not recall.

We sweetened the mixture in the beaker and spooned some down his throat. I smelled the green fragrance of the herbs, the heathery smell of the honey, the dark scent of the smoldering peats. After a time Eugenius fell into a fretful sleep and the MacNeil's wife straightened the kettle and utensils by the hearth. I watched my son sleep, drinking in the rising and falling of his breath.

Amie then showed me a place to leave my things, in an anteroom off their own bedroom. A curtain hung to separate the two rooms. She gave orders for Eugenius to be moved there and had two pallets prepared, one for my son and another for myself. A man brought a stool and table in; it was not so far from her own bed that she could not help with nursing the boy herself if needed. Yet we had some privacy. Then my hostess left to see to things in the Great Hall and the kitchens, as there were others still to be fed that day.

I sat on the stool and gazed at my son after we were settled in the new space. He dozed feverishly, at times opening glazed eyes. For all that Amie had claimed we looked alike, I saw little of myself in him. I thought of the lad's father, and shuddered.

He slept on, this son that I did not know. I set my store of herbs on the table and spread my mantle at the foot of my pallet; folded my clean shift and put that and my comb away in a kist. I changed the poultice, but Eugenius did not wake. I sat on the stool and watched him sleep. Perhaps I dozed myself.

A knock sounded on the arched stone doorway separating this small room from the great bedroom. I looked up to see Amie. "How does he do?" she asked.

"Still feverish, but sleeping. Fitfully. Hopefully the willow bark will help soon."

She walked over to the bed and gently smoothed Eugenius's forehead. My son seemed to relax a bit under her touch. I bristled a little, then told myself it did not matter. He knew her as his mother, and had for the past three years.

Amie turned to me. "I am thinking his forehead feels a wee bit cooler." She smiled. "Are you hungry?" she asked. "But of course you must be. Forgive me. I was so worried about this one."

"As am I. He's my own son."

I watched her face tighten. "Well, there is food and drink in the hall, and a place for you, if you are wanting something. There are other guests here as well, on business with my lord. Or I can bring something to you here."

"I'll not leave him." Nor did I want to eat, although I told myself her words were meant kindly. I thought better of my refusal. It would not do to alienate my son's foster mother at all, most certainly not on my first day here. "Perhaps you could send something, when there is time. But I've no wish for food now."

Amie looked at me a moment and then stepped away from Eugenius's pallet. "As you wish. I will check back later, then. After the meal is over."

"One thing. Where is the tonic the herb-wife was leaving?"

"It is just here. Let me get it." Amie went into the larger bedchamber. I watched her open a small kist, finely carved from walrus ivory with interlaced design work on the panel. She picked up a small pottery vial from within and brought it to me. "I'll just leave it here on the table." Then she turned and left me again.

I wrung out a fresh poultice and replaced it on my son's chest, then waited while her footsteps crossed the outer room. Then I heard the door close. Still I waited, until I couldn't bear to watch my son any longer and finally I reached for the flask.

This did not seem like a childhood fever. He'd been vomiting, and had the flux. And yet he burned with fever and his eyes had a glazed look, the pupils wide and unseeing.

I unstoppered the vial and sniffed. Bitter, earthy—a scent of dark roots and dark berries, gathered on a night with no moon. Not like any of the fever remedies I knew. I put a bit of it on my finger and touched it to my tongue, and after a moment felt the numbness spread through my mouth. Black henbane. Dog's mercury. Wolf's bane. Perhaps even hemlock. All of them poisons, and just one would have been enough to do the job. But no, someone had wanted to be sure. Triply sure.

My son had been poisoned. Here, on this isolated castle in the far back of beyond, where we had thought Eugenius would be safe, someone had tried to murder my son.

CHAPTER 2

For three days I stayed in that small cramped room with Eugenius, afraid to leave him for a moment. I did not know whom I could trust and so I told no one of what I'd found. I hid the vial deep in my pouch. Surely Amie and Murchard would not have poisoned Eugenius. But a rime of cold fear froze my tongue and kept me from speaking of it to Amie, or even from asking where the herb-wife might have gotten the vial, or what reason she might have had to give it to my son. If indeed it had been her at all. I even feared asking Amie about the woman who had prepared the remedy. What reason might some woman on Barra have to poison my son? Or could a different person have given the vial to Amie?

I gave my son purgatives, and treated him with a bezoar stone. I murmured prayers and incantations by his side while he tossed and turned and sweated out the poisons under the hot poultices I applied. Amie tried to help me with the nursing but I told her there was no need. When I slept, it was only after the snores from the great bed in the adjoining room sounded loudly, lulling me into a few moments of snatched slumber before I would start awake again, fearful someone would try and poison Eugenius while my eyes were closed.

On the afternoon of the third day my son opened his eyes. The hot, glassy look had vanished, and instead he regarded me with interest as I came towards his pallet with a basin and more poultices. "Who are you? Where is my mam?"

His words knocked into me like a gust of sea wind, the weight of the unexpected, innocent question catching me off balance. He did not remember me. How could he? He had been so young when he left me.

"Your foster-mother will be back soon. Eugenius, you have been very ill."

"I do not know you. Who are you? And how do you know my name?" my son asked, and I did not know how to reply. His grey eyes were so like my father's…I twisted the fresh poultice in my hands, feeling the wet roughness of the linen against my skin while I thought of how to answer him.

"I am a healer. And I am your own true mother as well. You know, do you not, that your mam is but your foster-mother?"

My son looked at me curiously. "I want my mam," he said after a moment. "And I want Finn."

"Finn? And who is Finn?"

"My cat."

I smiled, remembering the large tabby cat that had kept vigil with me for the past three days. "Your mam will be here soon enough. And would this be Finn?" The big cat, which had been sleeping on my pallet, got up, yawned, and then jumped up onto my son's bed, settling himself on the covers between the boy's side and his arm. Eugenius smiled and moved a bit, making room for the beast and hugging it close, but he kept his eyes on me, solemn, watchful.

"You've been ill," I told him again. He stared at me, serious. "Do you remember?"

My son shook his head. "I went with Da and the other men to Cille Bharra. To see the well. They said it would be running with blood but it wasn't." He looked disappointed. "On the way back to the boat the dogs got a hare."

"Did they indeed? Well, that was some time ago. More than a week gone, it is now. Who went with your da and you?"

My son turned his head fretfully. "Just the men. The churchman wanted to see the well." He closed his eyes. I could see his weariness in the dark circles underneath them, and the pallor of his cheeks.

"Here, drink this. It's sweet with honey." I fetched a cup of medicine from a table nearby, then sat down next to him and lifted his body so he could sit up and drink easily. Finn, annoyed, jumped down and walked a few paces away, then sat, regarding us with amber eyes. I watched my son's throat move as he drank the remedy down. He smelled of sweaty child, mixed with the green scent of the poultices and the dark smoke of the peat fire.

Eugenius swallowed the last of the drink. I heard the outer door open, then soft steps as Amie came closer.

"Mam!" The undisguised joy in my son's voice sliced deep in my heart, sharper than an iron blade. I stood up as Amie flew to the boy's bedside.

"Och, white love." Amie hugged Eugenius, locking him in her arms while I watched, an outsider. She turned to me, her face glowing like the flame of the candle that flickered on the sideboard. "He's better! You've cured him!"

"Nature made the cure," I replied, falling back on one of my grandfather's aphorisms. "Nature along with the blessings of all the saints. But yes, he is much improved." My face relaxed with relief and I almost smiled. "Although he is still weak and must rest for some days."

"Indeed you must," said his foster mother sternly. "And you must mind all that Mistress Euphemia says. She is your own true mother. Do you not remember her?"

Eugenius looked at Amie, then at me, then he turned his head away. "I'm hungry, Mam." Amie looked at me awkwardly, embarrassed.

"It is no wonder he does not remember me. But Eugenius, your mam is right. I am your own true mother, but it has been a long time since I have seen you."

"I remember my grandfather," Eugenius said. "He visits here, at times. But you are my mother?" I murmured yes and he glanced away again. "I'm hungry," my son repeated.

"Well, there is some good broth that Morag just made today. Good broth with some beef and barley in it. We will get it and I will give it to you myself." Amie turned to me. "I would be happy to feed him. Will the broth suit?"

"He should eat cooling foods for a time, as his humors have been so hot. Perhaps a chicken broth instead? Or some white meats and milk? And a little of the broth you spoke of will do no harm," I added, as I noticed the pucker of worry appear on Amie's forehead.

"Indeed," Amie said after a moment. "We can easily get a chicken. And you, yourself, are you hungry? You've barely touched a bite these past three days, and have hardly seen the sun at all, cooped up in this room as you've been. Not that we are not grateful, Mistress," she added.

We watched Eugenius while his eyes closed and sleep, stronger than his hunger, overtook him. "Do you wish to go to the hall and eat with the others?" she asked me after a few moments.

"I don't know," I hedged. I felt loath to leave Eugenius. Amie's eyes lingered hungrily on my son while I looked at her, thinking of my son and his safety.

"You're not wanting to see other folks? You've been here alone with him these three days."

"I live by myself," I retorted, then regretted the sharpness of my words. "No, no, I can go to the hall. There's no need to trouble yourself." Perhaps she wanted some time alone with Eugenius. My hands instinctively went to the pouch that hung from my belt. I had secreted the poison there; could feel the vial through the soft leather. Eugenius would be safe if I kept the poison with me. And surely Amie could not have knowingly poisoned my son. Her affection for Eugenius was palpable. "If you do not mind sitting with him, that is. He should not be left alone."

Amie looked relieved and I knew I had been right. "I am happy to stay for awhile. The hall is to rights and Morag can handle everything there."

I rose, letting her sit on the stool near Eugenius's pallet, and slowly straightened my dress I patted my hair, unaccountably nervous at the thought of entering the Great Hall. My life had been overly solitary these past years. Not that the years in the convent before that had been festive. Although there had been order at the nunnery on Iona, and community, of sorts. I swallowed and fiddled with my mantle, pinning it properly, and adjusted my coif. I looked at Eugenius one more time as he slept on, and then stood, still irresolute, for a moment.

"They will be eating soon," said Amie. "The steward, MacMhuirrich, will seat you. A tall old man, with blue eyes. He wears a green and grey mantle. You will find him easily; he carries the rod of his office."

I thanked her and left the chamber, the sound of my racing heart filling my ears.

Folk milled about in the courtyard, getting ready to enter the hall. The MacNeil's *luchd-tigh* jostled one another. Surrounded by water here at Kisimul, I could not flee. I adjusted my mantle again, took a deep breath, and stepped into the throng, picking my way through the men. One man from the birlinn crew flashed a smile at me, but I caught other whispers and some of the guard stared openly.

I neared the hall, a largish stone building butting up against the wall on the far side of the watchtower, freshly thatched. I smiled a little. The MacNeil seemed intent on refurbishing his new holding. I tried to remember what I'd been told. The castle had come to the MacNeil when he'd married Amie, some five years earlier. Before that it had been held by the MacRuairis.

The wooden doors to the hall stood open. I stepped over the threshold, leaving the brightness of the courtyard for the gloom of the hall, despite the candles and torches that burned within. My nostrils filled with the scent of peat smoke and roasted pork.

Slowly my eyes adjusted to the dimness and I saw the chief's own table set on a dais, with two other tables standing below it, all set for the meal. I raised my gaze. The beams supporting the thatch were richly carved in intertwining designs of animals, newly painted, not yet soot covered. At the head table I saw one man I judged to be the MacNeil in conversation with another figure.

I felt queasy, as though I were still on the birlinn. I could not mistake that stance. I swallowed down bile and turned to leave the hall, to run back to my son and to safety. But the MacNeil noted my movement and called out to me.

"It will be Mistress Euphemia, will it not?" Murdach MacNeil was a dark-haired man, tall, with a decisive chin and a determined look to his green eyes. "How does your son?" he continued. "It was good of you to come this long way."

Warily I approached the two men. A young woman stood near them, but I scarcely noted her except for the fine clothes that marked her as a guest, not a servant. "Yes, my lord," I greeted him. "I am only glad I could make the journey. And, praise all the saints, Eugenius is much improved."

"We have other visitors here as well, mistress," continued the MacNeil. "You were at Iona, were you not? You may remember the man yourself, although doubtless you led a quiet life there." He turned from me to face his companion. "This is Euphemia, the daughter of Muirteach MacPhee, of Colonsay. Her father keeps the records for the Lord of the Isles. Mistress, this is Fingon MacKinnon, the abbot of Iona. And his daughter, Morainn."

My neck felt as taut as a tightly strung sail. "Indeed, we have met."

The abbot stepped forward. He looked older than I remembered, I noted with grim satisfaction, although I had not seen him for close to five years. More wrinkles scored his face; a larger paunch filled his rich robes. He extended a jewel-encrusted hand, as though he expected me to kiss his ring like some pontiff. I inclined my head slightly and stood my ground.

"And so it is Sister Beathag," Fingon said, his voice as slick as thick cream. My blood curdled at the sound of it.

"I go by Euphemia now."

"But your vows cannot be forsworn."

"They were a novice's vows only. But call me Sister Beathag, then, as you wish. Although I would not speak with you of broken vows." For although he was a churchman, and the abbot of Iona, Fingon kept a concubine, and his several children by her, including this Morainn, living in a fine house and lands that should have been the abbey's. He had even dowered Morainn's sister with abbey lands on Tiree.

The MacNeil looked on curiously but I said nothing else. He finally continued speaking. "The abbot had business at Trinity temple, on North Uist, and thought to break his journey here. He has been with us for some days now. Since before your son took ill."

Did the abbot know of Eugenius? I wondered. Of course, he must know. The identity of the mother of the MacNeil's foster son would be no secret. How often did Fingon come here? And why? The Green Abbot was not a man to take action without something of advantage for himself involved.

My thoughts churned like the waves outside the castle walls while I waited to be seated by the steward, but I schooled my expression, refusing to give Fingon the satisfaction of knowing he'd discomfited me. Whether he suspected

Eugenius's parentage or not, nothing could be proved. I had never admitted the father's name, and after all, most considered me but a wanton nun, little better than a whore. So I remained quiet and took the seat the steward indicated, at the high table, although the far end of it. Then I watched as Fingon, his hand possessively on the small of his daughter's back, steered her to the place the steward indicated and then took his own place with an unctuous smile at his host.

Fingon sat at the MacNeil's right hand and his daughter on the MacNeil's left. To her other side sat a handsome, ruddy faced, blonde haired man, dressed in fine clothes, who I learned from the man sitting next to me was Amie's cousin, Angus MacRuairi. I sat close enough to see Morainn smile pleasantly and say something in an undertone to the MacNeil. Her words must have pleased her host, for he grinned back at her as he drank from the mazer before him. She then turned to engage Angus in conversation, and the MacNeil looked less pleased. I shifted my gaze away when I caught Fingon MacKinnon's eyes upon me.

The food should have tasted good. It seemed the MacNeil's pretentions extended to his cook, for all was spiced to a rarity. There was even a blancmange, after the salmon in sauce and the pork, and other subtleties. It was much finer fare than I was used to, but I could not enjoy it. A lump in my throat and an unsettled feeling in my stomach made it difficult to swallow. The Green Abbot's presence at the table took any appetite from me, and I only hoped his business with the MacNeil would conclude quickly.

And whatever could that business be? It was little enough I'd heard of recent politics, but I knew well of the rebellion Fingon had instigated some years earlier. The Lord of the Isles, Donald, had a younger brother, Iain Mór. And Fingon's daughter, this same Morainn, had born a child to that Iain; they had met when he'd come on some business of his brother's to Iona.

The Green Abbot had encouraged Iain Mór to rebel against his lord, along with the chief of the MacKinnons, Fingon's own brother. The rebellion had come to nothing, and the MacKinnon chief had been executed. Iain MacDonald had not been hanged, but had made it up with his older brother, swearing fealty to Donald as the Lord of the Isles.

I looked curiously at Morainn. I had not met her during my time on Iona. The torchlight glinted on her auburn hair and flashed on the rings she wore on long and slender fingers, and the large brooch that pinned her mantle. She had beauty enough, I thought, to entice any man. But it seemed she had not kept the heart of Iain Mór. I'd heard Iain had cast off Morainn and had since married an Irish heiress, Margery Bissett, but I could not remember what had happened to the child Morainn had borne him. Fingon himself had somehow emerged unscathed from the affair, his wings but a little clipped. I had understood he was not to leave Iona, but perhaps that decree had been rescinded. I had not heard much news the past three years on Jura.

Still, there were other reasons I could not be easy seated at the same table with the Green Abbot. I resolved to plead Eugenius's illness and avoid future meetings until I could be assured Fingon MacKinnon was well away from here, and I prayed his boat would sink and drown him as he returned to Iona.

By the time the final remove had been presented I felt sick in earnest, my stomach uncomfortable as I picked at the subtlety. After that, a harper played. I tried to listen to the chords and empty my mind of all else, but my thoughts as well as my gut roiled like the Correyvreckan itself. The music lasted interminably and I felt only relief when at last the man stopped playing.

Finally, the MacNeil rose and I could leave. I muttered some excuse about needing to return to my charge and scurried from the hall, heart thudding. I almost collided with a large bulk as I neared the doorway, and looked up into Griogair's hazel eyes.

"Surely the music was not all that bad?" he observed.

"No, it is just—I must get back to Eugenius."

"How does the lad do?"

"Better. Well, somewhat better. But I must go to him."

He cocked an eyebrow. "Well, that is good. That he has improved."

I shifted my weight, ill at ease, wanting to be away from the hall, the crowds, the clamor. "Now I must go."

"As you will," Griogair said. I felt his eyes on me as I walked across the courtyard, back to my son. Hot acid filled my throat and I nearly retched, but pushed the bile down and fought for calm as I entered the antechamber.

Amie sat next to Eugenius on the small bed, singing a counting song to him. When she got to the last little piglet, she wiggled his toe and Eugenius responded with a contented laugh. It was a happy scene and I almost smiled to see it. Amie looked up and saw me.

"And are they finished now? How the time has flown! I must be getting over there to check on Morag; unless, that is, you want me to stay here."

"There is no need," I replied. "Do what you must. We will be fine here, will we not, Eugenius?" I looked at my son, who nodded, a bit uncertainly.

"And did you enjoy the meal? All was to your liking?"

"Indeed." I kept a smile on my lips until she left and Eugenius quieted, and finally drifted off to sleep. Then I went to the basin in the corner and vomited up all of the MacNeil's fine feast.

CHAPTER 3

Later that night I lay, unable to sleep, listening to the blessedly even breathing of Eugenius in the darkness. I had saved my son's life, but what now? I could not leave him here, not with his life endangered. Not until I learned who had poisoned him, and why.

I lay rigid under the blanket, not even tossing or turning, my limbs stiff and wooden. Amie and the MacNeil had retired to their great bed in the room next door, and the servants slept. The castle was still, silent, most of the guard no doubt snoring in their barracks on the first floor of the watch tower. It seemed everyone in the whole world rested easily, except for myself.

I heard a little scrabbling sound in the back corner, then the noise of a stool overturning, as Finn seized his prey.

"Murchard, what was that?" The sound was muffled, coming through the curtained bed in the next room, yet all else was so quiet I could hear most of what was said.

"That damned cat—"

"Och, Murchard, the lad loves it so."

"It could do its hunting elsewhere, all the same." I heard a yowl as Finn announced his catch, then a crunching sound from the corner of the great room.

"Murchard?"

"Hmm?"

"What did Fingon tell you of my cousin?"

"Nothing." The MacNeil's tone suggested there was something, all the same. "Nothing to concern you, my heart."

"I know Angus is impulsive, but—"

"He is ambitious. He wants this castle."

"He is young and hot-tempered, it's true."

"It's naught to us. Not if you give me a son. But now, give me a kiss for keeping me awake so late."

I heard some muffled laughter, then the creaking of the great bed. At length that noise ceased and soon after I heard the faint sound of Murchard's snoring.

I rolled over, trying to find comfort in my own bed. If the MacRuairis fought amongst themselves, it was nothing to me. Nor did I care if the MacRuairis and the MacNeils came to blows–except if they did, my own son would be in the heart of it all. I wanted nothing more than to spirit Eugenius back to Jura, fosterage agreements or no. Although a lonely cave on a hillside was no fit place to raise a child. But who had tried to poison my son? And what was Fingon MacKinnon doing here? Stirring the pot, no doubt, and to no one's benefit but his own. What of his daughter? What part did she play in this, as she flirted with both the MacNeil and Angus MacRuairi?

I felt a soft thump at my feet. Finn made his way up the bedclothes and, purring, butted his head against my face. I smelled a faint odor of blood on his mouth and remembered the mouse. I had not foreseen that death. Despite Finn's purrs I pushed the cat away and lay tense in the darkness, waiting for the dawn, remembering.

The first vision I recalled had come to me on a summer afternoon. I must have been about five and had been helping my mother in her herb garden, or playing while she weeded, more likely. I wandered into a wilder back section of the garden, outside the walls that kept the herbs confined and ordered—the fragrant pennyroyal, the pretty foxgloves with their flowers like the dresses of fine ladies, the lavender, and the rue. I saw a white hare and followed it as it bounded away over the heather until, wearied, I plopped down in a patch of soft bracken, green and smelling of the earth, and gazed at the deep blue of the sky and the clouds scudding by, losing myself in the shapes and making up stories about them as I sometimes did with my mother.

However, this day as I gazed the sky seemed to quiver in an odd way, and suddenly I saw the sea, and rocky cliffs, with a little village and a tiny strand of beach. A few timbers, wreckage from some craft, were strewn on the sands. I heard the sad cries of women keening.

Then my mother's voice called and a hand reached out to shake me gently.

"Euphemia! Euphemia!"

I looked into my mother's face. The vision dissolved, and I saw only her concerned blue eyes. "The boat is lost, Mam. The women are crying."

"Sure and you've been dreaming, my pet. Come along now and help me carry this feverfew back to the stillroom."

But later that day, when my father returned from Finnlaggan, he brought a tale of a birlinn wrecked outside of Port Oa, with most of the men from that village lost.

My mother glanced at me, but I was intent on the little rag dolly my father had brought back to me from his trip and I thought little enough of their words until later that evening, when they believed me fast asleep. I overheard my father speak again of the wreck.

"Muirteach," my mother said, "Euphemia saw it."

"Saw what, *mo chridhe*?"

"The birlinn. She said something about a lost boat and women wailing. I thought it was a dream she was having."

My father sighed. "Perhaps it was but a dream. Don't look so pained, Mariota. If Euphemia has the Sight there's nothing to be done for it." And I heard them say nothing else of the matter. But I remember thinking before sleep claimed me, *Of course I have the sight, Father. I can see as well as anyone, far better than old Morag. You're always telling me what sharp eyes I have—of course I can see.*

The next day Eugenius appeared well enough, and Amie seemed set on having me join the others for the midday meal. I suspected she just wanted to spend time with my son, and his face brightened whenever he saw her, in a way it did not when he saw me. That cut me to the bone, but I smiled pleasantly enough and acquiesced, leaving my son with his foster-mother whilst I joined the company in the hall. I found myself seated next to the Green Abbot's daughter, Morainn. The woman was but a few years older than myself. We were not un-alike, both having borne bastards. And more alike perhaps than that, although I thought she did not know all of it. Still, I forced my face into a grimace that I hoped would be taken for a pleasant smile, as we sat next to each other and listened to the bard entertain the party a bit while we ate.

"And what brings you to Barra?" Morainn questioned me, as I picked at my salmon.

I thought I might well ask her the same, but I did not. "Amie sent for me when Eugenius became ill. He is my son," I said to her, although doubtless she knew that well enough already.

"Yes, and you have some skill as a healer, do you not?"

"My grandfather was Fearchar Beaton," I admitted, "and both my mother and I studied with him, before my mother died. But my grandfather died when I was at Iona, some five years ago."

Morainn looked at me speculatively. A shaft of light shone on the gold and agate ring she wore, and the look of it teased at me. Something I could not quite remember. "Yes, I had heard you were at the nunnery. Why did you leave?" Morainn asked, as though it was the most innocent question in the world.

"My grandfather died, as I have said. And while I was on Islay, I discovered there were reasons I could not return to Iona. My son. The same reason that called me here."

"Yes, we are both mothers, are we not? With sons in fosterage. My own son stays with the Largie family. But I took no vows."

Bile rose in my throat. I swallowed it down. I saw Morainn's father watching us from across the hall. "It is my licentious nature, I fear," I whispered to her in a confidential tone. "I am a sinner, a wanton and weak woman." I smiled at her. "I have not the benefit of a religious father."

"And yet you live alone, on Jura, I have heard."

I hated her in that moment. "Yes," I said, as though I had no cares in the world. "I live like a hermit, as penance for my sins." I prayed the meal would end, and turned away to Amie's cousin Angus, who had been seated on my other side, hoping he had not overheard our conversation. But Angus seemed intent on drinking his ale, and had little enough to say to me, although he flashed many a smile at Morainn, who smiled back at him. When the interminable meal ended, I left the party as quickly as I could, grateful to return to my son in the little room off the MacNeil's bedchamber.

Another day passed. Eugenius grew stronger and it became difficult to keep him abed. So, despite my fears, he dressed and we went into the castle courtyard. He wanted to see the dogs. Especially after Amie told him one of the bitches had whelped while he'd been ill. "Can I go, Mam? Please?" Eugenius begged. His face was a little flushed and he still had a slight fever, but he'd eaten well both that morning and the day before.

"Do you see any harm in it?" Amie asked me, her brow wrinkled with worry. "He's fractious with boredom. And it's not far to the kennels—just across the courtyard."

I wanted to keep Eugenius from whomever might harm him—and I had no idea who that might be—but I could think of no plausible reason to forbid a visit to the kennels. So I forced a smile and said he might go, just for a short while, and that I myself wanted to see the pups as well. I still had not spoken of the poison. Who here could I confide in? The castle priest? Not if Fingon MacKinnon was his confessor. Amie? Yet she had brought the remedy from the herb-wife on the island. Not Murchard, who wanted a son of his own, not merely a foster-son.

We dressed Eugenius warmly and set out across the courtyard. My son blinked at the light outside, reminding me of a little owl fledgling I'd found once in Jura. Although the day was blustery and overcast the strong walls of the castle did not let the wind in. The kennels sat at the far end of the courtyard. Eugenius walked sturdily, holding on to Amie's hand, and everywhere folk stopped to greet him. He was clearly a favorite here and my heart warmed a little to see it.

The kennels smelled of wet dog and musty straw. A large deerhound bitch lay in one stall, nursing five pups. They butted against her teats, vying for a turn to nurse. One of the pups' eyes had just opened, but most of them squirmed blindly against the warm bulk of their mother.

Eugenius squatted in the straw to see the pups, petting the largest of the litter. "I want this one."

"Eh, we shall have to talk to the MacNeil about it all and see what Himself is saying about it," Amie replied.

A shadow blocked the light from the kennel doorway. "And who was speaking of me?" a jovial voice boomed. We looked up to see the MacNeil, accompanied by the Green Abbot, his daughter, and several attendants. Amie smiled at her husband and he grinned back, a proud man entertaining his guests. "And how are you today, young man?"

"Sir, I want one of Mairead's puppies. Please? This one?" Eugenius smiled into his foster father's face.

"Well, we shall see. I promised the abbot here the pick of the litter."

"Come, child," said Amie. "Let us go and leave the men to it."

"Ah yes," said Fingon gravely. I shuddered. "I heard that you were sick, young man."

"I was," asserted Eugenius, "but I'm better now." The adults laughed. "Aren't I, Mam?"

"Thanks to Mistress Euphemia. And the help of the saints," Amie added, looking askance at the abbot.

"What fine pups," said Fingon, picking up the largest pup, the same one Eugenius had petted. "This one, I think, Murchard. He'll make a fine hunting hound."

Eugenius's face crumpled. "But that is the one—"

"Shush, child," interjected Amie quickly. "You must excuse us, my lords. I fear the boy still tires easily, does he not, Mistress?"

"Yes, we do not wish him to do too much just yet."

We turned to leave the kennels. As I squeezed past the abbot, I fancied he brushed my body with his hand but his face gave nothing away. I shuddered as though I'd just glimpsed an adder in my path. No one else seemed to take any notice.

We emerged from the kennel into the brightness of the outer courtyard. "Come along, Eugenius," Amie chided him. "You're no baby, to be so upset over a wee pup."

"Mam, I don't feel so well."

"What is it?" Amie replied, looking at him closely.

I stared also, for Eugenius had gone pale. Then he fell to the yard floor, shaking and shuddering in a fit, taken with the falling sickness.

CHAPTER 4

Amie screamed. "Get something for his head, and quickly," I said, my voice taut as a whip. I knelt on the hard stones of the courtyard beside my son. He looked white as a shroud in the throes of his fit. I took off my mantle, wadded it up, and managed to place it under Eugenius's head while his limbs still jerked violently.

The shadow of the Green Abbot fell over my son. "He is afflicted with demons," he observed. "How unfortunate."

"It is no demon, but the falling sickness," I returned through gritted teeth as the convulsion quieted a bit. The abbot stood by while the MacNeil called for his men and Amie hovered anxiously, surrounded by her maidservants, who had come running when they heard her cries.

"He will sleep now, I think, now that the fit is over," I said to calm her. "Let us get him back to his chamber."

"Here, let me." I heard a man's voice and looked up to see Griogair. "Come, my boy."

Eugenius had lapsed into sleep, and Griogair lifted the boy up as if he weighed no more than a tuft of wool. "Has he ever been taken with the such a fit before?" I asked Amie. "And you did not send for me?"

"No, never." Amie's eyes were round and she bit at her lip as she followed Griogair and I towards the lad's chamber.

"I have heard of such cases after children have had a bad fever."

"Will he have another fit?" asked Amie, her face still pale.

"I've no way of knowing," I snapped at her as we made our way into the small chamber. "Lay him down here, on his bed."

Griogair placed Eugenius gently on the pallet. Now that the fit had passed, my son slept soundly. Griogair left Amie and myself with the boy, and at length the room grew quiet.

Amie broke the silence first. "Surely you have some remedies. Something to help him."

"There are a few things I can try. Here, let us first get him out of these soiled clothes." My son barely stirred as we removed his shirt and small clothes. He had wet himself during his fit, and his little linen shirt was dirtied from the mud in the courtyard, the saffron color stained with brown muck.

Amie started to cry. I stared at her, my own eyes dry, my throat raw and my breath ragged. "Amie, your tears will do him no good. Stop it." She stared at me. "There is more to this than you know, and we will both need to be canny and quiet."

"What is it?"

I hesitated a moment. Could she truly be trusted? Could I tell her of the poison? But I needed an ally, and I knew she loved my son. "Eugenius did not have a usual sickness. Someone tried to poison him." I took out the pottery vial and set it between us, a silent accusation. "With this."

"But that is old Murdina's remedy. She would not have poisoned him."

"Then who did?" I glared at her. "This is dog's mercury, and wolf's bane. Black henbane. Any one of them would have been enough to kill a child. It is a wonder indeed that Eugenius survived at all."

Amie's eyes widened in the dark room. "And I myself gave it to him—" She crossed herself. "You must believe me, Mistress, I had no idea." She swallowed, trying not to weep. "I believed it to be Murdina's remedy. I would never knowingly bring harm to Eugenius."

"Who gave you the remedy?" My voice was hard as flint.

"When he returned from the trip to Cille Bharra with Murchard and the others, I did not want to leave him. He had a fever."

"So who brought you the remedy?"

"I sent Morag, with some of the men to row the boat, over the bay to the village to see Murdina and fetch the remedy. For mine had not worked. That would have been the second day of his illness. Before we sent for you." Amie looked thoughtful. "When he first fell ill it seemed not too serious. And it was after I began to give him Murdina's remedy that he grew worse. That is when we sent for you." She shuddered. "But who could have wanted to poison him?" she repeated. "He's but a child!" I grew afraid she might cry again.

"You are here. You tell me."

Amie looked at me, her eyes wet. "You are harsh."

"It's my own son's life that's at stake here. Would you have me be soft? Now, who would wish to harm him? That is what we must discover," I said, finding her tears annoyed me. Or perhaps I was just afraid that I too would fall to weeping, and then could not do what I must to save my son.

"Everyone here dotes on Eugenius," Amie said, flustered. "He is the light of Murchard's eye."

"What of your guests? Who visited here then, two weeks ago?"

"Let me think." I watched Amie bite on her lip. "Angus was here. He is my cousin from Gamorgan, with some of his men. They were on their way up north, to Dunvegan, to treat with the MacLeod. The MacLeod has a daughter he's wanting to marry off. You met him, I think. He was here just now, on his way home again."

"Aye. And who else?" Eugenius stirred in his sleep and Amie waited a moment to answer, perhaps fearing he would wake. But he did not.

"The abbot and his party, on their way north also, to Trinity Temple in North Uist. They were the ones wanting to see the well that day, the day Eugenius took sick. The abbot said it would be miracle of God, a well running with Christ's blood. Though I have heard that it is no miracle, but a sign of war, when the Tobar Bharra runs red. They have lingered here and did not go on to Uist, although I believe they will leave today. But surely none of these folk would wish to harm Eugenius. He's but a lad."

"Aye, but his grandfather is one of the MacDonald's trusted men. And Lord Donald of the Isles himself is the boy's godfather."

Amie looked worried. "Angus was ever resentful that his father's claims to the Lordship were put aside in favor of Donald's. For Angus's father was a son of the old Lord of the Isles, by his first wife. But Angus would not strike at a child. How would that serve him?"

I remembered that Donald, the current Lord of the Isles, had several older half-brothers by his father's first wife, another Amie. In fact, my hostess had been named for that woman, her aunt. So Angus must be the son of one of those men. In addition, he felt his rights to Kisimul had been overlooked when the castle came to Murchard. I was not so sure Angus would not strike at a child but attacking Amie's cousin at this point would not serve. "Morag fetched the remedy from Murdina, you said?" I asked.

Amie nodded. "She knew Eugenius, knew what his symptoms were. She went into Castlebay and saw Murdina."

"Fetch Morag here," I demanded, "and let us ask her about it all."

Amie stared at me a moment, then turned and left to find Morag. I watched my son sleep and tried to think of what remedies might serve him, should he be taken with another fit. But I thought more on who might wish him harm.

A cradle sat in the far corner of the great bedchamber. Glancing at it through the doorway, I saw it covered with a black pall. I shivered. Did I see a shroud for Murchard's son, or my own? Thankfully, when I looked again the vision had vanished and the cradle sat empty as before. My heart thudded sickly in my chest as I sat in the dim room, waiting for Amie to return.

Morag's light blue eyes flicked anxiously at me as she followed Amie into the little room; a woman old enough to be Amie's mother, with brown hair going grey. Her thin, spare figure minded me of a crane I'd seen once, nesting on Islay.

"So herself said you wanted to speak with me. But how does the poor babe?"

"He is resting now." I was in no mood to discuss the health of my son with this woman, not until I knew her to be innocent. "What did your mistress tell you, when she sent for you?"

"Just that you must speak with me. But my lady looked aye upset." Morag said it with the air of an old and trusted servant who had watched her mistress grow up.

"And well she might be," I replied. "Was it you who fetched the potion from Murdina for Eugenius, when he first took ill?"

Morag shook her head. "That would be two weeks gone? Some days after the abbot and his party came. Was it not?" She turned to Amie, who nodded in agreement. Morag thought a moment. "I did not go to fetch it."

I saw Amie's eyes widen. "But I thought it was you who went! I asked you to go!"

"And how could I go, with the abbot and all his entourage here, and Himself wanting everything of the best, and you busy with the poor sick lad? No, I had too much to see to in the kitchens, and so I sent that lass, Murdina's own niece, Brona, the one that helps here. I told her the lad's symptoms, and what she was to tell Murdina. The lass seemed happy enough to go and see her auntie, although I'm thinking she has some sweetheart there in Castlebay she wanted to see as well; the lass has been looking like a cat that's got into the cream these past days." Morag stopped speaking a moment, and the two of us stared back at her. "Why?" she asked, after another moment. "Was there some problem with the remedy? What has happened?"

Neither Amie nor I answered her question. "Fetch the lass. Now," Amie commanded, her tears gone. She seemed once again well in control of herself, the mistress of a fine castle. Morag gave her a searching look, then left.

"I did not speak to her of the poison," Amie confessed awkwardly after the old woman had departed. Eugenius still slept soundly and we waited, uncomfortable with each other, listening to his breathing, for the few moments until Morag returned with Brona in her wake. I judged the girl to be well into her teens, comely enough to have a dozen sweethearts indeed, with curly dark hair and blue eyes and a rounded form many men no doubt found pleasing.

"So, Brona," Amie began, "Morag told us it was you who went to Castlebay to fetch the remedy for Eugenius."

"Aye, Mistress," Brona replied, her eyes flashing a bit despite the dutiful speech.

"And it was this vial you brought back from old Murdina?"

Brona glanced briefly at the pottery vial. "Indeed it is. How does the sweet lad?" she ventured to ask.

"He does well enough," Amie replied in a tone that did not encourage additional questions. "So you would swear that this is the vial you got from your auntie," and again the lass nodded. Amie thrust the vial towards her, in the light. "Look closely, lass." Her voice was stern.

"But how can I remember?" exclaimed Brona, sounding very young all of a sudden. "It was over two weeks ago that I brought it from my aunt's. It was just a wee pottery vial, like this one. Although perhaps not quite so round," she mused, as she looked more closely at the little vial Amie held.

"And what did you do with it when you brought it back here?"

Brona thought a moment, and then flashed a smile. "I left it on the shelf as you go into the kitchens. For I could not find Morag. I had my own duties to see to, Mistress. Then later, when I did see Morag, I told her where I had left it."

Amie turned towards Morag. "And when did you take the vial from the shelf?"

"As soon as ever I saw it there, and didn't I bring it to you just as soon as ever I could! It was well before the feast, but the meat was all prepared, I'm thinking. For Griogair had brought some hares from the island for the feast, that he got from that Hamish Beag, and I saw to them before the lass found me."

Amie turned back to Brona, who fidgeted under her mistress's iron gaze. "What else did you do in Castlebay on that day? Did you see anyone else at your auntie's? Tell us everything, lass, and quickly."

Brona cast a glance sidewise to Morag, who also glared at her, and the girl dropped her eyes. "My lady, Griogair rowed me over. He left me near my auntie's on the shore near her house, then he said that he would go and see Hamish Beag who lives over on the other side of the bay, whose mother makes such fine ale, and that he would return for me soon enough. So I went in and visited with my auntie, and told her of the lad and how he'd taken a chill the day before, just as you told me to, Morag, and then my auntie gave me the vial."

"And what else did you do at your auntie's? No doubt Griogair took his time returning. Did anyone else visit your auntie that day?"

I saw Brona glance at the floor, and then at the rafters, before she replied. "One of her old cows went wandering off into the hills. So I set out searching for her and found the cow too, across the burn. By the time I brought her back I saw Griogair crossing the bay, so I bade Auntie farewell and walked down to the beach to meet him."

"And no one else came to your auntie's that day?"

Brona shook her head. "I saw no one."

Amie sighed. "Get back to your duties, then. Morag, you go with her. I'll be there, as soon as I can leave here, to help set things to rights for the feast this evening." I saw Morag sniff, perhaps at the suggestion that her kitchen might not already be in good order, but she left with Brona. After they had gone, Amie and I stared at each other, confounded.

"We must ask Griogair," Amie said. "He may know something, or have seen someone."

"You do not think he could have poisoned my son?" I asked. I had thought Griogair pleasant enough when he fetched me here; he seemed a kind man. I remembered how he had carried Eugenius back this morning, after my son took ill. But perhaps all that meant little.

"I'd trust him with my own life. He has been my lord's man since they were boys together. And he has always liked Eugenius. But he could have seen someone. Or something."

"And what of the kitchen? Someone could have switched the vials while everyone was busy. No one was watching."

"Then it could have been anyone. Anyone in the kitchens at all. Any of the servants. But they'd have no reason to wish harm to the lad. I cannot believe it of them."

"Someone did it. And I mean to find out who it was. And protect my son."

"Are you thinking I do not want to protect him, then? What are you saying?'

"No, no, of course not." I had the beginnings of a headache as I spoke with Amie. "I did not mean that. I can see the care you give to my son, and he loves you indeed. But he is in danger, and now with that fit…" My voice trailed away. I had seen some infants taken with the falling sickness, during a fever. Sometimes it did not return. I crossed myself and prayed that would be the case here. Although Heaven does not usually favor my prayers.

"I will send for Griogair," Amie volunteered. "Perhaps he knows something of it."

But it happened Griogair had gone with the MacNeil, to visit some holdings on the far side of Mingualay, and they were not expected back until the evening. Although Amie confided that the abbot and his party planned to depart that day, and that news gave me joy. There remained the rest of the kitchen staff to question, as well as old Murdina. I did not feel comfortable leaving my son, and Amie and I agreed to leave the visit to Murdina until the next day. "And one other thing,"

I cautioned her, as she left the room to summon the rest of the kitchen staff. "Do not speak of this with your husband."

"Not tell Murchard? But why ever not? He must know; and he'll see justice done."

I realized too late my mistake. "I just thought perhaps we should investigate a bit more, and speak with Griogair, and see what he has to say about it all. Before we trouble your husband. He has so much on his mind. If we are not careful and canny, the poisoner, whoever they might be, will have warning, and then we might not be finding him."

Amie bit at her lip. "Well, I suppose a day or two can do no harm. He's preoccupied, what with the abbot here and all."

"I thought the abbot was not to leave Iona, after he made his peace with His Lordship."

"I do not know of that. He told Murchard he had business up at Trinity, and broke his journey here. Perhaps His Lordship of the Isles does not know of the abbot's journey."

I thought that very likely indeed. "Well, he would not be pleased. Nor am I thinking he'd be pleased with Murchard for treating with the abbot. I have heard that the man gives poor advice."

"Och, Murchard is canny. He'll not be seduced by fine words. And," Amie said, looking at me with a little resentment, "my husband can keep a secret. He cares for your son, as I do. But I'll not speak with him of it until after we talk to Griogair tomorrow." She gave my son another fond glance. "Now I must go. Shall I bring you something to eat?"

I shook my head no. "I am not hungry," I replied.

Amie frowned a little. "You do not eat enough. I will bring something to you when I return. Some fresh cheese. If you do not want it, give it to Finn." I laughed a little bit with her as she left the room, the cat following her out, then I sat by my son and tried to work on some sewing while I worried, both for my son and for fear I had offended my hostess. But what was that compared to my son's safety?

Amie returned presently with some oatcakes and fresh cheese for me, and the two other kitchen workers to be questioned. Neither Clara nor Elen remembered anything or anyone unusual in the kitchen on that afternoon two weeks earlier; they had both been busy, with Brona away and the exalted company, and there had been much to do. Clara had been preparing a special broth that the Green Abbot's daughter had requested. "I was told she had a sour stomach, and wanted some white broth for it," Clara said. "So there was that to do, in addition to everything else."

"And did the woman come to the kitchens herself to get the broth, once it was finished?" I asked.

"Oh no, Mistress. I am thinking she sent her attendant. I did not take it to her. And Brona and Elen were busy, as was Morag."

"Morag, did you know of this?" Amie asked sharply.

"I knew the lass felt poorly," Morag replied. "So we made the broth for her, and she seemed well enough that evening."

"Who took it to her?"

"She sent her attendant for it. I myself gave the bowl to the girl. She came into the kitchens, I gave her the bowl, and she left right enough." Morag bristled a little. Amie dismissed her and the other two women, and went to search for Morainn's attendant, but we were too late. The Green Abbot and his daughter and the rest of their party had finally taken their leave, continuing on to Trinity Temple in their fine birlinn, the saffron sail trimmed with a large green cross. The sun shone on the waves like jewels, and the oars of the crew splashed in the water as the party made their way out of the bay and turned north towards the Uists. I watched them leave with a thankful heart.

The next morning Eugenius seemed not much the worse for his fit. He woke early, wanting breakfast, then played quietly in the corner with some carved wooden gallowglass after he had his porridge. I tidied his things, waiting. Amie had told me she would bring Griogair to speak with the both of us. Which she did, very promptly; I could just see the sunbeam making its way across the floor of the great room as she entered the little room with him.

Griogair's bulk filled the smaller chamber. His head nearly touched the rafters, and finally Amie motioned for him to sit on the stool. He looked around and flashed a smile at me where I stood awkwardly by the table.

"Your pardon, Mistress," he said, and disappeared into the outer room a moment, then returned, carrying a small bench, which he set down at the foot of the bed. "There, my lady," he said to Amie. "Now we can all be comfortable."

Amie and I seated ourselves on the bench and Griogair sat on the stool. His long legs stretched across the tiny space between us. Eugenius threw aside his wooden soldiers with a clatter and greeted Griogair with a grin.

"Och, come here, you rascal," the man said, as Eugenius clambered into his lap. "Now," Griogair said, after the boy was settled, "what's amiss? How does the lad?"

"He's well enough," I replied, "as you can see."

Eugenius wriggled out of Griogair's lap and went to get his toys. "Play quietly, lad," admonished Amie. "We must speak with Griogair." Eugenius obediently gathered his playthings and sat down by the stool, lining them up in opposing sides.

"What is it, Mistress?" Griogair asked. His keen hazel eyes looked at us. "What's amiss?"

"Are you remembering the day you took Brona over to Murdina's, the day Eugenius took sick?"

"Aye."

"What happened there?"

"I rowed the lass to the wee beach below old Murdina's cottage. She got out." He looked concerned for a moment. "She is a fair enough lass, although she has little sense. But she's done nothing wrong, has she?"

Amie shook her head, and Griogair continued. "Well, I left her there at her auntie's and then went over to Hamish Beag's. His mother had just brewed a batch of fine ale, and we drank some, and then we went out after some hares on Beinn Tanghabal. Once we returned, I rowed back over the bay, to Murdina's. Brona was waiting for me on the beach. We came back here. That was all of it," he added, as Finn came into the room and started to bat at Eugenius's soldiers.

They knocked to the floor with a clatter, and the cat settled down amongst them comfortably, and started to wash his face. Eugenius's face crumpled. "There, laddie," Griogair said quickly, "it is just a more powerful force that has won today's battle. You must rally your troops now." Eugenius brightened and began to pull his toys out from under the cat.

"After I've done speaking with your mother," here Griogair looked at both of us a moment, his eyes twinkling a bit. "Your mothers, I should perhaps be saying." He grinned. "But after we are done, I will tell you the story of when I was fighting for the O'Malleys in Ireland."

Eugenius seemed happy enough with that promise and Griogair looked at us both again. "Now, what's amiss?"

"We are thinking that this vial is not the one Murdina gave to Brona," Amie finally said.

Griogair looked puzzled, then his eyes narrowed. He glanced at the boy, then back at us. "Mistress Euphemia," he finally said, "you have seen little of the castle here. Let me show it to you, and we can talk as we go."

"Indeed, and that will be a fine thing," Amie said, giving me a little push while Griogair rose from the stool. "She could do with a little fresh air, shut up as she's been in this wee room for all these days. Don't worry yourself," Amie added, looking at me. "I will keep a close eye on the wean and call if anything's amiss. Now off you go."

Low clouds were spitting rain as Griogair and I made our way across the courtyard. "I've a mind to show you the watchtower," Griogair said as I wrapped my mantle closely around me. "There's a fine view, and no one to disturb us there."

I followed him up a ladder and through the guardroom, then up another stairway to the walk that ran along the curtain wall. The view of the bay made me dizzy and I reached out to grab at a parapet.

"Och, you're not liking heights, are you, Mistress." It was an observation, not a question. I shook my head no and bit at my lip, praying I would not fall.

"It's pale you are, but we can speak privately here. Come, there's a corner just this way and it's out of the wind. And there's a fine view of the island as well."

I followed him, holding onto the wall when I could as we made our way to a corner of the watchtower. Then I leaned back against the blessedly solid stone while Griogair faced me, blocking my view of the sea, and I told him how Eugenius had been poisoned, and the rest of it all.

"And now he is taken with the falling sickness," I finished, "and all of it is my fault."

"I am thinking it is the fault of whoever gave him the poison," Griogair returned. "But who would wish to harm a wee bairn?"

"A wee bairn with a powerful godfather," I returned. "Perhaps whomever it was wanted to hurt the Lord of the Isles."

"Not many would tangle with him." Griogair looked at me piercingly. "What of the lad's father?"

"I do not even know who my son's father is," I lied.

Griogair arched his brows. "And is that so, indeed?"

I did not meet his eyes, but stared stubbornly at my feet. "I found I was not made for life in the nunnery."

"They did not marry you off, once you were with child?"

"I had taken novitiate vows. Too early, it seems."

He let that pass. "Och, we all make mistakes. But that's no reason to live in a cave like a hermit. Interesting, Mistress, but it does little to answer who might have poisoned your son."

"Someone wishing to get at Amie? She loves the boy."

"Indeed she does. And he has a place in Murchard's heart as well. So harming him would sorely hurt the both of them."

"And who might that be?" Braced against the wall of the tower, I dared to raise my eyes and look out over the bay to the island beyond. I could make out village folk going about their lives, fishing boats coming back into the harbor with their catch, other men mending nets while women worked the querns outside, or sat and spun, gossiping with neighbors. All seemed peaceful, quiet, homely, and my heart ached for my lost innocence. Those days were gone.

"I have heard nothing," Griogair said in answer to my question. "None of the guards, or Murchard's own people. An outsider, bent on stirring up trouble."

"Fingon MacKinnon?" I said, and shivered, casting my eyes away from the view and lowering my gaze to the walk in front of me. "He's stirred up trouble many times before."

"But how would this evil profit him?"

"Revenge upon Eugenius's godfather. Donald, the Lord of the Isles. Who hanged the abbot's brother, the chief of all the MacKinnons. And Donald's own brother, Iain Mór, set aside the abbot's daughter to marry Margery Bissett."

"But all that was some years ago."

"I do not think the abbot is one to forget a slight. And if Eugenius were injured while here, if Murchard were to fall foul of his liege lord, then perhaps the abbot would have someone else to suggest, to hold these lands. One of his sons, perhaps." I had never seen the abbot's sons, but if they were anything like their father, I did not wish to ever meet them.

"But His Lordship would never listen to the abbot. He's clipped the man's wings before."

"And look at the abbot now. I'd thought him confined to Iona for his misdeeds. And yet he was here, on Barra."

"I'm thinking word has not reached Finlaggan of his voyage here." Griogair shrugged. "There might be others about with a grudge against the MacNeil. Some of my own clan, the MacRuairis, possibly. A branch of the family held the lands here until recently, when Amie married Murchard and the castle came to him. And if Amie does not bear an heir, the lands might well pass back to them."

"Are any of them foolish enough to listen to such poor councilors as Fingon MacKinnon? Perhaps Angus?"

Griogair looked at me, his eyes suddenly piercing. "What do you know of Angus?"

"Nothing. I just overheard Amie and Murchard one night. They mentioned him."

"Any ambitious man can be swayed by bad counsel," said Griogair. "And Angus is as ambitious as most men, perhaps more ambitious than many."

"He seemed to enjoy speaking with Morainn, I noticed," I said. "At the feasting. I saw them together the times I went to the hall."

"She is a bonny woman. Most men would enjoy speaking with her, I think." For some reason this comment annoyed me, but I said nothing. After a bit, Griogair continued. "Well, I will listen and see what I can learn. And you must guard Eugenius, and perhaps Amie will learn something else from her women." I shuddered and he noticed. "But Mistress, let us go back down. I think there's little left to glean at this point."

I agreed, and we made our way down. I felt the solid ground of the courtyard beneath me with joy, and was happier still when I saw that Eugenius had come to no ill while I had been away.

I sat on the bench in the little bedroom and told Amie what Griogair and I had spoken of. She looked concerned. "Och, Murchard is aye flattered that the abbot and his entourage stopped here. He'll not remember all that came of listening to the man. But now they have left, and may the saints speed their travel. And we've nothing to accuse the man of. He was most certainly not in the kitchens that day."

But what of his daughter, I wondered. Who could have wanted to poison my child?

Amie left me with my son soon after, to see to the meal. I told Eugenius a story, something I had made up about a puppy, and that made him remember the pups he'd seen in the kennels the day before. His fever had left him, and so, against my better judgment, we ventured out to the kennels. But all went well this time, the lad petted the pups while their mother Mairead watched easily, even giving my son's hand a friendly lick as he replaced the little one at her side. I chided myself for my worries as we walked back from the kennels. The earlier clouds had blown away and above the castle wall I could see the arc of a rainbow to the east.

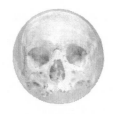

CHAPTER 5

The next morning dawned darkly, with rain drizzling down from a sullen grey sky. Despite the weather, Griogair rowed me across the bay to Murdina's early in the morning. I wrapped my *brat* tightly around me, hugging its woolen warmth, and said little as the shoreline come closer. The village of Castlebay sat near the harbor, the stone cottages with their thatched roofs snug against the poor weather. As we neared the shore, Griogair turned the boat to the right of the bay and we landed in front of a blackhouse that stood alone, up the hill from the beach. We disembarked and I helped him pull the boat up onto the pebbles littering the shore.

"That is Murdina's dwelling, just up there," he said, gesturing to the cottage. "Do you want me to come along with you?"

I hesitated, unsure. Inside my pouch I felt the weight of the vial of poison I carried, heavy as lead. Undoubtedly it would be best to have someone with me who knew the village and the people who lived there. I found I had become accustomed to Griogair, and the thought of him going along reassured me somewhat. I gave him a short nod. "She does not know me," I said.

"Och, fine enough. I'll walk with you up to her door. You're a stranger, and the woman, although her heart is kind, can be as prickly as any thistle."

My shoes slipped a little as we walked up the muddy pathway leading to the cottage. The door faced the bay and on a fine day the view would have been lovely. A tumbled pile of peats sat near the front door, and smoke from the hearth made its way out through the smoke hole in the roof, hanging heavy in the air, the scent mingling with the cool smell of the rain. A couple of bedraggled chickens, their feathers wet, pecked at the ground outside, intent on some worms the moist weather had enticed to the surface. We approached the door and Griogair called out.

"Murdina?"

"Aye, aye. Whoever is it, then?" The door opened and I saw a tiny woman standing in the doorway. Wrinkled, wizened, and so short that she could almost have been one of the Good People, the fairy. Untidy grey hair peeked out from under the white kertch she wore on her head. She wiped her hands on a cloth as she stood there, blinking a little at the light outside.

"Och, it will be you, Griogair." She smiled in welcome. Most folk did smile at Griogair, I had noticed. He seemed to charm people without trying. "Whatever is bringing you here today? Is someone ill at the castle? And who is this you have with you? But you must come inside, out of the wet."

She ushered us into her cottage. Bundles of herbs hung from the beams above, and I could see steam rising from a cauldron that sat on the fire. I smelled whatever remedy she had simmering there, a sharp, sour scent, like the smell of wet earth in the autumn. On some shelves I could see various flasks and vials, all containing her tinctures and cures, I supposed. The crowded cottage seemed more like a stillroom than a home, but I felt comfortable amongst all the herbs and remedies, and homesick, for just a moment, for my own cave on Jura.

"You must sit down," our hostess said, and from some dark corner of the cottage she produced a couple of stools, moving the grey cat that had been sleeping on one of them and offering the stool to me. I sat down, feeling the warmth left in the wood from the cat's body, the sensation welcome on such a *dreich* day.

"Here, I will just get you some hot broth. I have it here on the fire. It's a raw morning, indeed it is. But what brings you here?" Murdina repeated, looking from one of us to the other with curiosity. Outside I heard some gulls cry, the sounds rapidly fading on the wind.

"This is Mistress Euphemia," Griogair said, introducing me. "From Islay. She is the mother of Eugenius, the young boy who is fostered with Himself and Amie at the castle."

"The lad that was taken ill? How does he do now?"

I inclined my head and watched her closely. "Well enough," I replied. "What was in the cure you made for him?"

"Och, just a few things for the fever. Ash bark, willow, and meadowsweet, that would be all of it, I'm thinking. Did it help the boy?"

None of those herbs had been in the vial of poison I now carried. I felt certain of that, at least. "We wondered if we might get a bit more of it, and I wanted to thank you for your trouble."

"Surely that was no trouble," Murdina replied, looking among the pottery flasks on the shelf. "Here it is. I'll just make some up and put it into a smaller flask for you. I am glad indeed to learn the lad is doing well, but this is a fine remedy to have on hand for children." She busied herself with her herbs, taking some tinctures from large clay bottles and mixing them together as she spoke.

"Your niece Brona came and fetched the remedy, did she not?"

Murdina's pale blue eyes looked sharply at me. "You'll know that yourself, for didn't Griogair bring the lass over here from Kisimul." Her gaze moved from me to Griogair. "Something is amiss. What is it?"

I sensed no evil in the woman, rather the opposite, and found it difficult to believe she would have given poison to my son. I glanced at Griogair as I retrieved the little round pottery flask from my pouch. "Did you ever see a flask like this?"

Murdina stepped away from her remedies and approached me, looking at the bottle. I wondered if she had a bit of the Sight herself, for I saw her shudder before she reached out and took it from my hand.

"That is not mine. The ones I get from the potter here have a lighter color. And the shape is different as well. Why?" She unstoppered the flask and sniffed, and her face grew solemn. "This is never any remedy of mine." As I myself had done, she put a tiny drop of the contents to her lips. Her eyes widened in shock, likely as the numbness made itself felt. "Where did you get this?" she demanded. "This is poison. Who gave it to you?"

"It was found at the castle," Griogair interjected, "and we were not sure what it was. Amie herself hoped you could tell us. As you have." He took the flask back and handed it to me.

Murdina appeared somewhat mollified. "Best be careful with that. Those dark herbs can kill."

I replaced the vial in my pouch, then pulled out the pot of honey and the cheese Amie had sent with us. "Well, Amie asked us to give you this. She also is grateful for your cure and your skill." I gave the cheese and honey to the old woman. Murdina took them, thanked us, and put them down on the table. She returned to her herbs and at length handed me a small bottle. It was narrower than the one that held the poison, and the clay an entirely different color.

"You've a great knowledge of herbs and medicines," I observed.

"I learned from my mother," Murdina replied as she finished her task, returning the large jars to their spaces on the shelf that hung above the table.

"I learned a bit from my mother as well," I said. "And from my grandfather."

"Indeed?"

"Yes, just a wee bit. Might you show me your stores? You've a vast collection of herbs here, and I'm sure you have much knowledge to go along with it."

Murdina looked pleased. "Indeed, I'll show you, Mistress. If Griogair won't mind the wait."

Griogair glanced towards the door. "The rain is pouring down. And it's fine and warm indeed here by the fire. I've no objection." He stretched out his long legs towards the fire.

Murdina showed me her store of herbs. I asked her simple questions, ones that I myself knew the answers to, and chatted. She seemed just a simple herb-wife and I sensed no evil in her. Among her herbs I saw no dog mercury. No wolf's bane. No hemlock. Only healing herbs, not poisonous ones. And, as she had said, all the vessels she used were of the light grey clay favored by the local potter.

"I am not seeing as much of my niece since she got the place at Kisimul," Murdina remarked as we finished our chatting.

"Aye, there's plenty to keep her busy there," Griogair commiserated. "I'm sure Brona enjoyed seeing you that day. No one else came by, while the lass was with you?"

"No indeed. We had time for a fine visit before you collected her, Griogair." Her eyes narrowed. "But why ever are you asking me about the girl? She has not come to any harm, has she?"

"No, no," Griogair said, soothing her. "But she did not meet with anyone else?"

"Why would I be telling you if she did?"

"She's a bonny lass and it would not be surprising me if she had a sweetheart."

"You're thinking I would condone that?" Murdina sniffed, then smiled and her eyes took on a sweet, distant look. "Och, I was young once, and indeed I can remember what that was like. But no, she met with no young man. She is a well-behaved girl."

"I did not say she was poorly behaved. Not at all. I just wondered if she had a sweetheart somewhere."

"Why? Are you wanting her for yourself, Griogair?" asked Murdina.

I watched while Griogair's face turned a bright pink. "No, no, I am too old for a young lass like Brona."

Murdina laughed. "You 'd be a fine enough catch, would he not, Mistress?"

I did not know what to say, and felt an awkward blush rise on my own cheeks. "We should go," I said, standing abruptly. "Thank you again for the remedy, and your care for my son." We took our leave, and made for the boat that would carry us back to Kisimul.

My son had another fit. This time he had no fever; he had seemed to recover well from his sickness and when the spell came, neither Amie nor I expected it. The shock of it caught us unwary, like a golden eagle swooping down upon a mouse.

Some days had passed. All guests had left, and Eugenius, feeling much better, had the run of the castle. I had begun to wonder about returning to Jura myself, for the lad seemed healthy, and at times I feared Amie thought me interfering. I had dosed him with herbs said to prevent the falling sickness, cuckoo flower and others, and he seemed to do well enough. We both agreed, relieved, that his fever caused the attack, and now that it had subsided there remained nothing left to worry over. But more days passed, and I could not bring myself to leave my son. Amie was too fine a hostess, and too kind a woman, to suggest it.

So his second attack came as a surprise. We had relaxed our guard. Eugenius, playing some raucous game, had been laughing and chasing the cat about in the courtyard. I sat on a bench watching him, working in a desultory fashion at my spinning. Of a sudden I heard a thud, then a silence, and then a thrashing sound. By the time I reached him he was in the throes of the convulsion, his limbs jerking and twitching violently. I sat helplessly next to him, cradling his head in my hands, until he quieted, then somehow carried him back to his bed where he slept heavily for some hours.

I thought I would not sleep at all that night, but I must have dozed off at some point for I woke with the remnants of a dream lingering in my mind. A vision of a skull, water running from vacant eye sockets like flowing tears, and as I rubbed the last of my slumber from my eyes I remembered. My old companion from Jura that sat, dusty and neglected, on the shelf in the cave I called my home. The skull of a suicide, that folk believed could cure the falling sickness.

It is said that the water from a holy well must be drunk from the skull at sunrise and sunset, for twenty-one consecutive days to effect the cure. The afflicted person must walk sunwise around the spring three times before drinking, before the sun rises in the east, and just after it sinks in the western sky. For the healing to be efficacious certain charms must be said as well. I did not know of any such springs on Jura, but certainly the holy well, Tobar Bharra near the chapel at Cille Bharra, would serve. And surely Amie would not complain if I stayed there for the three weeks with Eugenius, during the time it took for the cure to take effect.

I looked at my son, sleeping quietly, with the bulk of the tabby cat stretched out beside him. Surely the saints would not deny my son this healing. Surely this remedy would work.

The door opened and Amie entered, carrying a tray with two bowls of porridge. "How is he?" she asked. "I was just bringing you both some breakfast."

Finn roused himself and jumped down from the bed, then up on the table where he sniffed interestedly at the porridge.

"Get down, you," said Amie to the cat, who ignored her. She gave it a good-natured push off the table. "But how is he this morning?"

"He slept soundly. No fits. But I have remembered something—an antidote, perhaps." I told Amie about my dream and her face lightened considerably.

"Och, yes. And should you need to stay at Cille Bharra, there's a wee cottage near the spring that you could use. The old man who lived there died last winter, from the cough. I am thinking no one lives there now. Although there'll be people enough near by. But you go to Jura and fetch what you need as soon as may be. I'll arrange for your lodging and see that the house is made ready."

"And what of Eugenius, whilst I am away?"

Amie looked practical, and her eyes shone with hope. "You will teach me all of what I should know, if indeed he is taken with another fit. And I'll prepare all his food myself. He

will bide well enough until your return, I hope. I'll just ask
Murchard if he can spare Griogair and some others for a few
days, to take you to Jura to fetch the thing back with you." She
paused, then crossed herself. "It sounds fearsome, Mistress.
Will you want to have it blessed?"

"I do not think so." Then I shivered. "Although perhaps it
would do no harm."

"Well, the priest at Cille Bharra would do it. Father Isidor.
Or Father Uisdean here could bless it as well. And what else
will you need? Shall I send a maid with you while you are
staying over there?"

I shook my head. "I am used to doing for myself, and
Eugenius will be no trouble." In truth, the thought of having
my son to myself for three weeks enticed me. I realized, with
some guilt, that I did not wish to have another person intrude
upon that prospect. I glimpsed a precious chance for just the
two of us to stay together. Perhaps Eugenius would even come
to think of me as his mother.

"Let me go to Jura," I told Amie, "and fetch the thing back
with me, and we will see how Eugenius does while I am away."

So that very afternoon Griogair and myself, along with
a crew of five other men, left Kisimul and set sail for Jura. I
knew a little more of the men now, after my time at Kisimul,
and could put names to their faces. There was a wizened old
man, Bricius, an experienced sailor who served as captain.
Two brothers, Conall and Calum, both dark and tall, silent for
the most part, and so alike they could well have been twins.

The fifth man, Tormod, had red hair and a big hook of a nose, and constantly cracked jokes, most of which had to do with women. They did not seem quite as threatening as they had to me when we first voyaged to Barra, although my heart still beat faster as we left the castle, anxious for my son.

The wind blew pleasantly and the day, so close to midsummer, stretched long. The waves were mild. As before we stopped midway, on Mull, and slept on the beach for a few hours before resuming the journey early the next morning. We made good enough time, with a fair breeze filling our sails, and arrived at Jura that afternoon. I fairly leaped from the birlinn, anxious to retrieve the skull. I needed to see it, to hold it safe. Fanciful, I worried that it would have vanished. Or that something else would prevent me from healing my son.

"The men will want some food," Griogair observed as they hauled the boat up on the small beach. I turned to him, in a rush to climb the hill.

"Are you thinking I left all my larders full here, when you fetched me away those few weeks ago! I am sorry, but they will have to hunt for their dinner. Or fish for it." I stalked away, unaccountably annoyed, and started the trek up the path that led to the cave I had lived in for three years.

The place looked forlorn and neglected after my absence. And indeed, I found no food there; the mice had gotten into the small store of oats I had left. I thought of Finn, and how his tail would have twitched as he hunted the vermin. I saw the skull, sitting there on the shelf covered in cobwebs. I took it down, dusted it off, and found an old shawl to wrap it in. "There, you'll just come along with me," I said to it as I placed it in a basket. Now that I had Eugenius's cure in hand, I found I could relax a bit. The nagging fear abated just a little.

I wondered whose skull it had been, and what was the great unhappiness that had caused the owner to commit the mortal sin of suicide. But the Sight revealed nothing about that, and I looked around my dark and cramped dwelling place instead, seeing it critically after my time away.

Some things I had not taken with me when I'd left in such a rush earlier, and I must bring them with me now. I gathered them together, adding them to the basket. Herbs, vials of tinctures. Two clean shifts. Another mantle. I remembered a pin of my mother's I had squirreled away when I first came here. I had kept it but never worn it. I found the small casket and opened it. My mother's brooch, a large smoky cairngorm quartz set in silver, engraved with interlacing designs. I smiled, remembering her wearing it. On impulse I put it back in the casket and added it to my bundle.

That was all.

I smelled a fire from the beach and peered out the cave opening. Thick clouds had rolled in, and it looked as though rain would follow. The crew would be wet if they slept on the beach. Feeling dark shame for my harsh words to Griogair, and for my unkindness to the men, I searched the shelves and found a jug of uisge beatha that might serve as a peace offering.

I made my way down to the shore, where the men had caught some mackerel and were grilling them, spitted on sticks, over the fire. "Here," I said, awkwardly. "The mice got into the grains while I've been away, but perhaps this will go well with the fish." The gift was well enough received and the fish close to being done. As we waited for them to finish cooking a few drops of rain began to fall.

"You must come up to sleep in the cave," I offered. "It will be wet here on the beach. I've not much to offer there, but at the least it will be dry and out of the wind." Tormod made some joke about the wet weather and the two brothers quickly agreed. I did not look at Griogair, embarrassed by my earlier poor manners.

The downpour began in earnest and the crew pulled the birlinn further up the beach, and then followed me up the path to the cave, bringing their meal along with them.

The small space felt cramped, filled with men. I wanted to run away outside, but the rain fell steadily and I could not flee. For furniture I had only a small bench, a narrow bed, and a stool. I started a fire on the hearth and the air grew smoky and close, the men joking and laughing. But the fish Bricius had caught were tasty and the uisge beatha lent them savor. I picked at my mackerel and licked a crumb of it from my finger.

"Is that all you're having?" I heard Griogair's voice close by. "You hardly eat enough to keep a mouse alive."

"It is enough," I answered. Suddenly my appetite fled, and I looked at the half-finished food before me, wondering how

I could have thought it tasty. "Here, I can eat nothing else. Do you want this?" I asked Bricius.

"No, Mistress, I am well fed, but Tormod might take it off your hands."

Tormod glanced up at the sound of his name. "Aye?"

"Are you wanting a bit more mackerel? Mistress Euphemia is not liking your cooking."

"No, it is not that," I protested. "It is just that I am full."

Tormod laughed and took the food away. The brothers sang a couple of songs; they both had fine voices. There were other songs after the uisge beatha ran out, some of them rowdy ones I would not have heard at Iona. At length Tormod yawned, followed soon by the others, and began to talk of sleep. Outside the rain still came down in torrents.

"We will just lie down here, by the hearth," Tormod said. "There's room enough if we all turn over at the same time. Now watch, Bricius, that you do not miss the signal with your snoring."

Griogair had been sitting next to me, on the bed, and he rose to find his own spot. I still felt raw, ashamed for my earlier poor behavior and his comment about my appetite. Sleeping with the crew on a beach under the stars was one thing. Here, enclosed in the cave, it felt crowded. I could not escape. My heart began to pound. "Here," I said to Griogair. "You can take the bed. I'll sleep on the floor."

"With those louts?" he laughed. "No, Mistress, I'll not turn you out of your bed. I'm tired enough to sleep well on a bed of rocks tonight. And the dawn will be here soon enough."

"We'll all guard your virtue, Mistress," I heard Tormod say, and I thought I should say something jesting in return, but nothing came to mind.

"Och, well, sweet dreams to you," Griogair said after an awkward silence. He gathered his mantle about him and stood to find a spot on the floor. I wrapped my mantle around me but did not lie down immediately.

Soon all was quiet. Somewhat. Bricius did in fact snore loudly, and he was not the only one. Someone farted and another man belched. The noises seemed louder in this enclosed space than when we had slept out on the beach. I fought down panic. I found the air close, and did not sleep well, lying on my narrow bed, listening to the snoring of the five men about me.

The rain continued all night and into the morning. The crew slept late, but I myself rose early and left the cave, walking in the pouring rain up the hill to the burn where I got my water. I washed, although I hardly needed to as the rain fell in torrents on me. My head felt fuddled from the uisge beatha and unaccustomed guests; despite my time at Kisimul I was not used to close quarters. Finally, chilled and somewhat refreshed, I started back down the hill towards the cave.

Bricius stood outside, wrapped in his mantle against the wet and frowning at the clouds. "We'll not leave today, Mistress," he said. "Although this could clear this afternoon, and then perhaps we could reach the near side of Mull, since the days are so long now."

I assented, assuring him that he must know best, and asked after the rest of the crew.

"They are still in there snoring like the hogs they are. But they are a sound enough crew for all that. And tired, I think. They rowed hard to get here. What is it you needed to fetch again from this place? Griogair did not say."

"You brought oats, did you not?" I said, changing the subject, unsure how folk would feel to be rowing a suicide's cranium back to Barra. "The mice got into the grain I left here. Perhaps the men would enjoy some hot porridge when they rise."

Bricius agreed that they might and so I went inside, picking my way around the sleepers, found my old cauldron, and fed the smoldering fire. Despite the smoke and the noise I made, the oatmeal was sputtering and thickening before anyone else stirred.

Griogair woke first. He looked at me for a moment, amused by something. I scowled a little at his laugh and continued my cooking. A bit of porridge landed on my hand and I muttered a curse under my breath. Griogair chuckled as he stood up and wrapped his mantle around his shoulders.

"Shh. You'll wake your crew," I said, wishing he would go outside. The cave felt cramped, what with Tormud and the two brothers sprawled here and there on the floor, wrapped in their mantles, still snoring.

"Well, and it is time they woke, the lazy louts that they are."

"There's bad weather. Bricius does not think we'll leave today, at least not soon. You may as well let them sleep." Just then Conall made a snorting sound and sat up, rubbing at his eyes.

"Good morning, Mistress Euphemia. Griogair," he said quietly. Then he got up and went outside, looking to relieve himself, I imagined. I wondered why Griogair also had not gone outside. Surely the man needed to take a piss. Finally, Griogair walked over to the cave mouth and poked his head out.

"It's wet enough out there to be drowning the water horse himself," he said, flashing a grin before he stepped outside.

I shivered. My father had told me, once, of seeing the water horse on a trip inland. But I had no wish to see one, nor to joke about it. The porridge looked to be done, and I moved the pot off the flames and searched my shelves for some dishes. I found a couple of cracked wooden bowls and an old wooden mazer. There were also some larger bowls I used for making remedies. I searched for the small pot of honey and found it on the shelf, dusty and sticky. I wiped it off and put the dishes on the table, along with spoons, feeling unaccountably domestic.

By this time even Tormod and Calum were awake. Bricius, Conall and Griogair came back inside, shaking the wet from their mantles, and everyone took some of the porridge, sitting wherever they found a spot. The fire crackled cheerfully and Bricius and Conall even complimented my cooking, once they stopped eating. The feeling grew quite companionable, and of a sudden I missed my father.

My mother had died before I entered the nunnery, nearly seven years ago now. Since then, my father spent little time at the house they had shared on the Rinns of Islay. He was more likely to be found at Finlaggan, where His Lordship had his primary residence, or at times on Colonsay, where he had a small house and his uncle was clan chief of the MacPhees. I realized with a start that my father did not know of his grandson's illness. I had not thought to send word.

The men were telling stories as they sat around the fire. Calum had just finished a long tale, something about some strange crossing of the Minch near Lewis. I had only half listened as I washed the dishes and straightened my meager kitchen area a bit. Bricius put his head out of the cave.

"It'll still be coming down like the waterfall on Skye," he announced. "We'll not leave today."

I thought of my father. If he was on Colonsay, that crossing could be made if the weather cleared a bit. And even if he was not there, my great-uncle could send word to my father.

"Perhaps, if it clears, we could travel as far as Colonsay tonight," I suggested. "My father might be there; he has a house in Scalasaig. Or if not, the MacPhee could send word to him. He does not know of Eugenius's illness," I said, a little apologetically. "I was so taken with nursing my son I did not think to send a message."

"And you do not think that Murchard and Amie did so?" asked Griogair.

"She said nothing of it." I paused a moment. No one looked overjoyed at the prospect of rowing some twelve miles in a downpour. It was cozy and warm enough here. I felt deflated, like some child's pig-bladder ball with all the air gone from it.

It must have shown on my face, for Griogair got up and peered outside. "Well, I for one am bored with this rain. I'll take you across to Colonsay, Mistress, if it lets up. The crossing is not so far, and the others can stay here and rest, if they wish. Perhaps we'll get a breeze later if the weather lightens. If you have a selkie's skin hidden in the rafters, though, you'd best be putting it on, for you'll be getting soaked to the skin."

I looked at him. Although the MacPhees are sometimes said to be descended from the selkie-folk, I did not find his joke funny. "I have a warm mantle," I said shortly. "That will have to do."

CHAPTER 6

Bricius refused to let Griogair take the boat alone, and swore he did not mind the wet, and so the three of us set out for Colonsay in the late morning. Tormod and the twins, as I had started to think of them, looked relieved when Bricius said they were not needed, and Calum and Conall looked even happier when Tormod produced, from somewhere, another flask of uisge beatha. They would enjoy their afternoon. We arranged to return either in the evening or early the next morning, and then we would begin the journey back to Barra. I felt sure my father's people could provide some fresh provisions; the men would be glad of a change from mackerel.

A fair breeze helped us across the Strait of Jura and the rain let up. I watched as we came closer to Colonsay; I had not been raised there and so did not think of it as home, but my father grew up on the island. It is a lovely place, small and green, with little wildflowers on the machair, and I knew my father's heart felt at peace there. Yet as we sailed closer, and the salty breeze filled my nostrils, my nervousness increased. How could I have neglected for so long to send word to my father about Eugenius? I was a poor mother, indeed. And a poor daughter.

We beached the boat at Scalasaig and walked up the lane, past the alehouse and the few houses clustered there. My father's small cottage sat on the far side of the village. I saw the door ajar and smoke coming from the chimney, and realized my father must indeed be here at home, not at his lands on Islay. I hesitated, apprehensive, and Griogair nearly walked into me.

"What is it?"

"This is the house. And my father looks to be home."

"Well, fine. That is what we came for, is it not?"

I swallowed, feeling awkward, then knocked on the door. "Father? It is Euphemia." I pushed the door open.

I discerned my father seated at a table close to the doorway, working on copying something out, most likely for his uncle the MacPhee. He raised his head at my voice and a smile lightened his face. Rising, he walked towards me and embraced me.

"Och, it is fine to see you, lass! I had a feeling I'd see you, indeed. I dreamed of you, and of Eugenius. But you are so thin! What brings you here? And where have you been? Seamus sailed to Jura two weeks ago, and you were nowhere to be seen—we have been worried over you." His eyes traveled towards Griogair and Bricius. "And who are these folk with you? Welcome," he added to them. "Come in and be seated."

The two men filed into the front room, their bulk filling my father's small house. I introduced them, and my father offered them some ale and oatcakes and cheese. Guiltily I explained to my father what had happened, how Eugenius had fallen sick, and how I had left Jura abruptly for Barra. My father's face grew grave as he listened.

"I'd had no word of any of this. What was Murchard thinking, not to let us know of it?"

"Well, I knew of it, Father, and I was there caring for him," I said. Remorse settled deep in my gut like some lowering cloud. "I just did not think to send a message, with all of the worry over Eugenius. I am sorry. And Murchard had other guests as well."

"My grandson has recovered? He is well?"

Feeling even more contrite, I told my father of my son's falling sickness. My father's grey eyes, so like his grandson's, grew darker as he listened to my story. "And that is why we came," I finished. "These two are Murchard's men, and they brought me back to Jura. I have a remedy there that I hope will heal him. We would have left today, to return to Barra, but for the poor weather."

Father did not ask what the remedy was. He had married into a family of healers but was not one himself. He simply accepted my words. "Well, will you stay the night?" he asked, changing the subject. "I can make space here, or there's room enough up at the Dun."

I looked at Griogair and Bricius.

"It is not so late, and the days are long right now," Bricius said, putting down his mazer of ale. "And it looks to be clearing. I'm thinking we'd do better to leave and return to Jura this evening, and we can be on our way home early tomorrow. It should be a fair enough day. But if you, or the MacPhee himself, could spare a few fresh provisions, enough to get us back to Barra, they would be well received."

My father inclined his head. "Of course. You are welcome to whatever you wish, but my uncle will have better food at up Dun Evin. Perhaps Seamus could go up and ask what could be spared. You two might walk with him, if you wish. And then my daughter and I can visit a bit whilst you are about that."

Griogair and Bricius good-humoredly agreed, saying that a chance to stretch their legs would be welcome. And so Seamus, my father's friend who lived nearby, led them up to the fort on the hill outside the village, the stronghold of the MacPhee clan, while my father and I settled down for a chat.

"Can I get you something else to eat?" my father asked. "I've plenty here, and some ale."

"I am fine, Father. I am not hungry."

"You are too thin, Euphemia. And it will do your son no good for you to starve yourself."

I did not want to argue with my father, and accepted the oatcake he brought me, but I ate little of it, mainly crumbling it to bits as we sat and talked.

Now I told him all of it, how Eugenius had not just been sick, but how someone had tried to poison him. How someone, we did not know who, had switched the herb-wife Murdina's remedy for the poison. My father's eyes narrowed as he listened and I saw his jaw tighten.

"And Father, you know who was also at Barra?" My father shook his head. "Fingon MacKinnon, the abbot of Iona."

"He is not supposed to leave Iona." The anger in my father's voice did not surprise me.

"That was what I believed, but he was there, with his daughter—the one that got the son off of Iain Mór. Morainn. Some other churchmen accompanied them. Amie told me they arrived at Kisimul before Eugenius first fell sick, on their way to Trinity in Uist. But they did not leave for Uist for some time. They remained at Kisimul for well over a week."

"His Lordship will not like that news," my father said, his face grim. He did not know the half of the reasons we had to hate Fingon MacKinnon, for I had never shared them. But the abbot had instigated revolt against the Lord of the Isles some years earlier, in 1387. His brother, chief to the MacKinnons, had been hanged, but Fingon had merely been exiled to Iona for his part in the affair. A trifling punishment, as Fingon had taken over many of the abbey lands on Iona for the use of his common-law wife and his several children, whilst the church fell into disrepair. No, the Lord of the Isles would not be pleased to hear of this. Not in the slightest.

"Fingon is an evil man," my father said. "And he is devious. Poison suits the bastard, but he'd have no reason to injure my grandson."

"You wrote the edict that condemned his brother."

"Aye, but the sentence was passed by His Lordship. I merely acted as the scribe."

"Would that matter to Fingon?" I laughed, the sound bitter to my ears, and my father stared at me, wondering.

I continued. "Father, someone tried to kill my son. I am going back to Barra, and I will heal my son of this sickness. Then I will find out who it was that poisoned him. And then, perhaps, I shall kill that person myself." My words surprised me. I had not admitted that before, not even to myself. But I wanted whomever it was to pay. I wanted them to suffer.

"Who can you trust there?"

"I told Amie. I had to tell someone," I replied helplessly. "She and Murchard truly love the lad, I believe."

"Aye," my father agreed. "I have seen them with him, when I've visited. They dote on him."

"Griogair knows of it as well. Amie feels he can be trusted."

"His Lordship is at Finlaggan now," my father said, "and I shall travel there and tell him what you have told me. Doubtless he'll clip the abbot's wings fast enough."

"He'd best clip them to the bone," I said. "Until they bleed. The man did not look to be suffering to me." There was an edge to my voice and my father again regarded me curiously.

"Euphemia, I cannot believe the man would hurt a child."

I bit my lip and did not answer. My father's eyes seemed sad. Or perhaps I glimpsed my own sorrow reflected in them.

"I've something for you," my father said after a moment. He stood and went into the small sleeping area, partitioned off from the front room. I heard him rummaging in a chest for a moment before he emerged. He put something in my hand. I felt the delicate metal circle in my palm.

"Here, dear heart. This is for you. It was your mother's."

I glanced down and saw a fine gold ring, with the words *Mo chridhe* on the inside. The outside engraving, an interlaced design, had worn almost smooth over the years.

"But why are you giving it to me now?" I asked, turning it slowly in my hand. I remembered my mother wearing it; she had never been without it. My mother had been gone for close to seven years. I had entered the nunnery soon after her burial, my decision fueled by grief and the idealism of a young girl. But I had left Iona two years later, and my father since that time had surely had many opportunities to give me the ring. My eyes filled with tears, and I obstinately blinked them away. But the tears proved more stubborn than I.

"I did not want to part with it, dear heart," he said, "and so I kept it. Perhaps I am a selfish old man. But I think you need something of your mother's about you now. Be canny,

Euphemia," he continued. "Be very careful. I have lost your mother. I do not want to lose you, or my grandson."

I nodded, my throat suddenly full, and slipped the ring onto my finger. It fit snugly there; the feel of it soothing and comforting. I dried my eyes and managed a smile, and realized my father's eyes also were wet.

We heard a noise outside, and Bricius and Griogair entered, followed by Seamus, a tall lanky man in his thirties. Griogair carried a sack of provisions. All three men appeared to have been well fed at my great-uncle's stronghold, and to have had plenty to drink as well.

The sun was still far from setting, and most of the rain had blown away. My father and I said our good byes, while Griogair and Bricius readied the birlinn. I felt a pang of homesickness as I clambered back into the boat, and watched my father wave to us from the shore while we departed. I wished to be a child again, safe back in Islay with my father and mother. But my mother was dead, and I had no real home now, just a cave in the hills. And a child of my own. A sick boy. That thought, like some pestilent demon, crushed any ease I had found with my father, and my stomach grew anxious as I worried for Eugenius, wondering how he had fared the past few days. I caught a whiff of my own sweat, tense and sour, before the boat pulled away into the freshening breeze of the Sound.

We crossed easily enough back to Jura, and found the crew well rested. In fact, we heard Tormod's snoring before we entered the cave. Conall and Calum were playing dice at the table and they smiled at the sight of the provisions we brought. Tormod roused himself, unrolled his mantle, stretched, and made his way to the table to join us as we ate our evening meal of fresh bread, roasted lamb, and cheese that my great-aunt at Dun Evin had provided. It smelled fine enough and the men enjoyed the feast. I barely tasted it, anxious for the night to pass, waiting for dawn and our trip back to Barra.

The sun rose in a clear sky the next day, and we set out for Barra with a fair breeze behind us, but the wind died down midmorning and the crew got out the oars. The sound of the *iorrams* the crew sang while they rowed rang over the water. Although we made fair enough time, I felt we crawled over the waves, and was glad when the wind picked up again. I reached out to feel the bundle at my feet, the skull that would save Eugenius, then checked its safety again a few moments later. At length we neared Mull and rounded the southern end, past Iona. I shivered a little. "Are you cold, Mistress?" Griogair asked, and I said yes, although the cold had not caused my shuddering. We travelled further and finally beached the boat, camping again on the far side of the island for the night.

I had thought I would sleep better there on the shore, with space around me, instead of crowded into a small room with strange men. Yet I did not. Horrid visions disturbed my rest. Water. A flash of whiteness in a pool. The skull, leering at me. As I awoke and rubbed the last vestiges of sleep from my eyes, I told myself it was just a dream, brought on by our ceaseless sailing. Not a true seeing. Not the Sight. But I hesitated to board the boat as we set sail that morning.

We reached Barra by the afternoon. A brisk wind sped us on our way, and nothing untoward occurred, although as we approached the island Griogair showed me a large basking shark, a *cearban*, swimming nearby.

My heart leapt in my chest as we drew closer to the castle in the bay. Why had I ever abandoned Eugenius there, with Amie? I should have brought him with us to Jura, whether he had a fever or not. What if he had sickened again in my absence? My thoughts roiled like the choppy waters of the bay as we neared the castle and the guards raised the sea gate. With relief I saw Eugenius, standing with Amie, amid the folk who welcomed the galley into the boat slip. I fairly flew out of the boat and hugged my boy closely to me. He squirmed a bit at my embrace. I released him and he moved nearer to Amie, shifting his weight from one leg to another, restless, while I greeted his foster mother.

"How did he do?" I asked Amie, as the clamor died down and people began to disperse.

"Not a single fit did he have." She smiled fondly at the boy, who had run ahead of us across the courtyard. "As good as gold, he was, my heart's darling." She scanned his direction; Eugenius had headed towards the kennels. "He'll be wanting to see the dogs again, that will be it. It is all he thinks of these days."

My heart sank a bit. My son had not missed me while I was gone. And why should he, really? He had spent the last three years here, with Amie and Murchard. This was my son's home, and a litter of new puppies were of vastly greater import than a strange woman who appeared with foul tasting medicines, claiming to be one's mother.

"And you," I asked Amie rapidly, turning the subject. "You have been well?"

Amie patted her stomach protectively. "Well indeed," she said. "But I'm thinking soon I'll be as great in size as those huge cearban that swim around in the bay."

"No," I said with a laugh. "You're not as big as all that. We just saw one as we neared the island." The huge black fin and body, as long as our own boat, had somewhat unnerved me, but Bricius had assured me they were peaceful creatures and did not even possess teeth.

We followed Eugenius to the kennels, chatting as we walked. I carried my bundle carefully, well aware of the strange medicine it contained. Perhaps, if Eugenius had no more fits, we would not need to use it.

We found my son settled by the pups, their eyes now open. The kennels smelled of straw and wet dog. The puppies still jostled at their mother's teats, but in between feeding they played with each other. I wondered if Murchard would still give the largest pup to the abbot, or if he might relent and let Eugenius keep it. As Eugenius looked happy enough kneeling by the dogs, I did not raise the topic. After awhile Amie left Eugenius with me, and went to see to something in the kitchens. I watched my son start to fidget and decided it was time to go. As we walked back across the courtyard to his little room, off the great bedroom, I realized I had not thanked the crew, not even Griogair and Bricius. They were nowhere to be seen now, most likely returned to their families on shore, and I felt shamed again by my rudeness.

I stowed my bundle carefully away in the chest, burying the skull under my clean clothes. Eugenius played with his toy soldiers nearby, lining them up into rows and trying to coax Finn into attacking them. For his part, the cat seemed more interested in getting in my way, as I tried to mix up a new remedy for my son from the fresh supplies of herbs I had brought back from Jura. After several attempts at knocking the herbs and vials onto the floor, the cat retreated, with little grace, and sat at the far end of the table, watching me with challenging eyes. When Eugenius tried to move Finn down on the floor, to play, he said, the cat jumped back up on the table and nearly overturned the vial I had just filled. I swore under my breath and then saw my son looking at me, his grey eyes wide.

"What is the matter, Mother?" he asked.

"I did not want the cat to overturn the vial. And he did not," I continued, managing a smile, "so I shall put these away for now. I have finished."

"I am hungry."

"Well, let us walk to the kitchens and see what we can find for you to eat. Can you put those soldiers away for now?"

Eugenius complied readily enough, and we crossed the courtyard. The kitchens were busy, and Amie in the thick of it all, her cheeks flushed from the heat as she and Morag ordered Brona and the other two kitchen maids about. When she saw us, she readily found some cheese and bread, and even a sweet cake for Eugenius. We left the kitchens and walked back, and I told Eugenius about the large cearban we had seen.

"How big was it?" my son demanded.

"Longer than the boat itself. There was one big black fin past the front of the boat, and the tail fin a bit behind."

"Truly? Mother," Eugenius pleaded, "let us go up the battlements. I know how to get there, I've climbed up before. I am sure we could be seeing the cearban from the walls, if it is in the bay."

I shared none of my son's certainty. The Sight had shown me nothing of *cearbanan*, nor did I wish to climb up on those high walls again. But my son had a stubborn streak, and darted across the courtyard as I ran to keep up. Before I could catch him, he had started to clamber up the ladder that led to the guardhouse. "Eugenius, wait!" I cried, breathless, but he ignored me, laughing, and climbed higher.

I cursed for the second time that day, hiked my skirts up a bit, and began the climb up after him. The courtyard was empty, most people having gone into the hall for the evening meal. I could see Eugenius's feet just above mine, but did not want to reach for them lest I throw him off balance and he should fall to the floor. Suddenly my son let go of the ladder and tumbled back onto me, throwing both of us to the ground and knocking the air from my lungs. I sat up, slowly gasping for breath. With sick dismay I felt something wet on my gown, and my son's limbs jerking against my legs. Eugenius lay sprawled across me where we had fallen, in the throes of another fit. He had wet himself, and that urine soaked my skirts.

We had no choice. I showed Amie the skull. It stared, mocking us with its toothy grin, as we made our plans that night. Eugenius had lapsed into a sleep after the fit ended, and he did not wake again that evening. Amie told me again of the small house near the holy well at Cille Bharra. She had already made it ready, but had hoped we would not need to use it.

"What I have heard," I told her, "is that water from a holy spring must be sipped from the skull of the suicide, both before the sunrise and after the sunset, for twenty one days. And there are certain prayers that must be said as well. After that, surely he will be cured."

My hostess shuddered a bit. "Are you sure this skull belonged to a suicide?" I watched her try to hide her fear and wondered at her innocence. I found even the skull of a suicide did not bother me overmuch these days; I felt comfortable with dark deeds and dark thoughts.

"I found it in the cave when I moved in there," I answered her. "But the folk on Jura told me it was the skull of an old woman who killed herself after her family died from the plague, some forty years ago. And the woman who lived there long before I did dug up the skull from the grave during the dark of the moon."

I watched Amie shiver again, and wondered why it was that I took some pleasure in frightening her so. I did not know how the old woman who had lived in the cave had come by the skull, in truth, and had only heard it was the skull of a suicide. I knew nothing of the grisly cup's history, not really.

"I am certain it will work," I told her, feeling my chagrin sink like a lump of lead in my gut. "It must. And while we are there, alone, no one shall get near him to do him harm."

"Aye," Amie said, and a shadow crossed her face. I felt even more guilt then, for reminding her how Eugenius had been poisoned in her own home.

"I will pray to Saint Barre and the Blessed Mother for you both," Amie continued. "Eugenius is but an innocent bairn. Surely, they will answer our prayers. And we shall make sure you and Eugenius have whatever you may need, while the cure is undertaken. You only have to ask. The priest at the church there is Father Isidor. It is but a short walk up the hill from the spring. He will not refuse Murchard anything, for my husband is his lord. We shall make sure he keeps watch over you both while you are there."

So, after a day of preparations Griogair ferried Eugenius and myself up to the north end of the island, where we found the small cottage next to the spring, just as Amie had promised. Eugenius looked on it all as a great holiday, although he clung tightly to his foster mother a moment before he got into the boat, as she did to him. The sun was sinking in a blaze of dusky purple and brilliant orange, off to the west side of the island, and the shadows lengthening as we beached the boat on the northern part of the island and tramped to the small blackhouse, a short walk from the well.

Amie had been as good as her word, not that I'd been in doubt of that. The house looked in good enough repair, the beds freshly made up, with mounds of soft bracken and wool blankets to sleep on, and peats for the fire sat piled up by the door. I unpacked the clothes and food we had brought with us, and set the skull, wrapped in a shawl, beside my bed, while Eugenius ran about outside. From the sound of his cries as he chased the birds from the rushes, he thought it a grand adventure. I heard a croak and stepped outside. A pair of ravens, with a fledgling, perched on the peat stack and watched us curiously.

"Och, so you'll have company here, Mistress," Griogair said, indicating the birds with a smile. "I'm away now. Is there anything else the two of you are needing?"

All of a sudden I did not want to be here, alone with my child and the skull. "It is getting late," I said. "Do you not want to stay and go back to Kisimul in the morning?"

"I've time enough to get back," Griogair replied, "and duties to attend to in the morning. So I'll leave you. But Amie will send men to see how you are getting along in a day or so. I'll be surprised if she's not coming herself, for she'll miss the lad sorely. And, should you have any need, Father Isidor is just up the hill at the church." He pointed out the church to me, up on a rise, and then walked off, whistling, back to the strand where he'd left the boat.

I watched the shadows grow even longer and listened to the croak of the ravens. Despite the sound of my son's voice behind the blackhouse, I felt surprisingly bereft. I wished we had brought one of the puppies from Kisimul with us for company. But they were still too young to leave their mother.

CHAPTER 7

E ugenius slept well, but I did not. I tossed and turned, feeling every twig hidden in the bracken. The smoored peats glowed faintly on the hearth and the full moon shone in through the doorway as I lay there, wakeful. I prayed the cure would work, and worried if I remembered it all aright. Long before the sky grew light I shook Eugenius awake, wrapped him in his plaid, and hurried him outside. The setting moon gave just enough light to pick our way. I shivered, but my son just rubbed at his eyes, sleepy and silent, while we made our way to the well. I had told him the water there would stop his seizures and, childlike, he did not question me.

The dew lay thick and wet upon the rushes and bracken that grew near the spring, but the path to Tobar Bharra was clear. The site looked often visited by the islanders, and a carved wooden cup sat on a flat rock nearby. We walked around the well sunwise the prescribed three times, and then we stopped and I brought the skull out from beneath my mantle. I saw Eugenius's eyes widen and he opened his mouth. I shushed him and knelt down, dipping the skull into the spring. "Now, drink from this," I whispered to him, handing him the grisly cup, "and then stay quiet whilst I say the charm."

He did as I asked, and obediently followed me as we walked three times around the spring. I repeated the charm. "I trample on you, seizure, as a whale tramples on the foam. Begone from this body, in the name of the triune God, and the Blessed Mary, and all the saints." Although why I believed Mary and the saints would listen to my prayers, I did not know; I had not found her responsive earlier in my life. Still, I had my son to think of now. I would fight all the demons of Hell to bring back his health, and pray to the Virgin and all the saints in heaven as well, if necessary, whether they heeded me or not.

We completed our circuit and I glimpsed the morning star shining brightly in the east. We returned to the cottage. Eugenius remained quiet, but he nodded when I asked if he was hungry, and he watched me silently while I put the skull away, built up the fire, and started cooking porridge. I wondered if I should say something to him of the skull, but he did not ask, and I did not know quite what to tell him. I set his breakfast before him, feeling awkward. At least I had made his porridge myself; I knew what was in it. Oats. Water. No dog myrtle. No wolf's bane. No hemlock. It had scorched a bit, but my son ate without complaint. Finally, stomach full, he asked to go outside and play, and when I said he might he left the house quickly.

I ate a few bites myself, feeling the lumpy mealy texture of it in my mouth and tasting the bitter burned flavor, and berated myself for my poor cooking. While I straightened our bedding, I realized again that I had never been alone with my son before, just the two of us. He had been born on Islay, but my father's household was there, and my father himself when he was not attending His Lordship. And then Eugenius had been fostered, and I had left Islay and gone to live in the witch's cave on Jura. I did not really know how to be a mother to my son, especially not when Amie seemed so capable, everything I was not.

I heard the ravens cawing and stepped outside. Eugenius had set his wooden soldiers upon the peat stack, charging some of them up the mountain while he made the noises of some great battle. I watched, smelling the breeze that carried the scent of the ocean on it, and listening to the cries of the gulls and the gannets on the wind. A rowan tree grew near the house. Whoever had lived here before must have planted it, perhaps for protection from the Good People. The raven perched on one of the branches for a moment, then landed on the ground a bit away from me, watching the scene.

"Mother, we should name the ravens," Eugenius said.

"Oh?" I replied. "And how would you name them?" My son shrugged, thinking, his little brow furrowed slightly.

"Dubh," he said, his decision made. "For they are black."
One could not argue with that.

"And what of the other, and the young one?"

Eugenius bit at his lip. "Well, perhaps Dorchadus for the
female. And the fledgling can be called MhicDubh."

I agreed those sounded like fine names. Darkness, and
Black's son. "Who won the battle, there up on the peat stack?"
I asked.

"Murchard, of course."

"And who was he fighting?" I asked.

"The MacRuairis. He was fighting for the castle. They are
not wanting to give it up."

"Kisimul?"

My son nodded. "Here, I'll show you." I followed him over
to the mound and he climbed to the top, where he had built a
fair tower, using some of the fuel piled at the top. Although he
had crumbled many peats in his vigor.

"It is a fine castle indeed," I told him. "But have a care
and don't crush the peats when you're playing. I'm thinking
it would be better to play on the ground. Here are some rocks
you can use to build a better tower, if you wish."

My son did not argue but climbed down, and so I felt my
motherly admonishment not a total failure.

The next few days passed well enough, although I had
strange dreams: visions of long red hair and white limbs

floating in deep water. But I heard of no shipwrecks, and no one brought bad news to my door, so I prayed my nightmares were merely fancies and not the Sight. Eugenius and I gained some measure of closeness, just the two of us, and as the days were long so near to midsummer, and the housekeeping easy enough at the cottage, there were plenty of hours to fill. The sun shone brightly on the island and the sea; the days grew unusually warm. I played battle with my son more times than I could count, and he tramped with me over the hills as I looked for herbs. I taught him a few songs I could remember from my own childhood. We both swatted at ever-present midges. But the days were delineated, both morning and night, by our trips to Tobar Bharra, our circumambulations about it, and my son's draughts of the holy water from the suicide's skull. And in between, always, swimming just under the surface, like the great cearban I had seen on the boat returning to Kisimul, lurked the constant thought: *Who had poisoned my son? Who had wished to do him such harm? And why?*

I wondered if I could even trust Amie, or if the food she sent was poisoned. I took to washing everything—even the oats and barley—before I cooked them. A little spring ran close by to the cottage—not the holy spring, but a simple burn that ran sweetly nearby, and I brought buckets of water back to the house for washing the plates and the food we ate, trying to keep my son safe.

And Eugenius seemed to thrive. He had no seizures, and I dared hope his illness had finally left him. But we continued our treks to the spring at Tobar Bharra, both morning and night, for I had heard the cure must be undertaken for twenty-one days, and I wished to leave nothing to chance. Until one day something changed.

It had been a black night. The faint crescent of the waning moon set in the evening sky, for we had already been at the cottage for close to two weeks and the moon had waned with the times. I slept poorly, my dreams troubled—a woman crying, someone in the water—much like the dreams I'd had previously. Despite my troubled night, I overslept and rushed to rouse Eugenius. We hastened from the cottage and started down the path. The sky had begun changing from black to a greenish color in the east that promised a fine, clear day. My son rubbed at his eyes sleepily, and held onto my fingers warmly with his other hand. We had left a little later than I'd intended, and I feared the sun would rise before we reached the well.

"Eugenius, hurry along," I said, as I quickened my own steps. My son did not reply but kept pace with me as we made our way down the path. I heard a blackbird begin its early song and walked faster.

"Mother, go slower. I can't keep up."

"We must get there before the sun rises. We've been sad slug-a-beds today."

"Why must we even go?" Eugenius complained, still sleepy and fretful. "And why must I drink from that skull? It frights me."

"It is so you will not be taken with the fits. You do not like them, do you?"

My son shook his head no, and I paused for a moment. We had neared the spring, but as I took another breath, I saw someone had been here before us.

"What is that, down by the water?" Eugenius asked. I had seen it too, something white and something dark, growing ever more visible as the sky lightened. I saw no movement. An inert mound of white cloth and darker cloth, covering—what? My gut roiled.

"Eugenius, you stay here. I will go down and look." My son opened his mouth to protest, but I forestalled him. "You must be the sentry. Keep watch. I will be back as soon as I can be." Somewhat mollified, my son agreed, and I made my way down the path that led to the well.

The blur of dark and light resolved itself into a white kertch partially covering a woman's body clothed in a linen shift and overdress of green. She lay face down with her head in the spring. Strands of her hair, unpinned and loose, floated idly in the water.

I touched her shoulder. Her body lay next to the spring, at an awkward angle, as though she had been bending down to fetch a drink. The wooden cup floated in the water where she must have dropped it. The woman's flesh felt colder than the chill air. She was most definitely dead.

I suspected I had seen that auburn hair before. Feeling sick, I yanked her head out of the spring and, with some effort, rolled the body over to look at her face. And then I recognized her. Morainn, the daughter of Fingon MacKinnon, whom I had last seen smirking at me at Kisimul. The mother of Iain Mór's bastard son, whom he had then spurned to marry Margery Bissett.

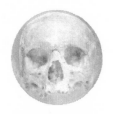

CHAPTER 8

I vomited the little my stomach held in the rushes near the spring. Then I closed the corpse's sightless blue eyes. I murmured a quick prayer, and remembered the crows. It would not do for them to get at the body. The woman's mantle lay in a heap nearby, a fine one of richly dyed green and brown wool. She must have taken it off before bending down to fetch a drink.

And then what? Had someone drowned her? I smoothed her hair some, for all that she could not feel my touch, and tried to repin the long reddish strands to neaten them somewhat. I could find only one hairpin, of silver with some filigree decoration at the top. I looked at the back of her neck and, in the growing dawn light, saw discoloration there. Bruising, finger marks, as if someone had held her tightly by the neck and forced her head under the waters of the well. Another prayer came to my lips. I ordered her garments somewhat, covered the corpse with the mantle, and returned to my son, who for once had done as I had asked and remained at the top of the rise.

"We will not be going to the spring this morning, Eugenius," I told him, "but we must go and speak with Father Isidor at the chapel."

"Why?" my son asked.

"A poor woman has died, and we must tell the Father. He will say prayers for her, and give her a blessing. And he will want to be sending someone to your foster-father. Murchard will want to know of it."

"Who is it? How did she die? Was there blood?"

I thought perhaps I should have told my son the woman slept there, but the time had passed for that stratagem. I took Eugenius's hand, glad of his youth and warmth, even glad for his incessant questions, which mirrored my own. I drew strength from him as we started towards the chapel.

We trudged up the hill. A black and white dog sleeping outside of a cottage barked at our approach but let us pass into the churchyard. I knocked on the door of the priest's house just as the first bright rays of the rising sun shone over the eastern horizon. Father Isidor came to the door, rubbing the sleep from his eyes. He gestured for us to come in. I saw a flask of uisge beatha on the table and guessed the old man had not risen early to say matins. We stood awkwardly, Eugenius shifting his weight back and forth while I told the priest what we had found at the spring. I watched Father Isidor's hands shake a bit as he reached for the flask and poured another drink into a wooden mazer.

"Are you wanting any?" he asked. I realized I was trembling myself, and thankfully acquiesced. He handed me the wooden cup; I took a swig and handed it back to him.

"Och, this will be a bad thing, I am thinking, a very bad thing indeed." He took a longer drink and drained the mazer without offering me another sip. "You are saying it is the daughter of the Green Abbot himself who lies there? And you did not see anything, or hear anything last night? You are close to the spring down there in that wee cottage."

"No, I heard nothing. We have no dog with us there to raise an alarm, and we slept soundly. Didn't we, Eugenius?"

My son agreed, his face solemn.

"Do you have a man you can send to Kisimul?" I continued. "The chief will need to know of this. And the poor woman will need burial."

"Here?" Father Isidor's pasty face turned even paler for a moment. "They'll not bury her here; not an important woman like that. Surely they'll send her back to her folk in Iona, that will be the way of it."

"And for that you'll need to send word to Himself at Kisimul." I grew impatient with this priest. "So who can take the message?"

Father Isidor picked up the flask again. Nothing came out when he tried to pour the contents into the mazer; the flask was empty. He went outside to the small cottage we had passed earlier. The dog started up at the priest's approach. "Iain," I heard Father Isidor call. "Stir yourself. There's been murder done, and we must be letting the chief know of it."

Iain emerged yawning, a big man with a rumpled head of greying hair and bits of bracken clinging to his plaid. "Murder?"

"Aye," replied Father Isidor. "A woman, down by the holy spring. Mistress Euphemia found her early this morning. Go, take the boat and rouse the chief at Kisimul." He thought for a moment. "And on your way, tell the villagers at Saltinish to gather here; we'll need men to fetch the body, and women to lay her out. I'll go and make things ready." With that he turned and went into the chapel, leaving Eugenius and myself alone with Iain.

Iain quickly left, accompanied by his dog, and was soon out of sight. I wondered if he would detour to the spring to gape at the body. I lingered at the church with Eugenius, unsure what to do next. No doubt Iain spread the news at Saltinish on his way to his boat, for it was not long before village folk began to appear at the church, gathering in the open yard before the building. They stared at me curiously. I had not met most of them, although I recognized one man and his wife who lived near our cottage. Eugenius and I had not sought out company, although this northern part of Barra was well enough populated.

News travels fast on an island. I was certain folk knew me to be a disgraced nun, with a son fostered at Kisimul. That my father kept the records for His Lordship of the Isles. That we had come to cure my son here at the holy spring, and had found the body there. A young woman with a toddling child pulled him back when he started crawling towards Eugenius. I glared back at one older woman until she lowered her gaze, and did not speak.

Talk hummed like the buzzing of summer bees, rumors about the poor corpse that had been found, and undoubtedly rumors about the woman who had found her. I closed my ears and tried not to listen, concentrating instead on tending to Eugenius, although he behaved well enough amidst the confusion. His initial energy had given way to solemn quiet as he watched the goings-on, his eyes large with curiosity.

Father Isidor emerged from the church and spoke to the villagers. "We must fetch the poor woman and bring her here to holy ground," he said. "She is not one of us, but our chief will want her to be well cared for." Apparently, the drink earlier had calmed his tremors; his voice came steadily enough now. "You, Domnhail, and you, Roderick, see to it. Take whomever you may need."

My son fidgeted by my side and pulled at my arm. "I'm hungry," he complained. The sun had risen high. And I found myself eager to escape the speculative glares of the villagers.

"I will walk with them," I offered, "and show them where she lies. Then I shall take my son home and feed him. If I am wanted, you can find me there."

The priest assented, and we followed the men down the track that led to the spring. Once again I asked Eugenius to play sentry, and the men surprisingly helped me out, saying they had need of sharp eyes to keep watch. Eugenius, flattered and proud to help such big men, complied. "It's not right for a bairn to see such things," Domnhail muttered to me as we left Eugenius and made our way down to the water, and I gave him my thanks.

Morainn still lay where I had left her, next to the well. No one appeared to have disturbed the corpse, although the hooded crow watched us curiously, cawing once or twice. The men had brought poles and cloth for a stretcher and while they saw to that, I glanced once again at the body. I had seen the bruises on the back of her neck, and now I noted a scrape across her collarbone. Rocks ringed the spring, and I guessed Morainn had struggled against whoever held her head down in the water. Whoever the murderer had been, I saw no trace of him now.

The men returned with the stretcher and I walked up the rise to where Eugenius waited. I watched them hoist the inert body onto the stretcher and start to carry it away. One arm trailed gracelessly off the stretcher as they began walking and I saw them stop a moment. Domnhail awkwardly folded the arm back in place across the woman's chest before they continued their way up the hill.

"Was that the dead woman, Mother?" my son asked. I nodded yes. "Can I go see her?"

"No, you may not," I said, and immediately regretted the sharpness of my words. Eugenius's lower lip trembled a little and I felt even worse. He was but a child, overexcited and hungry. "Let us go and have some breakfast. You must have a fine large appetite by now. It was a fine thing you did, to guard the spring while the men took her away. You were very brave. Did you see anything, while you were keeping watch so carefully?"

"Well, the crows were cawing by the cottage, and I saw some rabbits."

"And anything else?"

"Some footprints."

I had not thought to look. "And where were they?"

"Going from the holy spring. I'm hungry. Mother, I did not drink from the spring this morning. Will I have to drink twice tonight?"

"Indeed, that is a good plan, Eugenius."

I wanted to look at the footprints immediately, but we had almost reached the cottage and I knew my son was famished and tired. "Perhaps after we've eaten, you can show me those footprints you found, before the cows get into them."

My son followed me into the cottage, where I quickly found and served us the last of the oatcakes from yesterday, with butter Amie had sent, and a bit of honey. Eugenius wolfed his breakfast down and complained of still being hungry. I stirred up the fire and began making fresh ones. While Eugenius played with his toy soldiers outside, I mixed the dough and patted out the cakes, as thoughts buzzed in my mind like the great bumblebees we had passed on our way home, busy at the flowers on the machair. *Who had killed the Green Abbot's daughter? And why? Was this yet another threat to the safety of my son?*

As soon as the oatcakes were baked, I fetched Eugenius inside and watched impatiently while he ate another, the butter melting into the warm crust of it. "These are good, Mother," he told me, and I felt a sudden rush of tenderness for him. I vowed no one would harm even the tiniest hair on his sweet head while there was breath in my lungs.

"Thank you." I smiled. It was not often that anyone complimented me on my cooking. "But now, let us go and look at those footprints you found earlier. It will be an adventure."

So we set off, back towards the spring, and there, on a muddy patch of the path at the top of the rise where my son had waited, we found the prints easily enough. Large prints, made by a man, and delicate prints that must have been Morainn's. Both wearing shoes. And then one set of prints, the man's, going the other direction, returning to the beach.

Sheep and cows often roamed here from the nearby farms and I feared they would obliterate the prints before we could show them to anyone, to Murchard, or whomever he might send to tend to the corpse. I left Eugenius keeping watch, to make sure no animals disturbed the tracks, while I ran to the cottage and fetched a piece of linen, the same length I had used to wrap the skull, along with a piece of charcoal from the fire. I rushed back. Eugenius watched while I carefully traced the outline of the man's foot on the linen, and the woman's as well.

We followed the footprints towards the east but found nothing else; the tracks petered out and then ended abruptly at the beach. The tide had come in; if a boat had been there the night before, and if footprints had led to it, there was nothing to be seen of it now. But coming up the coast we saw a small birlinn flying the MacNeil's standard. As we watched, it turned in towards the land, the smaller islands in the Sound and the hills of the Uists visible behind it.

"That is Da's boat," Eugenius said, jumping with excitement. "My da's boat! And he must be on it, for the standard is flying. Were you knowing, Mother, that they only hoist the standard when he himself is on the boat?"

I said no, I had not known that, although I doubted my son heard me. He had already run ahead, shouting and waving. I followed him over towards the landing. The boat was now beached and several men had disembarked, Murchard and Griogair among them, along with other retainers and crew, and a few men at arms. Murchard greeted his foster-son with a smile and hoisted him up on his shoulders. "I've missed you, you young rascal! And you, Mistress Euphemia," he said, turning to me. "How have you both been keeping?"

"Eugenius does well, and myself also. We've been doing the cure, and he's had no fits."

"And what of this morning?" the MacNeil asked, his face suddenly grave. He set Eugenius down and my son ran over to watch the men store the oars.

"Today we did not take the cure. We found a dead woman lying in the well. Fingon MacKinnon's daughter, Morainn, the same one who visited Kisimul with her father. But I believe that is why you are here."

The MacNeil inclined his head, agreeing with me, before his eyes swept the land in front of him and the chapel on the rise of the hill.

"Yes, Iain Gillecrist brought word of it. I am thinking he is now drinking in Castlebay, telling others of what was found today, and word will be all over the island before the sun sets tonight. He told us a woman found the body." His eyes narrowed. "You?"

"Yes, and Eugenius found some footprints. We set him to look out while the men carried her up to the church, but I did not think he'd actually be finding anything. I just did not want him to see the body. At least he did not glimpse it from close up," I said, wanting to explain to Murchard that I was indeed a good mother to my son.

"Well, Amie will be glad enough to hear that, for she'd not be wanting to deal with nightmares once the lad comes home. But no doubt he was eager to view it, most boys would be. I'm surprised he obeyed you, at all." The MacNeil gave me a quick grin and then his face sobered again. "Still, this is a bad business, and the abbot will not be happy to hear of it."

"What parent would?" I returned, although my perception of the Green Abbot was not that of a kindly father. "I did not know her well," I said after a moment, thinking of the woman, and her sly comments to me. "We only met at Kisimul when she visited with her father last month."

"But you knew the abbot, I believe?"

"I was at the nunnery on Iona, as you know. And he is a powerful man there. So I met him, once or twice." I tried to keep a neutral expression on my face as I swallowed down bile. What the MacNeil did not know was none of his concern, and it would be best for everyone if he never found it out.

"Where is the poor lassie now?"

"They took her up to the church this morning."

"Well enough. We'd best go and see her. And I'll send some men to look at the spring. Griogair!" he called. I turned, and watched as Griogair strode up to his chief. The sun shone on his hair, bringing out some russet lights in the chestnut color.

"Griogair, go with Mistress Euphemia and look at the spring where she found the body. I'll go up to the church and speak with the priest. If it is indeed Morainn, we'll need to send word to her father. Is he still at Trinity?"

"I am not sure," Griogair replied. He sometimes had a thoughtful, considered way of speaking that reminded me of my grandfather. "I heard the abbot and his party were to stay there for some time. Trinity is not so far away. Morainn could have travelled here from Uist. If indeed the body is Morainn's."

"It is Morainn," I said, annoyed. I knew the woman well enough to recognize her. "We found footprints," I repeated, "Eugenius and I, leading from the beach to the spring and back. They must belong to the murderer. And to Morainn." I explained about the two sets of prints walking to the spring and the one set returning to the beach.

"Griogair, you go and look at them as well. Take my foster son and his mother; they'll show you. And I'll go up and deal with Father Isidor." Murchard scowled. "He'll be pestering me for endowments for the church, with all this trouble." Then he called two of his men to him, and they began the walk to the church on the little rise above the beach, striding rapidly across the machair.

"And what of these footprints?" Griogair asked me as we watched Murchard and his men. Eugenius had tired of watching the crew secure the boat and rejoined us. "You found them, yourself?" he said to Eugenius, with a smile. "It's sharp eyes you have, indeed. Can you show me where they are?"

Eugenius eagerly assented, his grey eyes alight with a sense of importance, and he stood a little straighter. "This way," he said and led us back along the path we had traversed a little earlier. The tracks were still there, but some sheep had passed by and marred them somewhat.

Griogair knelt to look at them while I unfolded the cloth with the tracings I had made. "Whatever made you think of that?" he said. "Indeed, it was a fine idea."

I felt my cheeks grow hot, and muttered something about my father. He had at times investigated for the Lord of the Isles, when certain matters needed to be seen to, and I had remembered him speaking of some similar stratagem when I was a young girl.

"Well, so I will just give all the credit for that idea to your father," Griogair said with a laugh. "Remind me to thank him the next time I see him." He stood up and stretched his back a moment. "But let us look around a bit, and see if there is anything else that might help us discover who the killer could be."

We walked down to the spring with Eugenius and I showed Griogair where I had found the body. There we stopped to examine some mud, along with crushed rushes and bracken where the body had lain. We could just make out some depressions where Morainn's companion must have knelt, holding her head under the spring until she drowned. "She had bruises on her neck," I told Griogair when Eugenius was not listening.

"She struggled."

I shivered, not wanting to think of it. "Yes," I agreed. "I imagine she did." My dream came back to me—long hair flowing in water, and the grinning skull—and I shuddered, feeling the struggle for breath, the rush of water into the lungs, the horror of death by drowning.

"Mistress Euphemia!" Griogair's voice came from far away. "Mistress Euphemia!"

The vision cleared and I shook my head, shaking the last of it away from me. "It is nothing," I said. "It would be a horrid way to die, that is what was coming to me."

"My brother died of drowning," Griogair said. "He was close in age to your son when it happened. Where we lived, on North Uist."

I waited. I heard the hoodie crow caw from her nest near the spring, but Griogair did not volunteer anything else, and after a moment I said, "I am sorry."

"Och, it was long ago; I was but a bairn myself," Griogair replied. "Come, let us see what else we might find here. And then I must meet with Himself up at Cille Bharra."

"Mother, Griogair, come look!" Eugenius called. He was bending over the spring, looking down with great intensity, and I feared he might topple into the waters—that my vision had not been of Morainn's death at all, but of my son's.

"Get away from there," I cried, and hurried to where he stood, reaching out to him.

"It is the water, Mother. Look! The spring is full of drops of blood!"

CHAPTER 9

Little flecks of red floated in the spring, its clear water now rusty and ruddy. Eugenius reached out and I pulled his hand back.

"Do not touch it," I warned, and crossed myself out of an old instinct.

"*Dhia*," Griogair said, standing behind us, staring at the water. His face, usually ruddy, looked pale under his tan. "It is true, then."

"What is true?" I snapped at him, fearful for my son. I moved him away from the spring and took a step back myself.

"My granny in Uist used to say that the spring here would run red with blood when there was to be a war."

"There is no war now," I said.

"No, but when the abbot hears of his daughter's murder, I'm thinking there could well be some fighting. The MacKinnons will blame Murchard for the death. The MacNeil holds this island, as you know. The MacKinnons could well take up arms against the MacNeils, and no doubt the MacRuairis would join them. They've been itching for a reason to contest Amie's marriage, saying Kisimul, and the entire isle, should have gone to her cousin."

I recalled the conversation I'd overheard between Amie and Murchard when I had first arrived at Kisimul. They had spoken of Amie's cousin Angus. Wasn't this something the Green Abbot would delight in, another chance to sow discord and weaken the Lordship of the Isles?

"About Angus... I heard Amie speaking one time. With Murchard. About Angus. I told you of it, there up on the watchtower. What do you know of him?"

Griogair shrugged. "A hot head that lad has, but that's no secret. He is full of bluster. I think he would be happy enough to try and take Kisimul back from the MacNeils. Fingon MacKinnon knows that, and he's always been a man to set others to fighting. Look at the trouble he caused the Lord of the Isles. It led to Fingon's own brother being hanged."

"Yes, and he himself was not to leave Iona," I mused. "And yet he has. To what purpose? Not a good one, I'm thinking."

Griogair bent his head in agreement. "The MacNeils have been loyal to His Lordship. That is why Donald of the Isles himself encouraged the match between Murchard and Amie."

"And if Amie does not have a son..."

"It would be all that much easier. With no MacNeil heir, Murchard's position would be weak. But what can all that have to do with the murder of MacKinnon's daughter? She did not have any dealings with Angus MacRuairi."

"She was at Kisimul, right enough. And flirted with Angus a bit while she was there. I sat near them one night but I could not hear what they spoke of."

Griogair's eyes narrowed. "Yes, but whatever they spoke of, Angus would have no reason to kill her. Especially not if he hoped for help from her father. She was an attractive woman."

For some reason that remark rankled, a little, but I did not reply. I remembered, instead, that first night I had eaten in the hall, and how Murchard himself had leaned close to Fingon's daughter while they ate side by side.

Griogair said nothing else either, and we resumed our search of the area. There seemed to be little there. The day, close to midsummer, had grown warm, and a cloud of midges came out to torture us. We swatted at them and searched the bracken and rushes near the spring. Eugenius ran here and there, saying he looked for clues. Mainly I sensed he just needed to run, letting off steam like a pot boiling on the fire.

I saw some rags tied to a rowan tree nearby, gifts to the saints from folk hereabout, hoping for healing, and I wondered how many of those prayers had been granted. I went closer. I am not sure what I sought, perhaps to wish for my son's safety. Although the saints had shown no care for me over the past five years, I still hoped they might protect my son. I did not have anything to leave for the saints, but took a moment, and a deep breath, and I made my supplication.

I stepped away from the tree. I saw my son playing next to a whin bush close to the trail leading from the well. The hoodie crow circled overhead, anxious. I feared she nested there and he might disturb the fledglings, so I walked over to check on him. Eugenius scuffed his foot in the dirt when I approached. I looked into the shrub, and there, protected by the thorny branches, saw a nest, well hidden, with three chicks within. Their beaks opened. Perhaps they mistook me for their mother.

"Come here, Eugenius. Look. See the nest, look, just there. You'll disturb her, and her young, so come away now."

My son reluctantly complied, but I stopped. A dark bit of fabric hung from a branch, caught on the spiny twigs. It looked as though someone walking, or running, by, had caught their clothing on the thorns. And it had ripped. I retrieved the scrap and examined it. A triangular piece of well-woven wool, black in color. Perhaps from someone's cloak. I called to Griogair, while Eugenius pushed close to see what I had found.

"Perhaps the killer ripped his mantle in his haste to depart," Griogair said when he saw our find. Of course, that thought had already occurred to me. I carefully folded the cloth and put it in my pouch that already held the tracing of the footprints Eugenius had found.

"I should take these up to Murchard," Griogair said, and held out his hand.

"Perhaps I should bring them myself, with you," I retorted, for some reason reluctant to let them out of my hands.

"What of your son?"

I took stock. Eugenius seemed fit enough but he had not eaten since earlier that morning, and would be getting hungry now. I had oatcakes at home, and cheese. "We will just stop by the cottage and I'll fetch him something to eat," I answered, "then he can come with us. Are you hungry?"

Griogair's eyes lightened with his smile. "Yes, breakfast was a long time ago."

So he walked with me and Eugenius to the little cottage and waited while I got some food together. Eugenius ate hungrily enough, and Griogair joined him, eating quickly, but with pleasure. "Your oatcakes have improved, Mistress," he said. I started to take offence but my annoyance evaporated like the dew on a bright morning when I saw his grin.

I put my son's wooden soldiers in a bag and gave it to him to carry, thinking Eugenius could play with them while he waited for me at the church. We left the house and made our way up the hill.

The scene there hardly resembled the sleepy chapel I had left earlier. Several of Murchard's men lounged in the courtyard, while from inside the priest's house I heard raised voices. Murchard's, and Father Isidor's, I surmised. Several other local hounds had joined Iain's black and white dog, along with one of Murchard's deerhounds, and they all yapped at each other in a corner of the space. One of Murchard's men picked at his teeth, while two others diced in a corner. Another stood in front of the door to the chapel, presumably guarding the space where I imagined poor Morainn's body lay.

The men greeted Griogair and looked at me curiously. I recognized some of them from my stay at Kisimul, and they all seemed to know Eugenius, greeting him with affection. My son beamed back at them, and within a few moments was happily pestering the dogs, who wagged their tails and licked his fingers. Griogair flashed a smile and I felt less nervous; surely Eugenius would stay safe with all these folk about him.

"Come," Griogair said. "Let us see if those prints you have traced fit the feet of the poor lass."

I nodded and started to follow him towards the chapel, but just then the door to Father Isidor's house opened and Murchard and the priest walked out.

"Och, it is Griogair," said the MacNeil. "And Mistress Euphemia as well. I did not think to see you again so soon, Mistress." He looked around at his retainers, spied Eugenius, and gave him a quick wave. "Did you discover anything, there at the well?" he asked Griogair.

"Signs of a struggle, a few footprints—those Eugenius found," Griogair replied. "The lad has sharp eyes. But come, let us go where we can speak privately."

Murchard led the way back into the priest's house. With a final glance at Eugenius, I followed. Griogair told Murchard what we had found, and I pulled the tracing of the prints out of my pouch.

"And we found this," I said, unwrapping the scrap of fabric and showing it to him.

"It could come from anything," Murchard said, dismissing me. "Many folk use dye of that color."

That was true enough, and I wrapped the remnant up and put it away again. "I know Morainn accompanied her father to Kisimul," I ventured to say, "but when they left, two weeks past, where were they going?"

"She came with her father on their way to visit Trinity Temple," said Murchard, "before your son was taken ill. That was the time we brought Eugenius with us, here, to see the spring. They lingered at Kisimul, as you know, for some weeks before they left for Trinity, before you came here. The woman would have known of the spring, she came along that day. But why would she revisit it?"

"And lord," Griogair interrupted his chief, "that same spring now runs red with droplets of blood."

"*A Dhia!*" Murchard said, crossing himself. "I heard it ran red in my grandfather's time, but I have not seen it run red in my lifetime."

"I fear that if we do not find the killer of the abbot's daughter, there will be bloodshed, and the water's warning will indeed come true," Griogair said.

Murchard looked suddenly tired, his face overshadowed by approaching evil.

"You said Morainn came with her father on their way to Trinity," Griogair continued. "They departed Kisimul close to three weeks ago, although they were here when Eugenius had his first seizures, were they not?"

I murmured my agreement and looked at Murchard.

"I remember that day all too well," Murchard said to Griogair. "The abbot and his party left the day before you took Mistress Euphemia to Jura. They told me they planned to continue on to Uist for a time. Fingon wanted to confer with some of the monks at Trinity, about what he did not say. Then he said they planned to return to Iona."

"And you have not seen Fingon since? Or Morainn?" Griogair asked.

"This is my island. I would know if they had returned," Murchard shot back, his tone vehement. "I was happy enough to see the back of the slippery bastard, and was not looking to see him again," he continued in a calmer voice. "But, for all that the Green Abbot is supposed to bide on Iona, he remains a powerful man, and I did not want to make an enemy of him for no good reason."

"Could the abbot still remain on Uist?"

"I am not sure. I will send a messenger to Trinity to see. They did not stop at Kisimul if they returned. But I've heard nothing from him since they left."

"Nor have I, my lord. And my ears are long, as you know."

A pitcher of ale sat on the table along with a few pottery cups. Murchard picked the vessel up and poured himself a drink. He gestured towards Griogair and took a long swallow. Griogair poured himself a drink and one for me as well. I took a sip. My mouth felt dry and the ale helped.

Murchard emptied his cup. "So what of the well? What did you find?"

"You already know of the footprints," Griogair replied. "It looks as though she came to the spring with another person, a man. Both of them wore shoes. Mistress Euphemia traced the prints." I set my cup down, retrieved the linen with the tracings from my bag, and Griogair showed it to his chief, spreading the cloth out on the table so Murchard could examine it.

"Aye," the chief said, refilling his cup. "Let us make sure the smaller prints belong to Morainn. For all we know these could belong to some courting couple from the village." He turned to me. "Mistress Euphemia."

"Yes?" His voice startled me and I nearly spilled my ale. "You were at the spring last night, were you not?"

"Yes, just after the sun went down. Eugenius and I go every evening, and then every morning before the sun rises. It was still gloaming when we went last night. I brought Eugenius to the spring, he took the cure, and then we left." I remembered that dusk, the purple sky while the last bits of orange deepened into the darkness, the evening star gleaming in the west. Strange to think that had been just a few hours ago. "All seemed quiet, just as usual."

"And you heard nothing during the night? You saw nothing?"

"No, I slept restlessly, but I did not hear anything unusual. And everything looked as always until we approached the spring this morning."

"And the tides? Och, I'll ask Bricius about them. But I'm thinking a high tide came in later."

"The man's footprints led back to the shoreline," I told him. "But the tide washed them away, and there was no sign of a boat by the time we reached the shore."

"It would be easy enough to bring a coracle over from Uist," mused Griogair. "Although Trinity Chapel is to the north, and a longer journey."

"Aye, but what would Morainn have been doing on Uist?" I objected. "Unless her father is still at Trinity."

"We will know that soon enough," Murchard interjected. "I've already said I'll send a messenger."

"My lord," Griogair said. "Let us first make sure these are Morainn's footprints. Is her body in the chapel?"

Murchard nodded, and led us out of the priest's house and into the small chapel. A shaft of light shone in through the open doorway, but the rest of the chapel was dark. In the dimness, from where I stood behind Griogair and Murchard, I saw the shrouded corpse lying before the altar. I wondered who had laid her out. Women from the nearby village, most likely. I thought of the lass with the baby I had seen who recoiled from Eugenius and myself. Most likely some old granny had prepared the corpse.

Just then a shadow fell across the doorway and Father Isidor came in, pushing me to one side as he walked up to Murchard.

"My lord," he said. "What are you doing here?"

"My man found some footprints. Mistress Euphemia was canny enough to make a tracing of them. We're wanting to make sure they match the corpse," Murchard replied. Father Isidor did not question him further, but neither did he leave the chapel.

"Where are her clothes?" Griogair asked the priest.

"The women put them aside someplace. Let me just be getting them for you." Father Isidor now appeared eager to comply. He disappeared into a small side room off the chancel and emerged with a bundle, which he handed to me. "Here they are, my lord. Her shoes will be in there, I'm thinking."

Murchard turned to leave the chapel, but Griogair stopped him. "My lord," he said, "should we not take a look at the body?"

I spoke up. "I saw bruising on her neck. When I found her," I explained.

"Well enough," said Murchard, crossing himself. He seemed anxious to be away. "I'll leave you to see to it, Griogair. Mistress Euphemia can help you. Let me know what you discover. If anything." He wheeled around and stalked out, followed closely by Father Isidor, leaving Griogair and I alone with the corpse.

"Well, shall we take a look? You are the wise woman, after all," Griogair said. I swallowed, my throat dry. "Where did you see the bruises? Her neck, you said?"

The body had been covered with a linen shroud. We lifted it and saw Morainn's corpse, clad in her shift, her arms crossed on her chest. With some effort we turned her so I could show Griogair what I had seen. Although the corpse had stiffened since I found her, and the blood had settled on her back, the bruises on her neck were plain enough to see, the marks of large fingers and a large hand standing out against the back of the neck and the shoulders.

"I think she was held down in the spring," I said. "And by a man, the finger marks are clear enough."

Griogair looked at the discoloration on Morainn's neck. Or what had been Morainn. Her soul had departed the body and what we looked on was but a fleshly shell, inert and lifeless. I took a breath and continued. "The waters are not that deep, there, to be drowning. She could easily have gotten out, had she just fallen in."

"Aye," said Griogair absently, intent on inspecting Morainn's face and neck. "Look, Mistress," he said suddenly. "Look here."

I bent to see. In her mouth were some water weeds, some rathum. "She must have swallowed them as she drowned," I said.

"Aye." Griogair's voice sounded far away and I remembered he had said his brother drowned as a bairn. "Poor woman. She did not deserve this end, no matter who her father is. Or what she was. Well," he continued, pulling himself together. "Let us examine her shoes. Are they in that bundle?"

I fumbled a bit as I unwrapped the parcel of clothes. Inside I saw Morainn's garments: an outer tunic of fine green wool, her shoes, some hose. They had been wrapped in her mantle, a finely woven wool tweed in a plaid of green and brown. The shoes were made of fine soft leather, with laces, still somewhat muddy from the woman's last walk to the spring. The women who cared for the body had not seen fit to clean the shoes. I unfolded the tracing and held the shoe up to it. It fit perfectly.

"So that's that, fine enough," said Griogair. "The prints are hers, indeed."

"You were not really thinking it could have been anyone else's prints?" I asked.

Griogair shrugged. "There are many people who live on this end of the island. They could even have been your prints, Mistress, although I am thinking your feet are much bigger than those dainty ones."

I sputtered, then saw Griogair's face and realized he was teasing. Embarrassed, I mumbled something and put the shoe back, making a great show of looking through the garments and folding them, so as not to have to face Griogair. I saw a small leather bag. "Here is something," I said. "Her pouch, I am thinking."

Griogair's grin vanished like the sun disappearing on a cloudy day. "Let's see what she carried inside it."

I untied the laces, opened the pouch, and peered inside. There was a comb, a little vial, a gold ring with a red agate stone. I wondered if it had been a gift from the father of her child, John of the Isles. A handkerchief. A brooch that I remembered seeing her wear at Kisimul. I wondered if the woman who had laid her out had taken it off her mantle and put it in the pouch. Nothing else.

"Does the ring fit her?" Griogair asked.

"It looks small enough." I held it out to him. The look of it nagged me, but perhaps only because I had seen her wearing it on Kisimul when she had flirted with Angus. Now, just a few weeks later, here Morainn lay, cold and dead, flirting with no one. Griogair took the ring and held it against the corpse's finger, but did not try to put it on. The dead fingers had grown stiff. Griogair shrugged and handed the ring back to me, and I replaced it in the pouch. Then I picked up the vial.

I un-stoppered it and took a sniff. Then another. The acrid scent teased at my memory. I put a little of the liquid inside on my fingertip and touched it to my tongue, felt my tongue tingle, and remembered in a rush. This vial held the same poison I had found in Kisimul, the same poison that had been given to my son.

My hand trembled as I managed to replace the stopper and put the vial back in the pouch. The last faint tingles of the aconite faded, along with the bitter taste of dog's mercury, and I fought down the urge to vomit. I saw Griogair regarding me curiously. "What is it? What's wrong?"

"This is poison, the same one that someone left for my son," I managed to reply, then turned away and started for the door of the chapel. Griogair followed quickly behind me and I felt his touch on my arm. Startled, I whirled around to face him. "What is it?" I demanded.

"You must be canny. What do you plan to do?" he asked me.

"She poisoned my son. It must have been her. She was there, at Kisimul, when Eugenius took ill. And now the same poison is here, here in her very own pouch. She tried to poison my son, the bitch that she is, and I'll leave her here, dead and cold, to rot in Hell." I had been shouting in my fury. I bit at my lower lip to stop the trembling, to keep from shouting more.

"Aye, and what will come of making this known to everyone now? What if someone planted this on her? And what of her father?"

I took a ragged breath, then another. The air felt as though it would tear my chest apart. "Her father is a randy bastard, with a viper's own heart. He'd poison his own son if it would gain him anything; he led his own brother to the hangman's noose and danced away as free as you'd please."

"I'll agree he is not a kind man. He is canny and sly. But why would either of them have cause to hurt Eugenius?" asked Griogair.

The man had no sense of Fingon's evil, I thought. He had no idea. I filled my lungs with a steadying breath and tried to stop my shaking.

"Because the boy's grandfather is close to the Lord of the Isles."

"But to strike at a child?" Griogair's puzzlement showed on his face.

"And because he is wanting to avenge himself on me."

"On you? But why?"

"Because—" I stopped. I could not disclose this to Griogair. I could not speak it at all. My chest felt tight and I could not breathe, as if I was shackled in iron chains.

"There is something else, Mistress. What is it?" Griogair repeated, looking at me with intent eyes.

When I finally found the words, they came in a rush. "The bastard raped me, on Iona. The prioress did nothing, she was afraid of his power. He holds the whole island in thrall. And I left, soon after that. My grandfather was ill, dying. I left, and when I was at home, I discovered what had happened. Beyond the rape. What he had done to me. I never went back to Iona. I could not go back."

"A Dhia!" Griogair's face paled. I thought he would move away from me, such was my shame, but he did not. "So the man is Eugenius's father?"

I couldn't say it, for the dark guilt of it, but finally nodded, avoiding his eyes. I took another searing breath. I felt wetness on my cheeks and realized I had been crying. Angrily I wiped at my cheeks with my hands.

"Who knows of this?"

"No one. I told no one what he had done. Not even my own father."

"But surely—your father!"

"No. Not even him. His heart was too full of grief over my grandfather. I let him think I'd been seduced, wanton, and refused to speak of it."

"What of the abbot? He must suspect."

"And that is why I am telling you, he would see his own son poisoned. He has, already."

"A Dhia," Griogair swore again, then said in a more considered tone, "The lad has a bit of the look of him, in the hair, and the set of the chin. But why would the abbot wish to poison Eugenius?"

"I told you, for revenge on me. And on the Lord of the Isles, and on my father as well. My father advised Himself somewhat, when the rebellion was put down ten years ago."

"Do you think the abbot kens Eugenius is his?"

"I doubt it would matter to him, the vile serpent that he is."

"And now his own daughter lies dead. And you, Mistress, found her corpse. I'm thinking you must be very canny indeed, for he'll no doubt want to put the blame for the murder on you."

My mouth went dry. I had not thought of that. "But what of the footprints?" I asked, my throat so tight I could barely speak the words.

"You could have planted the footprints."

"But you were with me, you saw them. And Eugenius found them, not I."

"Aye, I did see them, and I believe you. And Eugenius. I am just trying to think of what others, the abbot most like, could be saying of the whole affair."

"And what of the bruises on her neck? I could not have held her down... the fingers are larger, a man's hand."

"But who's to know of that, once the corpse is buried. In this heat they'll no doubt want her buried sooner rather than later."

I started to shake again. Any relief my confession had brought had now vanished. Griogair reached out and took my arm. I found the warmth of his grasp comforting and did not pull away, his touch a lifeline. "All I am saying, Mistress," he said, his voice gentle, "is that you must act wisely and hold yourself above reproach. And perhaps say nothing of what you have found in this vial, for now."

I inclined my head and moved my arm away. "What, then?"

Griogair thought. "We will tell them the prints match her shoes. And show the ring, to make sure it was hers. But say nothing of the vial of poison. You take it, and keep it hidden someplace."

"But what if it is found on me? They will accuse me of poisoning her."

"The woman did not die of poison. And you can say it is but a remedy. Most folk will not know. Only a wise woman would know it for a poison. But hide it, keep it safe."

Where, I wondered. Amongst all my other remedies? *What's another vial among so many others?* I swallowed and looked Griogair in the eyes. "All right. But what of justice for my son?"

"If it was Morainn that planted the poison for him, I'm thinking she did not act on her own. If we find her killer, I'm thinking we'll find who wanted your son dead."

"It was the abbot," I said, sure of that fact. "And he'd not kill his own daughter."

"If what you say is true, he tried to kill his own son. And you must have proof before you accuse him. But if indeed it was the abbot, he'll try again. Unless his wings are clipped for good and all. Now," Griogair said. "Can you think of anything else we could learn from Morainn's corpse, before we are leaving?"

I wanted nothing more than to run out of the chapel, take my son, and spirit him away with me to Jura, where we could be left alone. But there were other things to consider. Fosterage agreements that could not be broken. Poisoners to bring to justice. Murderers to be found. So I went with Griogair and looked the body over, searching for some sign from the dead.

There was little else to see. Some water weeds and slime beneath her well-kept fingernails, where she must have fought, pushing against the edge of the spring in an effort to free herself.

I thought of her struggling to breathe and shuddered, feeling as though my own lungs were searching for air and sucking in only water instead. But as I replaced her arms across her body I found one thing, a few short dark hairs caught between the middle and ring fingers of her right hand, as if she had pulled them out from someplace.

"Look!" I showed them to Griogair. "These could be her killer's." We wrapped them up in a bit of cloth, along with the ring and the pouch, and put it with the tracing of the shoes, to show to Murchard. I hid the vial in my own pouch, and together we left the chapel.

CHAPTER 10

Outside the sun shone through scattered clouds and the day had grown warm. I filled my lungs and smelled the scent of the summer flowers and from further away, the tang of the sea. I felt relief to smell fresh air rather than the faint odor of corruption that filled the chapel from Morainn's corpse.

"Mother, look!" I turned to see my son with Murchard's men-at-arms in the courtyard. They had been play wrestling with him, showing him some holds and throws.

"Were you badgering the men, Eugenius?" I asked as he came up to hug me. "I told you not to bother them." I gave him a quick hug, to show I was not really angry.

"It was no trouble, Mistress," said one of the men. I recognized him from Kisimul. "The young lad and I go back many years. We've missed him at the castle. Will he be returning soon, do you think?'

I muttered something vague. Griogair stood next to me, and looked anxious to find his chief. "We must speak with your foster father, Eugenius. And then we will go home."

"Home? To Kisimul?" My son's voice tore a little hole in my heart. Home was not with me.

"Not yet. Just to the cottage, for the now. You'll want some supper, will you not?"

Eugenius nodded, and I saw him scuff his feet as I followed Griogair into the priest's house, where we found Murchard pacing like one of his own restless deerhounds.

"And what did you find?" he demanded. He gestured at us to sit down at the table, and then he did so himself, perching lightly on a stool as if he might fly off it at any moment.

"The footprints we traced matched her shoe," Griogair said. "They were Morainn's. So she walked to the spring with someone, a man by the size of the prints."

"And what else?" asked Murchard.

"There was a ring in her pouch. And we found these." Griogair took the cloth from me, unwrapped it, and showed the dark hairs to Murchard. "They were between her fingers. They could well be her killer's." The hairs lay on the table, an accusation. Who? "Her neck showed bruising on the back," Griogair continued. "A man's hand, by the look of it."

"So they came by boat, and visited the spring. The bastard left after the deed was done." Murchard sighed heavily. "And now the spring water flows red, and the whole island jabbers of nothing else. And when the abbot hears his own daughter is murdered, all the whole isles will run with blood indeed."

"Unless, my lord, we could discover who killed the poor woman before her father hears of it."

"I have already sent a messenger to Trinity," Murchard said. "And one to Iona. He'll learn of it soon enough, wherever he is. No doubt he'll want to take her body to Iona for burial."

I had no desire to see Abbot Fingon MacKinnon again, and the thought of him returning to Barra chilled me to my marrow. I must have shuddered, for I caught Griogair looking at me, but I did not meet his eyes.

"Will he want to see the body?" I asked. "Or should the women shroud it for burying?"

"We'll leave her as she is for the now," replied Murchard. "He might want to see her. Although it is warm, and in the heat..." He paused a moment. "It is a sad thing, she was a bonny enough woman."

"And what of Iain MacDonald?" asked Griogair. "The father of her child, the one fostered at Largie?"

"Och, I'm thinking now that he is married to that Bissett heiress he'll not be overly upset."

"Would he have had her killed? Morainn?"

Murchard chewed on his lower lip. "Well, it was all settled right enough, before he married. And in Morainn's favor." He poured ale from the pitcher on the table into a beaker and took a swig, then continued. "Morainn received some money from him, and lands on Mull, to provide for the child. The lad had a good enough fosterage. So I'm not thinking Iain Mór would have any reason to kill the lass. The lands will not revert back to him; not now. I'm thinking the abbot will hold onto them tight enough."

"Aye, he's not one to let anything out of his clutches," I said softly, and Murchard looked at me curiously. "I must take Eugenius back to the cottage. He needs to eat, and will be tired as well. It has been a long day. How is Amie feeling?" I asked Murchard, as I stood to leave.

"Och, she misses the young boy something fierce. But she feels well enough, although she's large as a well-fed porpoise, and growing fatter by the day."

"Yes, her time will come soon enough. Another month?"

I could see Murchard try to hide a satisfied smile, and fail. "Yes, and then my son will be born."

I nodded, hoping he would have a healthy son. The day felt bleak enough, despite the sun outside, and I did not want to mar what joy he might find in it.

"Well, Mistress, good day to you then. Och, I almost forgot, Amie sent some supplies for you. Uisdean will have them. How long do you intend to stay here?"

I hesitated. Now that the spring was fouled with blood, I hesitated to continue the cure. There was no real reason, then, that Eugenius could not return to Kisimul. And I could return to Jura, to my solitary life there. Or to Colonsay, or Islay, if I wished. But I found I was not eager to part from my son.

My greed for him consumed me, the sweet smell of him, the freckles on his face, the swirl of his hair—and the funny bit that would stand up no matter how I tried to smooth it down. So I said to Murchard, "Let us wait a few days. If the spring clears, we will continue the cure."

"Aye," put in Griogair. "And while you are here, on the north of the island, you might check with anyone living near where we found those prints. Perhaps they saw or heard something in the night, that might lead us to the killer."

"That's not a bad idea," Murchard said thoughtfully. "I sent some of my men to ask today, but no one admitted to seeing anything. But they might say more to a woman."

I doubted, somewhat, that the local folk would tell me much. I was a stranger. I did not want to face their questions, their curiosity, their sly stares and suggestions. Staying quietly at the cottage, playing with my son, that was what I craved. But I could not refuse. Murchard had my son in his care. He was the lad's foster father and it would not do to alienate him. So I made my agreement and took my leave, heaving a sigh as I crossed the threshold and left the priest's house behind me.

I found Eugenius watching, spellbound, while two of Murchard's men sharpened their daggers. I collected the provisions from Uisdean and then collected my son, despite his protests. The promise of a fine dinner softened his complaints somewhat, and we made our way down the hill from the church, past the spring, and towards the little cottage that had begun to feel like home, at least to me, if not to my son.

The clouds had built up to the west, behind us, and a breeze gusted from the far side of the island. It looked as though the spell of fair weather might be ending.

When we reached the cottage, I hurried to unpack the basket Amie had sent. A big round cheese, and fresh oatcakes, as well as loaves of fine manchet bread. A leg of venison and some jugged hare. We would eat well for some days on this bounty. I thought of Amie, her frank face and warm-hearted nature, and smiled at her kindness. Outside I heard Eugenius playing. Despite the horrid discovery of Morainn's corpse— could it only have been that same morning?—I felt at peace, and perhaps even happy. I took a deep breath, enjoying the moment of grace, as delicate and ephemeral as a blue butterfly landing on a sprig of heather.

It began to rain in the night, and a gale set in. When I awoke, early the next day, I peered out the door and judged my son would be playing inside this morning; rain poured down in sheets and the air felt much colder. I looked at my son, his russet hair just visible above his blanket where he lay, deep in sleep, glad I would not have to drag him out of bed to walk to the spring to take the cure.

He had not had a single fit while we had been here. Cautiously hopeful, I busied myself sorting some of my remedies while my son slept on. I thrust the vial of poison deep in the bottom of the little kist I stored them in, wishing

I had not agreed to keep it. The skull, shrouded in a piece of cloth, sat on the shelf. Despite its covering I found myself too aware of its grinning presence. I wrapped my mantle around me tightly, feeling the chill with a little shiver, and started to make the porridge.

After my son woke and we broke our fast the day dragged. The storm kept on, the weather so poor that I doubted the abbot and his men would arrive today. Eugenius refused to play quietly and did his best to annoy me, succeeding all too well. By mid-morning the rain let up a bit, and when I suggested we walk down the path toward the beach Eugenius agreed readily. Thinking of the task Murchard had charged me with, I took our empty milk pail and the loaves of manchet bread along.

Outside we could see that the clouds had lightened a bit towards the west, and I thought perhaps the storm might blow itself out by the end of the day. We passed the place where Eugenius had found the prints the day before, today just muddy hollows in the ground. Nearer the beach a few blackhouses sat snug on the land as if they had grown there. I thought to stop and visit my neighbors, to see if any of them had heard or seen anything on the night of the murder.

The first cottage belonged to Una and Raghnall, an elderly couple. They had several cows and we had stopped there before to get milk. It seemed a good enough place to start. No one was to be seen outside, so I knocked on the door. I heard a dog bark from inside the house and after a moment or two Una appeared.

"Och, you both are fair drenched," she exclaimed. "The poor wee mite. Is it milk you're wanting, then? But you must come in, out of the wet. Come in, come in."

Inside the air was heavy and warm, redolent with the scent of the cows that shared the blackhouse. One end functioned well enough as a byre, and in the other end, separated from the livestock by a wooden partition, Una and Raghnall lived. A peat fire smoldered on the hearth and a kettle of soup hung above it, perhaps dulse and limpets by the smell of it. A tabby cat sat curled up near the fire, glaring at the black and white dog that came to greet us. The dog sniffed at us, apparently approving, and then settled by Raghnall's stool. The smell of the soup mingled with the peat smoke and odor from the byre, and we gratefully took the seats they offered close by the fire while Una set our mantles to dry nearby.

"I have fresh milk, if you're wanting some. Did you bring your pail?" she asked.

I gave her the vessel, along with some of the bread. She exclaimed her thanks, commenting on the fineness of the loaf. Raghnall said little, content enough to sit by the fire quietly with his dog, and I wondered if he had already been drinking a bit of uisge beatha to keep the cold out of his bones that day.

"Would you want a bit of soup? I'll bet the young one will not refuse me. Boys are always hungry; I should know, for haven't I raised three of them myself." She got Eugenius a bowl of broth, with a bit of bannock, and he began eating with a good appetite.

I listened while Una rattled on, loath to disturb her rambling with my questions, hoping perhaps she would speak of the murder on her own. It must be the talk of the whole island. Soon enough, she did.

"Did you know," I finally interjected, "that Eugenius here found the footprints, of the dead woman and a man, on the path near here yesterday."

Una crossed herself. "Are you saying they walked just this way? Blessed Mother! We could have been murdered while we slept!"

"You heard nothing?"

"Och no, but my ears are not as sharp as they once were. And Raghnall here, well he barely hears me."

Raghnall gave me a bit of a wink, and I found myself wondering if his deafness might not be somewhat selective, but I did not voice that. "Aren't you remembering, my heart," he said suddenly, "how the dog barked that night. It must have been late. I got up to make some water and heard them."

"I did not hear that," said Una, a little miffed. "Not at all."

"I did not want to wake you, my love," Raghnall said mildly. "But I needed to make water something awful, and I got up, and went outside, and the dog set to barking. It must have been near midnight, for the Swan was high in the sky."

"And did you see anything? Or hear anything besides the dog?"

Raghnall shook his head. "I saw nothing. I looked indeed, but then I heard a fox cry, and I grew afeared that the Good People, the fairies, were dancing near the spring, and so I called the dog back to me, and went inside."

"Och, you old man," said Una, "and so you left the hens unprotected, then, after you heard the fox?"

"The hens were fine, safe in the coop," Raghnall said. "And I think perhaps it was not a fox that I heard but the Good Folk."

"It might not have been the Good Folk," I said. "You might have heard them walking to the well. The woman, and her killer."

"Och no," Raghnall said, stubborn. "It was not that. It was the fairies that I heard."

"But is it true that you found the body?" his wife put in, her curiosity getting the better of her. "And the poor lad here with you?"

"She lay face down in the well," I said. "Drowned."

"What a terrible thing, indeed," Una exclaimed, eager for details. "Just lying there, she was? She must have slipped and fallen in. The poor thing."

I remembered the sight and shuddered. "I do not think she fell," I replied, wanting to keep the conversation going. "I think her companion held her under the water."

"Holy Mother!" Una cried, and crossed herself again. "What a wicked thing, indeed!" She fetched Eugenius another bannock, spread with butter and honey, and he settled back in his seat, appearing more interested in the dog and cat than in adult conversation.

"It is sad," I commented. "The poor woman, and her the daughter of the Green Abbot, from Iona. And what could have brought them here in the dead of night like that?"

"He is a wicked man," Una said suddenly. "Sure and the saints took his daughter from him in revenge."

I was shocked to hear her speak so strongly. "Why do you say so? What do you know of him?"

Tears filled Una's light blue eyes and began rolling down her wrinkled cheeks. Raghnall spoke for her. "She will be crying for our son. When Iain Mór of the Isles rebelled, His Lordship himself called for Barra men, and our own lord told us we must send our sons. And wasn't our youngest son, Eoghan, all eager to go, for he claimed that the life here irked him— you know what young men are like—and so he left us then, to go and battle for our lords. And just when he set sail, on a birlinn bound for Islay, there came a foul storm. A very wicked storm it was, indeed, and the boat went down, and none of the men survived at all. And my poor wife blames the abbot for it, for if it was not for his rebellion young Eoghan would never have been on that boat. She grieves for him still." Raghnall put his arm around his wife's shoulders. "There, there, my heart. Hush. Your crying will not bring him home."

"I am so sorry," I said, feeling awkward. "I did not know of this."

"Och, well, you've not been long on Barra," Raghnall said. "There were many Barra men lost that day. Many families lost their sons."

Una composed herself, drying her eyes and sniffing a little, then blew her nose. "He was a braw lad, my Eoghan. Big and tall, and strong. Was he not, Raghnall? And such a voice he had, such a fine singer. Och, the young girls were always after him, for the good looks of him, and his fine ways. Weren't they, my love?"

Raghnall nodded and looked sad as well. The two of them sat forlorn in their cozy home.

I felt we intruded. Or perhaps their grief, still so raw, made me uncomfortable. "We should take our leave. Perhaps the rain has let up."

"Aye. Do not forget your milk." Una handed me the wooden pail. "Here, fresh as you could wish, from this morning." She opened the door for us. The rain had lessened, and drops of water clung like crystals to the grass and bracken.

Eugenius and I bade her goodbye with thanks, but instead of turning back towards our cottage I suggested we walk on closer to the Traigh Ban. A few blackhouses sat nearer the strand, where the footprints had headed and the mysterious boat presumably had beached. Perhaps someone living there had seen something, although I did not know these folk at all. Murchard's charge weighed on me like lead. I regretted our isolation of the past few weeks, and feared our visit could prove awkward. But as we neared one cottage, I heard the sound of children playing and Eugenius's face brightened at the noise.

I recognized some of the children; I had seen them at the chapel the day before. They started clamoring at the sight of us, and one ran into the house for his mother. When she emerged, I could see it was the same young girl who had pulled her child away from me the day before. I swallowed, my mouth suddenly dry, wishing to take my son and run away. But there was nothing for it but to go on.

"What is it you are wanting?" she asked, clearly not pleased to see me.

"Good day," I replied. "We were just walking over to the beach, my son wished to play, and he saw your bairns. He has been lonely, while we've been staying over by the spring."

She looked at me, clearly not approving of my somewhat bedraggled tunic, the black of it now long faded to a rusty brown color. "Is it your son that's fostered with the lord at Kisimul?" she asked, although I felt sure she knew that fact very well.

"Yes indeed," I answered. "He is called Eugenius. And the lady there just sent some fine manchet bread yesterday." I got a loaf out of the bundle and offered it to her. "I'd be pleased if you would take a bit of it. You'd be doing me a favor, indeed, for she gave us more than we're able to eat."

The girl glanced at the bread, considered, then reached out her hand and took the loaf. "I thank you," she said, her eyes still guarded and her tone less than welcoming. "I am called Kenna. And you?"

"My name is Euphemia," I replied. "I come from Islay."

No doubt she knew that as well. "The wind is blowing something awful. Tam!" she called to one of the children, a lad who looked to be about Eugenius's age. "This will be Eugenius. He lives at the big castle in the bay, down to the south. He can play with you and the others for awhile."

The two boys looked at each other, sizing each other up. Then Tam gestured to my son. "Is it true you live in the castle?" he said. "And there are soldiers there?"

"Of course there are," my four-year-old son scoffed.

"Have you seen them?"

"Indeed, and they've shown me how to fight." Tam's eyes widened and the two boys walked off together, their mothers forgotten.

"Best you come in," said Kenna as we watched them rejoin the other children.

"That's a great deal of bairns," I observed. "Surely you are young to have such a large family."

Kenna gave a curt laugh. "No, they are not all mine. I live here with my mother-in-law, and some are her children. I have only one babe. Tam is my brother-in-law."

"And your husband?"

"Dead," she replied, and I wished I had not asked. I wondered if her husband had been another of the men drowned that Raghnall had spoken of.

"I am sorry to hear that, indeed," I replied, and followed her into the house. An older woman, the same one who had glared at me the day before, sat by the fire, spinning with a drop spindle. She glared at me again, but her fingers did not pause.

"Mother, this is Mistress Euphemia," Kenna introduced me. "This is my mother-in-law, Sorcha. The lady brought us some bread, Mother." She showed her mother-in-law the loaf and the woman's face lightened a bit.

"Indeed. Well, that is indeed kind of her, after she has been here on the north part of the island for so long, to finally think of us. Una told us you are staying there, near the spring."

"Yes, well, I did not want to bother anyone." I swallowed, nervous. "I saw you both up at Cille Bharra yesterday, did I not?"

The older woman nodded.

"Was it you who laid out the body of the lass that drowned? The poor woman," I said.

"Yes," Sorcha replied. "Not the first, nor the last, I've done that for. But it was sad, to do it for one so young and lovely as she was. And how did she come to fall into the spring? You found her, did you not?"

"You yourself must have seen the bruises on her neck," I countered. "Someone pushed her in and held her under. We found footprints leading to the spring from the Traigh Ban. It seemed they passed close by here. You did not hear anything that night? Or see anyone?"

I saw Kenna give her mother-in-law a sharp glance, and I wondered at it.

"No, no, we saw nothing whatever," Kenna said hastily. "Not until that Iain Beag came down from the church when the sun was already up in the sky, to tell us that Father Isidor had need of us. Could it not have been Iain's prints you found?"

"I do not think so. My son saw them early in the morning." We did not speak for a few moments, and the silence grew awkward. Kenna's toddler grew fractious and she put him to her breast, and I heard the soft sound of contented suckling, and the cries of the children playing outside the blackhouse.

"You laid out the body," I finally said to Sorcha, to break the quiet. "You saw the bruises. What was she doing here? Who do you think could have wanted to kill her?"

Sorcha shrugged her shoulders and reached again for some wool. She started the spindle turning, and pulled at the mass of wispy fibers on the distaff, which transformed under the motion of her fingers to a fine and delicate thread. "I've no way of knowing," she insisted as she worked. "The lass was not from these parts. I had never seen her before."

"Aye, she was from Iona." I stood. The noises outside had gotten louder and I heard the squeal of a pig. The other women heard it too, and turned towards the door. "I've taken too much of your time. No doubt you've much to do. But might Eugenius come and play at times with your son? Until we return to Kisimul? He gets lonely, and I'm sure the lord and lady there would appreciate the kindness to him."

Kenna appeared to soften a bit, and she looked in her mother-in-law's direction.

"Ach, I'm supposing it will do no harm," Sorcha finally said, winding the spun yarn onto the spindle and starting it whirling again. "You can bring him whenever you wish."

I thanked them and went outside where I found Eugenius caked with mud and muck, grinning widely. Tam stood behind him, equally dirty, holding a squirming pig, not fully grown. "You've been in the pigpen," I said, and looked around at the other children. "All of you."

Kenna must have heard me for she came out of the blackhouse and started yelling at the children, saying she was going for her switch. In the confusion I seized Eugenius by the hand and dragged him away from the cottage. As we walked away, I heard yowls from some of the younger children as Kenna came out of the house and the switch came down on their buttocks.

CHAPTER 11

You have been very naughty, Eugenius." I scolded my son as we walked home, trying to sound stern. Letting the pigs out and wrestling in the muck of the pigsty—surely Tam should have known better, even if Eugenius did not. My son was covered in black muck, and every breeze blew the scent of his unpleasant perfume towards me.

"But Mother, we were wrestling, and he landed on the gate, and it flew open, and then the pigs got out..."

"And now you've created extra work for Tam and his poor mother. Are you not ashamed?"

My son had the grace to hang his head a bit, for just a moment. Then he looked up at me and grinned. "But I won. I used the hold that Griogair showed me back at Kisimul. And it worked. I threw him, and didn't he fly and land in the mud, and push the gate open when he did. That's how the pig got out."

I bit my lip to keep from smiling and tried to keep my voice severe. "Well, for the trouble you've caused Tam's mother you'll need to make amends." I had to do something to punish the boy. "Tam's mother was saying that you could come back and play again with Tam," I continued, "but that was before this happened."

"But it was Tam who broke the gate, not me. And we caught most of the pigs," my son protested. "I want to go back and play again. Please? Tam told me that his sister, Kenna, saw a selkie."

"A selkie? Indeed? And when was that?"

Eugenius shrugged his shoulders. "He didn't tell me that."

When we reached home, I filled a pail with water and scrubbed my son clean, dressed him in a clean tunic and then set him with a pail of water outside to wash the bowls from the morning's porridge, while I filled another basin and wondered about what, if anything, we had learned. Someone had indeed passed by. Old Raghnall thought it might be the fairies, and whatever Sorcha and Kenna had heard or seen they were far too canny to tell me. But it seemed clear to me that they had all heard something. And what of the selkie Tam said his mother had seen? Had it been a selkie, or something, someone, else?

And who would visit Saltinish in the dark of the night, and come to the spring? And murder Morainn there? Where could they have come from? It must have been a small boat, from not too far away. I was not overly familiar with the islands nearby. Uist lay across the Sound. The smaller islands—Fuday, Hellisay, Gighay—closer by. Eriskay halfway across the Sound to Uist. But why, I pondered as I set my son's filthy tunic to soak in the basin of water, had the abbot's daughter come back to the area in any case? Why had she not returned to Iona with her father? Or did the abbot still linger on Uist?

Those were questions I could not yet answer. Perhaps Murchard's messengers would bring some news, or the abbot, when he came to claim his daughter's body, would tell us something else of his daughter's whereabouts. But that might mean I would have to speak with him, and that I had no wish to do. Perhaps Griogair could ask him, or even Murchard. I shuddered and suddenly felt very cold. I put another peat on the fire and wrapped my mantle tighter around me against the chill. But it was not the damp day that made me shiver so.

The storm continued in a desultory fashion through the night but cleared in the early morning, leaving cooler weather behind it. I rose early, started the fire, and set the porridge to cook. When I stayed alone on Jura I seldom had cooked so much. Now I had my son to feed, at least for a few days longer, until he returned to Kisimul. Eugenius still slept soundly and I stepped outside.

A pale sun strove to break through the remaining clouds blowing away towards the east. The air smelled fresh, and the hot weather of a few days ago had vanished. I pulled my mantle around me and stood by the peat stack a minute, enjoying the crisp air. If the water in the spring had cleared, perhaps Eugenius could continue his cure. Although he'd had no fits since we'd been here. I felt cautiously hopeful as I brought in a few more peats and added one to the fire, watching the flames catch and the fire strengthen, enjoying the warmth of it.

I heard Eugenius stir and turned to smile at him. "Did you have good dreams, my son?" I asked him. He smiled sleepily, but did not tell me what they were.

After we had eaten, I suggested we walk down to the spring. We left the cottage and made our way down the path, the mud squelching under our feet. My heart beat faster and I swallowed fluttering apprehension as we approached the spring, worried that something horrid awaited us there.

But nothing did. When we took the last few steps to the well all was quiet, except for the calls of the blackbirds and the whirr of insects. I bent down to look at the water, afraid it still ran with blood. A wave of relief washed over me when I saw the water, not red today, clear, just stained with peat. I smiled.

"Look, Eugenius, the water has cleared. We can continue the cure tonight," I told him, joy evident in my voice. But that proved short lived.

"Yes, Mother, and after that I will go back to Kisimul, won't I?"

I heard the croak of a raven flying overhead and felt my son's grin pierce me like a shard of broken glass, but I forced my lips into a smile. "Yes, and then you will go back to Kisimul. Perhaps five days from now, I'm thinking."

"Do you think the puppies will remember me?"

I did not have time to answer; we heard men's voices and footsteps. I thought I discerned Murchard's voice, with another voice I felt not so eager to hear. The sounds came closer and I realized the men approached the spring.

"Come, Eugenius, let us leave." But we were too late. They had arrived.

"Da!" Eugenius cried out with pleasure at the sight of his foster father, but Murchard looked preoccupied. Fingon MacKinnon accompanied him, along with a couple of Murchard's men and one of Fingon's own retainers. I pulled my mantle around me tightly and wished we had stayed at home.

"Mistress Euphemia," Murchard greeted me and gave his foster son a perfunctory hug. "The abbot has come to take his daughter home. Mistress Euphemia found the body," he explained to his guest.

"Sister Beathag," the abbot said. I felt my skin prickle. If his daughter's death grieved the man I could not tell so from his face.

"Sir. I am sorry. About your daughter," I managed to say, although I felt each word stick in my throat as I spoke.

"Yes, we are saddened indeed. But you found the body, you say?"

"Eugenius and I came to the well just before the sun rose, and found Morainn lying just here." I showed him the spot.

"Do you know," Murchard interjected, "how she came to be back on Barra? We thought she had returned with you to Iona."

So Murdach had learned that much, at least.

"Indeed," Fingon said. "But her mother has an aunt on Uist, in Cille Bhrighde, and the poor woman became ill. And my daughter went to tend her as we were close by, at Trinity, about two weeks ago. She refused to return to Iona with me, but stayed with her aunt. She cared so for the poor woman."

"It is not so far from Cille Bhrighde to Barra, just across the Sound," Murchard observed. "I can send a man over, to see what can be found out there, if you wish it."

"No, there is no need. I will stop there myself before returning to Iona. But Sister Beathag, how came you to be here? And with your son? I'd imagined him safe at Kisimul," the abbot said with a slight smile that sent shudders down my spine.

"We are here to take the cure at the well," I replied, fighting to keep my voice even.

"Did I not mention it?" Murchard said. "The lad has the falling sickness."

"Ah. Yes. I remember. How unfortunate."

Eugenius fidgeted, and I remembered that day in the kennels, the day the fits had first seized my son. I remembered the abbot's shadow landing on my poor child as he lay in the courtyard at Kisimul.

"We must go," I said, anxious and eager to be away from the man.

"We shall not keep you, Sister Beathag."

Eugenius and I made our goodbyes. I held tightly to my son as I hurried him up the track. As we walked, I wondered what Murchard had told the abbot. Had he mentioned the footprints, or the fingerprints we'd found on Morainn's neck? Although no doubt Fingon would see those for himself, if he viewed his daughter's body.

"Mother, stop! You are hurting my arm!"

I released my grip on my son and looked back. The men still stood talking at the spring, just out of sight. "I am sorry," I told him. "But aren't you in a hurry to get home? I am, indeed. Perhaps that hoodie crow has built her nest. You can go and see if you can find it."

My son rubbed at his arm and I felt even more remorse. "Come along, Eugenius," I finally said. "We've no time to dawdle."

"Yes, Mother," my son replied, and followed me dutifully to the cottage door.

The next day Eugenius and I watched from our cottage as the abbot's men carried the body of Morainn, wrapped and tied in a linen shroud, down from Cille Bharra, bearing the corpse to the galley. The sweet fragrance of incense did not entirely disguise the corrupt odor of the corpse as they carried it past. The abbot followed the procession, accompanied by Murchard.

As he approached, I fought down the urge to flee. "Ah, Sister Beathag," he said in greeting, his glance assessing and shrewd. "I carry my daughter's body back to Iona for burial." He stared at me a moment, his eyes hard. "Now, I've business to attend to." He turned from me, and spoke to one of his men.

I looked for Griogair, and saw him behind Murchard a few feet away. The abbot walked away from my cottage, following his men from the church, down the track that led to the beach. I saw Murchard bend to kiss the abbot's ring and the procession then made its way to the waiting galley. I did not leave my post, but stayed, my eyes on the galley, as the men loaded their sad bundle on board and the Green Abbot himself followed his daughter's corpse onto the ship. I remained as though on guard myself, waiting until I saw the party weigh anchor and raise the sail. The fabric filled as it caught the summer breeze that blew from the northwest, and the galley set sail down the Sound. But still I watched, not moving, until the boat vanished from my sight.

"Och, there you are, Mistress." Griogair's voice broke into my reverie. His glance followed mine, down towards the beach. "So, they have left now, gone back to Iona."

"They'll not stop at Kisimul?" I asked, still not taking my eyes from the coast.

"I think not," Griogair observed. "It is a fine day for sailing, the winds are fair, and, not to put too fine a point on it, yon corpse is beginning to stink. I think her father will want her buried sooner rather than later."

I finally looked away, the spell broken.

That afternoon I sat spinning inside the cottage while Eugenius played with his wooden gallowglasses. We had looked for the nest of the hoodie crow, and found it, a mass of sticks interwoven with strands of seaweed, with four little chicks in it already, almost ready to fledge. After that expedition we had returned to the cottage and I, anxious to make amends for my roughness with my son the day before, had made fresh oatcakes that we had eaten with honey, and another of the cheeses Amie had sent to us. We were relaxing after the meal, listening to the birds calling outside as the long afternoon drew to a close, the blackbirds near the cottage and, further off, the cries of the gulls from the Sound, when I heard footsteps. I tensed, wondering who it could be.

"Mistress Euphemia?"

"It's Griogair!" Eugenius cried, and he ran to the door to greet our guest.

"What brings you here this afternoon?" I asked.

"Och, I was out walking and smelled those oatcakes, and the scent of them drew me to your house like a lodestone. Have you any left? I've a terrible hunger on me."

"But that's not all of it, is it?" I asked him as I fetched him some oatcakes and cheese. I told him of the visits Eugenius and I had made to the neighbors, and what had come of that. "So I think they heard something, or someone, but are not wanting to say what. Raghnall is convinced he heard fairies. But the women at the croft close to the beach are keeping something back."

Griogair settled himself on a stool by the fire, near to where Eugenius was playing. "That could be, indeed."

I tried to keep my voice light and even. "Did you know the spring is running clear again? We can continue Eugenius's cure," I said, glancing at my son who was sitting on the floor next to Griogair. "Have you spoken with Murchard, or with the abbot, before he left?"

"Yes. The abbot still claims Morainn was in South Uist, in Cille Bhrighde, caring for a sick aunt. So the question is, how did she get here, and who brought her to Barra?"

"And killed her," I added.

"Aye. And killed her." Griogair sounded sad.

I thought back to what I had heard. "The abbot said he did not want Murchard to send a man over to Cille Bhrighde."

"And that sounded odd to me. Surely he must want to know what happened there."

"I heard him tell Murchard he would see to it himself."

"Aye, and Murchard said to me he thought it strange that the abbot seemed so unconcerned. Almost as if he already knew what transpired."

"Here. Eat." I handed him the platter.

"Your cooking is getting better," Griogair observed after he bit into an oatcake. I felt annoyed, although I knew I was no fine cook. "And the cheese is none so bad."

"The cheese came from Amie," I replied. "And if you do not like my cooking, do not be asking for it."

Griogair ignored this last comment. "I'm thinking, Mistress, that perhaps we should take a small boat over to Uist tomorrow, and see what we can find out for ourselves."

"But Eugenius—his cure—the spring runs clear now, and we must resume it. And what of the abbot?"

"The abbot has left, to take his daughter's body back to Iona. You saw him go yourself. Eugenius could come along with us. You'd like that, would you not?" Griogair said to my son, who grinned enthusiastically. "And it need not affect his cure. We've no need to leave before the sun is well up, and I'm thinking we'll be back well before it sets. It's not so far across the Sound."

"Do you know the name of Morainn's aunt?" I asked.

"No, but I can find out, I'm thinking, without too much trouble. Cille Bhrighde is but a small village, and everyone will know the woman who is kin to the Green Abbot."

I nodded. Yes, everyone would know that, indeed.

"Perhaps we can say you are Morainn's friend, come seeking her for some reason."

"Aye. But we cannot say we are from Barra. They will have heard of the killing already, and everyone here surely would know of it. So if I am seeking Morainn, I cannot be from Barra or I would have heard of it. And what if the abbot's man is there?"

"The abbot took his men with him when he left today. He'll not want to travel to Uist with a corpse on board, not in this heat. So we need not fear seeing him or his men at Cille Bhrighde."

I did not feel completely reassured by Griogair's reasoning, but the thought of finding out who had killed the woman proved a strong temptation. "We could say I'm coming from Islay. From Finlaggan. That is true enough. And the woman has been ill. Perhaps I'll bring a few remedies along. It might make it easier to see her, were I to offer her something."

Griogair nodded. "Mistress, do you have a different tunic?"

"Why?"

Griogair looked awkward. "It is just, if you are coming from Finlaggan you might be somewhat better dressed. And if Eugenius is introduced as your son, it might be best if you were not wearing an old nun's habit. People there may know of a child fostered on Barra with the MacNeil, whose mother was a nun."

"Amie sent some extra clothes, "I said, my jaw tight. "I might find something there that will suit."

"Well, that's settled then. I'll tell Murchard of our plan. He'll want this cleared up as fast as can be. I think we can borrow a boat from Iain Beag in Scurrival. In fact, I'd best go there now to see to that." Griogair stood, the tallness of him filling the room. "Thank you for the oatcakes," he said, grinning. "Very tasty, Mistress. I'll be coming in the morning to collect the both of you. We'll have fun, will we not, Eugenius?"

Eugenius looked up from his toy soldiers with a smile, and I wondered if we were making a mistake, to take him along. But I trusted no one here to look after him, and what harm could we come to, over on South Uist? Cille Bhrighde was but a small village, after all.

The sun rose surrounded by showers, and we rowed across the Sound to South Uist amidst rainbows arcing over the water, magical ribbons of light against the morning sky. Despite the rain the waves were mild enough and the boat, although small, had a sail. Eugenius chattered excitedly to Griogair while the man attended to the sail. I simply sat, enjoying the journey and the beauty of the day.

It is no far distance from the north end of Barra to the village of Cille Bhrighde, sitting as it does on the southwestern tip of South Uist. We skimmed past the little isle of Eriskay, and soon enough we landed on a little patch sandy beach, surrounded by grey rocks. Further down the coast we saw a stray cow, grazing on the seaweed that had washed up on the shoreline and further out in the bay some seals watched us with wide eyes, like selkies themselves.

We picked our way through the rocks, the purple dulse, and the golden bladderwrack, making our way to the little village of blackhouses that perched between the higher grey hill, a single rock formation, behind and the shore in front. Eugenius ran ahead and climbed from rock to rock, capering like some goat and ignoring my warnings to take care, which left Griogair and I to follow at a slower pace.

"You are from Uist, are you not?" I asked him.

"Indeed, from Howmore, a good bit north of here. Where the MacRuairi has his seat."

"And how did you come to serve the MacNeil, then?" I asked.

"We knew each other when we were young," Griogair said. "He was fostered in Howmore. And my mother had kin in Barra, although she herself comes from the MacVicars."

"And your father?"

"One of the MacRuairi's men, born and bred here in Uist."

"What do you know of Cille Bhrighde? And Morainn's aunt? Who might she be? Do you think she even has an aunt here, or could that have been another lie?"

"We'll find out soon enough," Griogair said as we neared the village. I called Eugenius to me and we entered the settlement, just a few blackhouses clustered against the rocky hill. A small parish church, thatched like the rest of the buildings but marked by a stone cross in the front and a stone wall marking the churchyard, stood at the end of the village. "I see the church," Griogair observed. "I wonder if there's an inn, or an alehouse?"

Some folk out and about stared at us curiously as we approached. Women sat outside their homes, spinning. One young woman ground oats in a quern, and an old man looked to be heading off to cut peats.

"Bide here," Griogair ordered, and Eugenius and I waited awkwardly while he approached the old man. They started to speak but from where I stood with my son, I could not catch the words. At first the man looked guarded but by the end of the conversation he spoke with Griogair in a friendly and animated fashion. They finished their talk and embraced, much to my surprise. The old man gestured towards one house, a bit larger and finer than the others in the village, grinned at Griogair and sauntered off. I watched Griogair as he walked back to us, a broad smile on his face.

"Good news, Mistress."

"And what would that be?"

"Well, it just turns out that that man, Padraig Dubh he is called, is my own father's cousin, through my grandmother's side. For his grandfather and my own grandmother were sister and brother. And he told me of Morainn's aunt. She is called Cristina, and lives in that big house yonder." He pointed to the larger house the old man had indicated. "And he also said," Griogair continued, looking pleased with himself, "that if we were hungry or thirsty, we might stop in to see his wife, in the little house yonder, the one with the red cow grazing in the back, for that is his own cottage and his wife makes good ale. She can give us some milk for the lad as well. Now remember, Eugenius," Griogair cautioned, "if anyone asks you, do not tell folks you are staying in Barra."

My son nodded, his eyes wide.

"Just tell them your mother is from Islay, as indeed she is, so you will be speaking the truth, indeed."

"But why am I not to say I live on Barra?" Eugenius asked.

"It is a bit of a game we are playing, lad," Griogair said.

"Like blind man's bluff?"

Griogair laughed. "Indeed, a bit like that. Are you ready? Let us visit Padraig's wife first."

We walked down the lane to the house with the red cow grazing behind it. An old woman sat outside, spinning.

"*Dhia dhuit*," she greeted us as we approached, a curious look in her eyes.

We greeted her in turn, and she continued speaking. "And who might you be? It is not all that often visitors come to this village. I saw you speaking with my husband, he's off to the peats."

"I am your husband's cousin, mistress. I am called Griogair and this woman is Euphemia. Her son, Eugenius."

"Your wife?"

"Och no, I am just bringing her over her from Islay. She is seeking Morainn, from Iona. She was told Morainn is visiting her aunt here."

The old woman frowned and looked at the bay. "That's a small boat to be traveling all the way from Islay."

"We left the large boat up at Howmore," Griogair replied easily. "I have kin there."

The woman relaxed. "And who might be this aunt be? Cristina? But I am forgetting myself, to my shame. You are kin, come inside, come inside. I've fresh milk for the young lad, and new-baked bannocks. And am I right in thinking some ale might not be amiss?" She ushered us inside and settled us by the fire. "I am called Annag. Now how is it that you are related to my Padraig?" she asked Griogair.

While Griogair satisfied Annag's questions, I let my mind wander just a bit. Annag's bannocks melted on my tongue, tasty and tender in a way that mine were not, and her ale was excellent. I finished half of a bannock, generously spread with fresh butter, and found I could eat nothing else. Eugenius ate his hungrily and I offered him what remained of mine. But Annag's quick glance caught me out.

"You do not like my cooking?" she asked.

I protested it was just that I had no appetite, and Griogair interjected, "Och, cousin, you mustn't worry over her. It is just her way. She scarce eats enough to keep a bird alive."

Annag looked at me dubiously. "Well," she sniffed, "she should be eating more, I think. Her clothes will fall off her, poor thing."

I felt strange, discussed like that by Griogair and a stranger, and tried to defend myself. "Truly, it was just the choppy boat that took my appetite. Your bannocks are tasty indeed; how is it you make them so fine?"

Annag softened a bit, and started to tell me her recipe. "I fear I'm no great cook," I told her. "Folks complain of my cooking all the time."

"It's not such a hard thing to learn, making bannocks. Did your mother not teach you?" Annag commented.

"She tried," I laughed, feeling self-conscious, "but I've no talent for cookery." I changed the topic. "But what of my friend, Morainn? She told me she would be here with her aunt, Cristina. That her auntie was ill and she was coming here to tend her."

"And why is it you've come so far to find her?"

"She is wanted in Finlaggan, at the court of Himself, the Lord of the Isles," I said, the lies coming readily enough to me. "They are wanting her for a betrothal, to a fine young man. And I wanted my son to see the western islands. So I volunteered that we would come to find her. My father is close to His Lordship, and has his ear," I added. That at least was true, as far as it went.

"You came so far in that small boat? And your husband did not come with you?"

"Oh no indeed," I lied. "My husband is dead, some years ago it was." I paused, hoping I looked appropriately bereft. "The sweating fever took him from me. I miss him everyday, but we wanted a wee adventure. Did we not, son?" I glanced at Eugenius, who nodded, his grey eyes wide as he listened to the tales I was spinning. I continued. "We came to Howmore in a grand galley, indeed, but the crew wanted rest, and so Griogair kindly brought us down here in the smaller boat."

"Aye," Annag muttered. "It's not so far from here to Howmore. But Cristina does indeed do poorly. She was struck with a fairy dart, some months ago, and now she coughs all the time, and seldom leaves her bed. She has Fiona to do for her, and Fiona's son, Fearglas. And a bonny lass was here for a time, your friend, I'm thinking she must have been. She came about two weeks gone, and such fine ways she had. A daughter to that powerful abbot from Iona, she is. But I've not seen her for some days, three or four, perhaps it would be. Since before we had that rain." Annag paused dramatically and lowered her voice a bit. "I heard the fairies took her! For no one has seen her since these past few days, not at all."

"Indeed? Perhaps she is just occupied with caring for her poor aunt," I said, and Annag grudgingly agreed that could be so.

We stayed for awhile longer, Griogair telling Annag details of his grandmother's side of the family and satisfying her curiosity about distant relatives. I wondered how he could always be so easy with people, and wondered even more at myself, sitting here with my son, dressed in another woman's clothes, eating this good woman's food, and telling her lies in return.

CHAPTER 12

After a time we took our leave, and walked towards the larger house where we'd been told Cristina dwelled. It looked as though it once had been well kept, but signs of neglect could be seen in the thatching, and the worn paint on the doorframe. As we approached, I saw a woman carrying a basin emerge from around the side of the house.

"Would you be Cristina?" I asked her, before she could go inside.

She turned and glared at us somewhat suspiciously, her eyes a remarkably pale blue. They stood out against her weathered complexion and her faded hair, brown going to grey. "What would you be wanting with her?" she demanded.

"It's not Cristina we're seeking," I explained. "I have come from Islay to seek her niece, Morainn."

"From Islay, is it?" The woman sniffed, not impressed. Her nose, large, matched her bulk.

"Indeed, from the court of His Lordship of the Isles himself."

"Well, you've come a long way for naught, I'm thinking. Morainn is not here."

"Oh no!" I cried. "She is my dearest friend! Where has she gone?"

"I'm not knowing, am I? But off she goes, four days ago, vanishing in the night. The fairies could have taken her for all I know." She crossed herself. "That's what folk are saying. Her poor aunt inside, near to dying, and so much to be done, and the girl runs off. Indeed, I did not think her to be as young and foolish as all that. Although she did not do much to help here, when it comes to that. She forever made eyes at Fearglas, my son. But he paid no mind to her, for all her fine ways." She spat on the ground. "Perhaps it is not such a bad thing that she is gone."

"Did you search for her?" Griogair asked.

The woman glared at him. "And who are you to be asking about her?"

"I told you," I put in, "I was sent from Finlaggan to fetch her back with us. Griogair brought us from Howmore, where a fine galley waits for us. But how am I to tell her father she has disappeared?"

"It's no problem of mine," the woman retorted.

"Please, might we speak with her aunt? Can she not make a guess as to where the lass has gone?"

"Did you not look for her?" Griogair demanded again, his voice more commanding this time.

"Ach, yes, of course we searched for her. The priest, Father Benneit, himself led the search. My son helped as well. They looked all over. Over the island, over to Eriskay, up the coast as far as Kildonan and over to the east towards Lochboisdale. But not a trace of her could anyone find."

I found myself surprised that Annag had not mentioned this. Surely a missing woman would have been news in a village this small. "We were just speaking with Annag, down the street, and she did not mention it at all."

The woman sniffed again. "Cristina is full of pride. She would not want the entire village to know the girl has disappeared. Father Benneit searched, along with my son. But there is no reason for the whole town know and be gossiping about the woman."

"But what of her family? What am I to tell her father?"

"Her father is a powerful man, indeed, and I do not know what you should tell him. Perhaps the Good People will send her back to us. But it is easier here with the lass gone away." She picked up the basin again.

"And where is your son today?" Griogair asked.

"He's away at the peats. And busy."

"We've come a long way," I said. "May we speak with Cristina herself? No doubt the abbot will want news of her, as well as of his daughter. You know she is his kinswoman."

"The fairies hit her with one of their darts," the woman cautioned us. "She speaks but poorly, and it is hard to understand her."

We made no move to leave and eventually the woman gave in. "I will just go and see if she is sleeping." She went back inside the house and returned a few moments later, carrying a basket of scraps. "She is sleeping, poor dearie," the woman said and set the basket down on the ground. "Ach, it is hard to get old." She rubbed her back a moment, then picked up her burden and headed behind the house, towards the hen coop.

"Well enough," said Griogair. "Perhaps we'll return later, and Cristina will be awake."

"And still not able to speak to us," I retorted, annoyed. It was a fool's errand we were on, and no mistake about it. "What do you advise we do now?"

"Let us go and speak with Father Benneit. Perhaps he can tell us something of Morainn."

"Yes, let's."

We found Father Benneit in the sacristy, a little space partitioned off from the main chapel. He was bent over polishing the cup for the Eucharist, his back to us. The gleam of the silver chalice shone in the dimness of the chapel.

"Who is it, then?" he said, without looking up from his task.

Griogair answered with a question of his own. "Father Benneit?"

The priest turned around at the unfamiliar voice. "And what can I help you with today?"

I stared. Father Benneit was young, with fine chiseled features, piercing brown eyes, and hair trimmed in the tonsure of his calling. For some reason I had expected an older man here in this tiny village.

Griogair introduced us, and explained how we were looking for Morainn. "This woman is her dear friend, come to fetch her to Islay, to the court of His Lordship. But now we hear Morainn has disappeared. The old woman yonder said you had searched for her."

Father Benneit nodded. "Yes, I did. I helped poor Fiona and Fearglas. But we found no trace of her. She just disappeared." He crossed himself. "It is ungodly."

"What happened?" Griogair asked. Eugenius and I stood back, letting him question the priest.

"Four nights ago, it was. She went out walking in the twilight, Fiona said, and never returned. We searched over as far as Lochboisdale and to the north." He looked away from us for a moment, perhaps remembering the hunt. Then he gave a sad shake of his head. "I'm thinking perhaps she just walked into the sea, and let the waves take her."

"Why? Was the poor lass distraught?"

"By all accounts, and from what I had seen, she was very close to her aunt. That would be Cristina," the priest explained. "And the poor old woman's time is close, I fear."

This did not exactly accord with what the old woman— she must be Fiona—had been telling us.

"So perhaps poor Morainn could not bear the thought of life without her aunt," he continued. This also did not accord with the Morainn I knew. "And I believe other things troubled her as well," Father Benneit added. "She had been handfasted and there was a child, I believe. But the man married an heiress and left her." That much at least I knew to be true.

"You know her father is a powerful churchman?" Griogair put in.

"Oh, yes, indeed. I knew him on Iona," Father Benneit replied.

"So what are we to tell him of all this? Women do not just disappear."

"I have told you what I believe happened. I believe the poor misguided girl took her own life. No doubt she walked into the surf. And the villagers, at least those who know of it, believe she was taken by the Good Folk, the fairies."

"But won't word get out? Sooner or later?"

Father Benneit shrugged. "That is not my concern. I saw her down by the shore that evening. No one else was about. She looked as though she had been crying, and—"

"What?" Griogair demanded.

The priest waved a hand. "No, it is nothing. Just that I had seen her with Fearglas, Fiona's son. He seemed quite taken with her. But he is young, and Morainn is a fine lady. She'd not have anything to do with him, so I doubt she cried over him. Is there anything else I can help you with? For I've things to see to, if you're not objecting."

We took our leave and stood outside the chapel a moment, wondering what to do next. The sun, high in the sky, had begun to move westward.

"That does not accord with what Fiona said of her son," I remarked to Griogair. "She told us he paid no attention to Morainn."

Griogair nodded in agreement. "Perhaps he paid more mind to her than his mother knew."

"I wonder what Cristina would say of the matter?"

"I thought she could not speak," Griogair said.

"Well, that was just what Fiona said. But I want to see her condition for myself. And am I not a Beaton, on my mother's side? Perhaps I can offer the poor woman a remedy."

"Indeed," Griogair said and then, after a moment, he spoke again. "That color suits you, Mistress. That dress."

I felt a flush rise in my cheeks. "It is just something of Amie's. An old kirtle she did not need any longer. Now, let us go back to Cristina's." Leading the way, I started back down the track to the old woman's house, Griogair and Eugenius trailing behind.

Fiona sat outside with her spindle, looking at us with narrowed eyes. "And so you spoke with Father Benneit?" she asked, as we approached her.

"Indeed. How is the poor lady now? Did she wake?"

"Not yet, otherwise I would be seeing to her. The poor thing cannot even get out of bed for her needs, and I must clean her up after she soils herself."

"I am a Beaton, on my mother's side," I interjected.

"Are you indeed?" Fiona seemed to thaw a bit. "Truly?"

I nodded. "And my grandfather was physician to the Lord of the Isles himself. He taught me a little of his skill. Perhaps, if I saw her, I could suggest a remedy to help her."

"Well, perhaps it would do no harm," Fiona said. "Come away in, now, and I'll just see if she is awake. And perhaps I can find some ale for your husband and something for your son."

Neither Griogair nor I corrected her assumption. We followed Fiona into the house, a large blackhouse with finer furnishings than most. The inside walls had once been whitewashed, but that looked to have been done a long time ago, and everything showed signs of age and wear and tear. A partition separated the outer room from the bedroom at the back. I followed Fiona into the back room, while Griogair and Eugenius, at Fiona's invitation, sat down at the trestle table by the fire.

"Cristina is the step-daughter of the MacRuairi himself, through his second wife," Fiona said to me as we walked into the bedroom. "But you know that already, no doubt, as close as you are to her niece." I nodded, thinking that explained the fine furnishings. I wondered if Cristina had ever married, and how she came to live here in Cille Bhrighde, but those questions would need to be answered later. Perhaps Annag would tell us.

Cristina lay in her bed, a real feather bed with a wooden frame and hangings, although the tapestries looked somewhat moth-eaten and faded, much like Cristina herself. Her wrinkled face looked pale, and at first I thought her to be asleep, but she opened her eyes as she heard us approach. Her eyes had clouded with age, but I could see they had once been a deep blue. She must have been a beautiful woman, in her prime. But age, along with the elf-shot, had taken its toll. The right side of her face drooped as she tried to smile, and some spittle dripped from the corners of her mouth.

"This woman is a Beaton," Fiona announced in a louder voice to Cristina. "Perhaps she'll have a remedy to help you."

I saw Cristina try to nod, but she looked a bit confused and I wondered if she had truly understood what Fiona told her. Fiona motioned to me. I approached the bed and took Cristina's frail wrist in my hand to try and read her pulse; it wavered like a flickering candle flame. A fit of coughing seized her, and I felt her struggle to catch her breath, wheezing and rattling.

"Perhaps a decoction of bramble, sloe root, and elderberry will ease her breathing. I have sloe root and bramble. Do you have elderberry on hand?"

Fiona nodded, staring at me intently, and I took a vial from my satchel. "Some poppy will keep her comfortable," I suggested. "Here is some. Just give her a little, not too much. And you must say this charm as you make the tea, and as she drinks it: 'I will heal thee, Mary will heal with me, Mary and Michael and Brigit, be with me all three. Thy strait and thy sickness be upon the earth holes, be on the grey stones, since they have firmest base.'"

As I repeated the charm Cristina seemed to relax somewhat and her coughing eased a little. I smiled at her and though she raised the left side of her lips in a smile, the right side of her mouth stubbornly drooped still. "Thann...thann," she said.

"There, there," I said. "I am Morainn's friend, come to fetch her back to Islay." She shook her head, fretful, and I felt bad for disturbing her again, now that she had quieted. "But I am also a Beaton, and those remedies should help you."

The old woman moved her head and tried to speak again. "Mor...Mor..."

"Morainn?" I guessed. Cristina nodded in answer.

"Faa, faab, vaan, aang..."

"Fearglas?" I asked.

She moved her head, restless, and I saw tears in her blue eyes.

"Do not fret," I said.

"Vuu, vuu, vaan..."

Confused, I looked for Fiona, but she had left us alone to go fetch the elderberry and some refreshment for Griogair and Eugenius in the outer room. "What is it?" I asked Cristina again. "What troubles you?"

"Mor..." Cristina repeated.

"Morainn? What of her?"

Cristina nodded yes, and I wondered what she had seen before Morainn disappeared. Although I knew what had become of the lass, and that news would grieve the old woman all the more.

"Was she alone?" I asked. Cristina moved her head, but I could not be sure if she meant to say no or yes. My confusion must have showed on my face, for all of a sudden the old woman's grip on my own hand tightened.

"Noo, vaan, bann..."

It was little use. I felt I had put the woman through too much with my questioning, and all I'd succeeded in doing was agitating her. "Rest quietly, do not fash yourself," I said to her. "Rest, and grow strong again." Cristina quieted, and her eyes closed. Eventually her breathing grew regular. When I judged her to be sleeping, I eased my hand from hers and quietly left the room.

As I entered the outer room, I saw another man seated at the table with Griogair and my son. This must be Fearglas, returned from cutting peats. A tall man, with broad shoulders and his mother's blue eyes, although he stood upright and strong where his mother stooped with age. He wiped his large hands on the towel his mother brought him and took the mazer of ale she handed him, draining it quickly.

"This woman will be a Beaton," Fiona said to Fearglas. "Come all the way from Islay, she is, searching for Morainn, with her husband and young son, here."

Fearglas's face darkened, and I saw his mouth tense as he reached down to touch the iron blade of his knife. "Ach, the woman has disappeared. I'm thinking she's gone with the fairies. We searched all over the island."

"But whatever shall I tell her father?" I asked. "He'll be distraught to hear of it."

Fearglas shrugged. "If the fairies took her there's nothing to be done for it." He crossed himself and I saw his hand move, seeking the protection of iron yet again.

I left a tincture of bramble and sloe root on the trestle table for Cristina, and a short while later, Griogair, Eugenius and I walked down the track leading to the beach. The sun was lowering in the west, and I found myself worried that we would not get back to the well in time for Eugenius's cure. I quickened my steps, and Griogair kept pace with me. Eugenius had tired, and Griogair finally picked up the lad and carried him the last bit of the way to the boat.

"Did you learn anything from the old woman?" Griogair asked, as I helped him to push the boat into the water. Eugenius now lay on Griogair's cloak in the boat, almost asleep, dreaming like a baby in a cradle, I thought. "Get in Mistress, and I'll just give it one last push."

I climbed in, and felt the boat take to the waves, and then another jostle as Griogair jumped into the boat.

"No," I answered him as we got underway. "She tried to tell me something, but the elf-shot has garbled her speech, and I could not understand. But I think she saw Morainn with someone."

"Her killer, most like," Griogair said. "Although who in that village would want to murder the woman, I do not know. Still, someone must have come with her to Barra."

"Could it have been Fearglas? Although he did not seem overly worried about her whereabouts."

"Because he knew well enough where she was; drowned in the spring on Barra," Griogair replied. I shuddered, and he gave me a smile that took a little of the sting from his words. "Here, there's a fine breeze this evening. I'll just hoist the sail and we'll soon be back."

The sun lowered in a blaze of crimson and vermillion to the west, behind Barra, as we sailed across the Sound. I wrapped my mantle around me, tight against the sea breeze, and picked up Eugenius, who still slept, enjoying the warm bulk of my son in my arms as Griogair steered the craft toward home.

CHAPTER 13

This time of year, the sun set late, but it had nearly sunk into the western sea by the time we reached Barra. Murchard's birlinn remained on the shore; he had not yet returned to Kisimul.

I hurried my drowsy son back towards the cottage, anxious to fetch the skull and get to the spring in time to continue with Eugenius's cure. But as we reached the place something felt amiss. Around the house the ravens flew, then alighted a moment, croaking, before taking flight again. The door hung ajar. Had I not closed it properly when we left that morning?

I smelled my own tense sweat, and sensed Griogair stiffen beside me. "Wait here," he commanded. I watched while he entered the cottage, my heart suddenly racing like some wild thing. I held Eugenius tightly by the arm, my fingers digging into his skin.

"What is it, Mother?" he asked. "Let go of my arm."

"Stay here," I hissed, and let him go. "But do not move until Griogair returns."

My son looked at me, his grey eyes wide. "What is it?" he repeated.

"I do not know yet," I said, "Griogair will tell us."

I do not believe much time went by before we saw Griogair emerge from the cottage, although it seemed like hours. I let the breath I had not realized I was holding out of my lungs with a rush. His face looked serious; no smile lurked on his face. "What is it?" I demanded. "Is all well?"

"You have had a visitor, Mistress," he said, his voice grave. "Come and see. It is safe," he added, as he saw me hesitate. "No one is there now. But I do not think you'll like what you find inside."

I bit at my lip to stop it from trembling and followed him into the cottage. The house had been ransacked, the stools overturned, the bedding thrown on the floor and the bracken from the mattresses fouled by urine. The pot I had left on the hearth with this morning's leftover porridge in it lay in the ashes, the porridge spilled among the peats. The chest where I kept my remedies lay opened, vials smashed on the floor, the earthy scents of the herbs and tinctures combined with the odors of ashes and piss.

"Who could have done this?" I cried, surveying the wreckage of what I had come to think of as home. Eugenius looked around and started to cry.

"Och no, lad," Griogair said, turning to Eugenius and ruffling his hair, then giving the lad a quick hug. "We shall have a fine time putting this to rights, and will pretend that the marauding O'Donnells have just raided us from across the Irish Sea. It's nothing to cry over, indeed it is not."

I managed a smile for my son, who took heart, and even began to smile himself. "Now, lad," Griogair said, "come and help me set these stools to rights, and this table as well, while your mother makes sense of her remedies. And then you and I will go outside and cut some fresh bracken for your bedding tonight."

The two busied themselves with the furniture while I surveyed the mess of my medicine chest. Most things could not be salvaged. Who could have done this, and what could they have wanted from me? Perhaps it indeed was a blessing that Eugenius and myself had been away from home this day; I shuddered to think of what might have happened if we had been here when they came. Whoever *they* might be. Although I thought I knew.

I nearly wept as I picked up masses of shards and carried them out to the midden. A few vials remained unbroken and those I carefully put away in the chest, noting what had been destroyed and what had been left to me. My inventory gave me scant comfort. I could not find the vial I had taken from

Morainn's pouch, and guessed it lay with the many other rare tinctures now soaked into the beaten earth floor of the cottage. Such a sad waste.

I found the skull rolled under one of the stools, a new, faint fracture line across the cranium. Perhaps the thieves had thrown or kicked it there. I picked it up and dusted it off, mentally apologizing to it for the indignity it had suffered. And what had the thieves been searching for? We had nothing here of value. I wore the ring my father had given me, my mother's ring, on my finger. My only other jewelry, the pin I wore on my mantle, was still securely fastened through the fabric. So what had they been after?

With a chill I saw a glint on the floor, something shiny. I bent to pick it up. A ring of gold, a ring with a red agate. I stood, frozen, as I recognized the ring, and my heart raced despite my inability to move. For I had seen it on Morainn, and now I remembered where I had seen it before. I had seen it on Fingon's hand as he had forced me, those five years ago. The ring had bitten into my lips as he held his hand over my mouth, stifling my cries. I relived the horror, lost in the past. The ring belonged to Fingon MacKinnon, the Abbot of Iona.

I heard a noise at the door and spun around, ready to flee. But only my son and Griogair stood in the doorway, their arms filled with fresh-cut bracken, the bulk of it nearly hiding my son from view.

"What is it, Mistress?" Griogair asked, dropping the bracken to the floor as he saw my face. "What is wrong?"

My throat closed and I could not speak. Mute, I held my hand out to him.

"A ring," he said, taking it in his fingers and examining it. "Morainn's ring. The one we found in her pouch."

"The Green Abbot's ring," I managed to say, in a faint voice. "I found it there, on the floor, under the stool. And the vial of poison is gone. He was here, Griogair. This will be his doing."

"The vial is not broken?"

"I cannot tell, it is all such a shambles. Look at these shards. What if he stole it back?"

"Would he have known what it was?"

"Indeed he would have, if he gave it to his daughter."

"Well, I am knowing where you got that vial, and how long you've had it. I can vouch for you well enough, should it be needed. But let us hope he smashed it, not knowing what he had."

I found that hope faint indeed, but there was nothing to be done for it now.

"Are you sure the ring is his?" Griogair asked.

I nodded, reliving the memory, and started to shudder.

"But why leave it here? To what purpose?"

I found my voice. "He is a devil; he will torment me simply because he can. He will torment me because I did not go running to my father, telling him of what happened those years ago. You are the only person who knows what really happened. And Fingon may not know who fathered my child, but he guesses. And so he plays with me, like a cat toying with a mouse."

"It is not safe for you to stay here," Griogair observed as he pocketed the ring. I felt relief not to have to see the hateful thing, so I did not object. "I will keep this, for now," Griogair added. "He need not know you found it. Perhaps that will confound him. But you should take Eugenius and return to Kisimul."

"Perhaps, but what of Eugenius's cure?" The sudden lump in my throat once more made it hard to speak. I felt as though I had swallowed a stone. I thought of my son, in the grip of the seizures, and hot tears filled my eyes.

"How many days does he lack? Only three? Och, the saints will surely grant the cure to the lad, rather than have him stay here with a madman on the loose. And he's not had a fit these many days, has he?"

"Not since we were coming here," I admitted, finding some comfort in Griogair's words, although I was not sure I believed them. I dabbed at my eyes with my sleeve, wiped at my nose, and took in a ragged breath.

"So, you see, they've already granted him the cure," Griogair continued. "The saints. You need not be afraid. And Amie will no doubt be happy to see the lad again, although her own time is coming soon."

And that also troubled me, although I could not even speak of it. Once we left here, I would lose this special time with my son. The agreement was that Eugenius be fostered at Kisimul, and that could not be undone. Not without great trouble, and insult to Amie and Murchard, allies of the Lord of the Isles who had only treated my son with the greatest kindness. No, nothing whatsoever could be done about that. Eugenius would stay at Kisimul, and I might visit sometimes, or he might visit me. But that was all there would be. I felt my throat would burst with the sorrow of it, and yet I could not even voice my sadness.

"All right, then," I finally said, making the decision. "Eugenius and I will return to Kisimul with Murchard, when he sails. And after Amie has her child, I will return to Jura." I looked around the little cottage. "But we'll have to sleep here tonight. Perhaps you could stay? I'm afeard they might return."

"Indeed, I think that would be wise," said Griogair. He bent to replace the bracken on the bed and then made a bed for himself before the door. "Rest easy, Mistress. No one will get in."

I did not think sleep would come easily to me, but as I listened to Griogair settling himself before the door and to the even breathing of my son, I closed my eyes, and slept soundly through the night.

Eugenius and I visited the well that evening, with Griogair following along, and made one more pilgrimage the next morning before the sun rose above the horizon. The dawn's rays sent fingers of light through eastern clouds. My son sipped his final draught of the holy waters, and I murmured the incantations one last time, praying to the saints to heal him, as the sun crested the horizon. We returned to the cottage, I gathered our belongings together, and we closed the door behind us. The ravens croaked at us, a farewell, I thought fancifully. Then I turned my back on the little house, and the ravens as well, and followed Griogair and my son past the spring and up the hill to Cille Bharra.

Eugenius chattered gaily as we walked, eager to be travelling on the galley with his foster father and anxious to see Amie again. I said less, and Griogair also did not speak much. We left two bundles containing our clothes near the doorway of the cottage, planning to fetch them on our way to the galley. We would pass close by on the way to the landing site, but I carried what remained of my remedy chest with me, along with the skull, not wanting to leave them unattended. For some reason I did not fully understand, I also brought Eugenius's wooden gallowglass soldiers that Griogair himself had carved for him.

The hoodie crow flew about us as we mounted the hill. I would miss her company, I thought, as we neared the church.

From the hill I could look over to the Sound and see Murchard's galley moored on the beach. The day had dawned fair, so most likely Murchard would leave today for Kisimul, and take us back with him.

We passed through the doorway in the grey stone wall that surrounded the churchyard. Inside, folk bustled with activity. I heard Murchard's voice. The door to the priest's house opened and Murchard emerged. "Och, and it is Griogair," Murchard said. "And my foster-son!" He gave Eugenius a quick hug and smiled at me. "And Mistress Euphemia."

"Eugenius's cure is completed," I said to Murchard, as my son ran off to greet some of Murchard's men, "and we hoped we might return to Kisimul with you when you leave."

"Indeed, and the sight of the boy will do my wife great good, I'm thinking. And you as well, of course, Mistress."

I inclined my head. "I will stay until your wife gives birth, then I plan to return to home."

Murchard nodded in agreement and then turned to Griogair, leaving me alone. I fancied I saw relief on his face. They spoke a few moments, then Murchard beckoned to me.

"Mistress Euphemia, Griogair has been telling me of your trip to Uist."

"Yes. Folk there had not yet heard of the murder. Some think Morainn has gone with the fairies. I believe the old woman, her aunt, knew something, but her speech is garbled, I could not understand it. And her aunt's servant has a son, Fearglas, who may know something of her disappearance. The priest says he saw her with the lad, and then later saw her crying."

Murchard's eyes narrowed. "That does not sound like Morainn. But perhaps all women are prone to tears. And the neighbors, here?"

"They told me nothing of much use. But I think the two women in the house closest to the beach, Kenna and Sorcha, either saw or heard something that night. One of the boys there said Kenna had seen a selkie, but it might have been something, or someone, else. And the old man, Raghnall, also heard something that night, voices, but he took it to be the Good Folk."

"And what will happen when the folk at Cille Bhrighde learn of the slaying?"

"We said I had just come from Islay. Which is true enough. So I would not have been knowing of it then."

"I'm not altogether liking that," said Murchard. "News travels fast on these islands. But there's nothing to be done about that now." He sighed, then straightened his posture. "And what is all this Griogair was telling me of thieves at the cottage?"

The reminder chilled me. "Someone seemed to be looking for something. They ransacked my remedy chest. But we had nothing there worth stealing." I did not know if Griogair had told his chief that the most likely thief was the Green Abbot, who supposedly had left the island, and I hesitated to speak of that myself, for that would lead to other questions I had no desire to answer. So I added nothing more, but stood and looked on as Murchard's men scurried about, preparing to leave Cille Bharra.

Griogair approached. "They are almost ready. We can walk down to the beach and pick up those bundles, and meet them at the galley."

"Where is Eugenius?" I could not keep my voice entirely calm, although I knew nothing could have befallen my son here.

"As safe as can be, with his foster-father's bowman. Pestering him to let him have a turn at shooting. But the men are far too busy for that, the now. Look, here they come."

I looked and saw a party of Murchard's men depart the entrance of the compound. Murchard's old captain had my son on his shoulders and Eugenius waved gaily as he passed me.

"So there, Mistress," Griogair said, "he is safe and sound enough. Shall we go and retrieve those bundles? We can meet them at the shore."

I nodded and set off back down the hill, past the spring, to the cottage. The hoodie crow, still there, squawked as we picked up our burdens. Griogair joked about the size and weight of his bundle but I barely heard him. The crow squawked again, and I bade her a mental farewell as I hoisted my own bundle and followed Griogair down the track. Soon enough, we stood on the white sands of the beach and watched while the men loaded the galley, stowing the small cargo and readying the sails.

Eugenius left Murchard's men, where he could only have been getting in the way, and capered around us, eager for the short voyage and to be returning home. The crew finished their tasks. And shortly after that, we, along with the remainder of Murchard's men and the chief himself, boarded the birlinn.

"It's a fine day indeed for a sail," Murchard said to me as the men bustled around us. I watched while the men hoisted the sails and stretched the ropes, tying the knots efficiently with skill that came from long practice. I took a deep breath, and smelled the salt on the breeze as the sails filled with the wind. " 'Tis just a short trip, as you know," Murchard added, watching me a moment. "We'll be back at Kisimul well in time for dinner."

CHAPTER 14

We reached Kisimul in good time and found Amie waiting to greet us, looking much larger than when we had left a few weeks ago. Despite her bulk the woman bloomed like some wild rose. Eugenius ran to greet her as we disembarked and she enfolded my son in her embrace. "Och, it has been so long since I have seen you, white love," she told my son.

"We went to Uist one day, and there were pet ravens there, too," Eugenius said, then rambled on in no particular order. "And the spring had red water, like blood, and then it cleared. And a woman died there."

"Were you seeing all of that yourself?" Amie asked, with a strange note in her voice.

"No, for Mother would not let me get close."

"And a good thing that was, indeed," I heard Amie say softly. I caught her eyes and she gave me a wink. "But come along, I'll see you to your room. Mistress," she said, turning towards me, "I have spoken with Murchard. Would you be willing to stay until my bairn is born?"

"If you would wish it," I said. "Eugenius's cure is complete. I am no midwife, but if you wish me to stay on, I am happy to."

"Yes, that would be kind of you. And Eugenius will enjoy it as well," Amie added, although I was not sure that my son cared, much. I myself had no wish to leave him and was grateful for the chance to stay a bit longer.

The next week or so passed quietly enough. I helped Amie prepare for the new baby, hemming linen for swaddling clothes and diapers. Eugenius stayed well, with no fits, and spent a great deal of time in the kennels. I allowed myself to hope that the cure at the spring had worked.

Murchard heard nothing else from the abbot about the death of Morainn; eventually he sent a man to Cille Bhrighde to see what the villagers knew of it. By this time folk there had heard of the murder, and the village was full of talk, but no one had insight as to who might have wanted her dead, nor who could have taken her to Barra. Fearglas swore he was innocent. Murchard's man also brought the news that Cristina had died. I was sad to hear that but, after all was said, the woman had been old, and ill, and elf-shot.

Snug in Kisimul as we were, watching Amie prepare for her new child during the long summer days, Cille Bhrighde and Saltinish seemed far away. Still, sometimes when I glanced at the cradle that sat in the corner of their room, by the grand bed Amie shared with her husband, I thought I saw a winding sheet thrown carelessly over the blankets. Not enough to completely cover the cradle, and at times I could barely see it at all. So I prayed, despite the omen, that things would go well with the birth and did not speak of it to Amie, not wanting to distress her.

My hostess flew into a fit of cleaning and set the maidservants to scrubbing every floor in the living areas, whitewashing the walls, and beating clean the curtains on the great bed. The cradle lay ready while Amie and I stitched a few final baby clothes. She had chosen a young maidservant to help her nurse the baby, when it came, and spent hours making sure the lass knew where things were kept and how she liked things to be done.

The July heat grew sultry and oppressive although Bricius, when I happened to ask him of it on one hot afternoon, swore that the weather would soon break. Even the gulls and gannets seemed enervated by the heat, sullen and warm.

He proved correct. That night a breeze played with the still air, lifting and freshening the atmosphere. The breeze soon became a gale and cooler winds swirled around the castle walls, while black clouds gathered overhead.

Amie, who had eaten heartily at the noon meal, complained of a bellyache that quickly turned to cramping, and then full-blown contractions. Despite the gale some men were sent to row to fetch old Murdina, who served as the midwife for Castlebay. While they were gone on their errand Amie vomited all the food she had eaten earlier, and kept vomiting, finally puking up a bit of green bile. Murdina arrived on the scene just as the rain began falling in sheets.

Although I remembered Eugenius's birth, I myself am no midwife and I met Murdina with relief. The old woman quickly took charge.

"Keep her walking," Murdina ordered me, while Amie groaned. I sponged her face and muttered prayers and incantations for an easy birth while Murdina made sure everything lay in readiness in the birthing chamber. Soon Amie's contractions came more quickly, and walking became impossible. It did not look to be a prolonged labor, and the babe was not, after all, her first. Murdina tucked an iron blade under the mattress, to prevent the fairy folk from stealing the babe and replacing it with some wan and scrawny changeling, and Amie lay down, gasping as another contraction took her in its wake.

"She'll not be much longer, I'm thinking," I remembered Murdina saying to me at some point in that long night, and her prediction proved correct. Close to daybreak Amie was delivered of a small but healthy boy.

I looked on as Amie, her eyes shining, took the wee bundle of her swaddled son from Murdina's arms and set the babe to her breast. The old woman then took a burning brand and carried it around the bed where Amie lay, sunwise three times, chanting a prayer to protect the new mother and child from the fairy folk. Then she took a small silver coin and tucked it in the baby's hand. He gripped it tightly.

"He's got a good, strong grip," Murdina said. "He'll not be letting the luck run through his fingers."

The castle priest came in and blessed the child and then Murchard was allowed in to see his son. Beaming, he held the boy, kissed his wife on her forehead, pronounced himself well pleased, and announced that the lad would be named Roderick. He poured a dram for the priest, one for the midwife, and me, then took one himself.

The sun rose over the eastern horizon, and the last of the clouds from last night's storm blew away to the west. I murmured a prayer for the safety of the new mother and her child and then went to catch a little sleep in the room I shared with Eugenius. I felt sure that my son would be demanding to see his new foster brother as soon as he woke and heard the news of the birth.

For now Eugenius slept deeply, curled up in his blanket like a puppy. I thought of the little wrinkled face of the newborn Roderick and remembered Eugenius's own birth, four years earlier on Islay. It had not been an easy one. My body had fought my son's arrival, struggling with shame and grief. But when the midwife laid my son in my arms, and he had opened his sea-grey eyes to me, I had fallen helplessly in love. As it seemed Amie had now done. I murmured another charm, this one for the safety of my own son, before I lay down and closed my gritty, tired eyes.

A few hours later I roused myself and neatened my hair, and glanced around the chamber. Eugenius's bed lay empty and I surmised that the scamp had snuck out to the kennels. I left to check on Amie, and to find my own son. The new mother slept peacefully enough, as did the babe at her side. Murdina told me that although the babe was small, he had a good suck, and had fed well enough. And questioning of Murchard's men revealed that Eugenius had indeed gone to the kennels, trailing after the groom. I went to fetch him and bring him back to meet the new arrival.

"He's small," my son announced as he stood on tiptoe to see the little bundle Amie, now awake, held in her arms.

"Aye, but he'll soon grow bigger," she assured him with a smile. "And he'll be a fine playmate, for now you both shall be foster-brothers, closer even than flesh and blood."

Eugenius nodded dutifully, but he looked unconvinced. "Can I go back to the kennels and play with the puppies again?" he asked, rapidly losing interest in the baby. Amie and I both smiled, and agreed that he might go.

The day progressed and Murdina announced herself pleased with Amie's progress. She began to speak of returning to her own home in Castlebay, perhaps even the next day, since I remained there to tend to Amie. In the midst of this conversation, I heard a commotion in the castle yard. Curious about the clamor, I left the room and ventured outside, to hear that the watch had sighted an approaching birlinn. That seemed common enough, for ships often stopped at Kisimul to treat with Murchard. I returned to Amie's chamber, where Murdina stood giving instructions to Amie's maidservant. Intent on listening to Murdina's advice, I paid little attention when the door to the bedchamber opened. One of Murchard's attendants, a young lad just a few years into his teens, came in, awkward and hesitant.

"What is it?" I demanded, most of my attention still focused on Murdina's instructions.

"Mistress, they are asking for you," said the lad, shifting his weight and averting his eyes from the bed where his chief's wife lay nursing the new baby.

"Why would that be? Tell him his wife and son are resting and should not be disturbed."

Shadows filled the doorway and several armed men entered the room. I glanced up in alarm. They were not Murchard's men, although a few of the faces seemed familiar.

"Mistress Euphemia." I heard Murchard's voice boom from outside the door. "Come away into the courtyard. We need you there."

"Whatever can it be, then?" I responded foolishly, as I moved through the doorway and outside. The men came behind me, and I felt surrounded, hemmed in, but my first thought was of Eugenius. Had he suffered another fit? "Is all well with my son?" I demanded, my voice shrill with concern.

"Mistress, it is not that," Murchard said, and even his normally confident voice sounded hesitant. "These are the abbot's men. And they are accusing you of the murder of Cristina, the old woman from Cille Bhrighde in Uist."

I stared at Murchard. My heart stopped dead still for an instant, then began pounding furiously. "But that cannot be! It is preposterous! I saw the woman only one time—how can they accuse me?"

"They say, Mistress, that they have proof against you."

"What proof? There can be no proof, for I did not harm her."

"But you did see her?" Murchard asked.

"Aye, and left a vial of poppy and another of coughing remedies with her servant. Fiona, the woman's name was."

"These men claim you left poison for the old woman. And that she died thereafter." One of the abbot's men interrupted Murchard, and spoke to him urgently in a low voice. I could not catch the words, for I only heard the hammering of my own heart. The courtyard seemed to have shrunk to a narrow tunnel, and I was barely aware of two more of the abbot's men drawing closer to me, one on either side, as I watched Murchard and the first man.

The man stopped his whispering, and Murchard continued, speaking gently to me. "They say that the abbot himself has the vial of poison, that he obtained it from the old woman's servant. He insists these men bring you to Iona, for trial, both for the slaying of his kinswoman, Cristina, and for plotting in the death of his own daughter."

"No, it was poppy I gave to her, only poppy. And sloe root, and bramble, for her coughing." I laughed, a strange laugh that came from fear. "Why should I want to poison an old woman whom I had never met before, or the abbot's poor daughter, for that matter. Morainn was not killed by poison—she was strangled and drowned. You saw the bruises on her neck yourself. They were a man's hand."

"Indeed. A fair question, that is," Murchard replied, but the two men on either side of me reached out and grabbed my arms. I shrieked with terror and tried to twist away, but they held firm despite my panic. Or perhaps they enjoyed that, and gripped me the tighter for it.

"Let her go!" roared Murchard. "This woman is my guest!" I saw some of his own guard advance upon the visitors. With relief I felt the men release me. Somehow, I remained standing, and did not sink into a groveling heap on the floor.

"I'll not go back to Iona," I managed to say. "I'll not go there, to that man."

"And the old woman herself was from Uist, from Cille Bhrighde, so why would the Gorrie at Lochboisdale not have jurisdiction? What has the Green Abbot to do with all of this?" Murchard asked the abbot's men, reasonably enough. He considered for a moment while I stood, not breathing, watching him like a rabbit watches the fox.

"No, I'll not send her with you," Murchard finally said to the abbot's head man. "She's a guest in my hall. I'll hold her here, and if the abbot seeks to show her guilt, he can bring the proof here himself."

"I am innocent. There is no proof," I repeated, helplessly.

"I have heard you, Mistress, and you are our guest, as I have said."

The abbot's henchman whispered a few words in Murchard's ear, and the MacNeil's face darkened. The man withdrew to where the others from Iona stood, hands near their broadswords. Murchard stared at them, and then at his own men, who stood tense and at the ready. Then he spoke again.

"However, with a wee babe and my wife just recovering from her birth, and you an accused murderess, I can take no chances. You must understand. So I will keep you under guard until this matter is resolved." He glared at the men from Iona. "You may assure your master of that."

"But I am innocent," I repeated. "I've done nothing wrong."

"The abbot says he has proof, Mistress, and until that has been dealt with, heard and adjudicated, I will take no chances

with the life of my wife and my son. You understand, of course."
He turned to the abbot's messenger. "You and your crew will
stay and dine with us, before you leave."

My wits left me and fear turned my tongue to lead. I
could only stare at my son's foster father as the abbot's men
grudgingly assented, while two of Murchard's men stood close
by me.

Then I remembered. The vials, smashed and missing from
my remedy chest, when the cottage had been ransacked.

I had hoped it was broken, the vial of poison that had been
used on my son, the noxious liquid soaked into the earthen
floor of the house and the fragments of the vial smashed, now
lying on the muckheap. But that hope had proved vain. The
vial had not been destroyed, it had been stolen. To trap me.
And there was the ring, the abbot's ring that he had left behind,
to taunt and torment me. Still, Griogair had kept the ring, had
proof of who ransacked the cottage and could have stolen the
vial. Griogair could speak for me, and prove my innocence.

I had forgotten Griogair in my fear, but now my eyes
darted over the faces of Murchard's men, scanning desperately,
looking for him. I did not see him, and belatedly realized I
had not seen Griogair for some days. With the preparations
for the birth, and the storm and Amie's labor I had been busy,
preoccupied with women's matters.

Frozen in my panic, I could not ask for him now. Two
of Murchard's men, their faces sympathetic but their force
unassailable, ushered me, not back to my own little chamber

near Amie's birthing room, but to a small room off the guard tower, with a door that could be locked and a tiny slit window that let a single ray of light into the darkness. And there they left me, alone.

CHAPTER 15

I heard the metal bolt clang shut behind me and collapsed in a heap on the straw covered floor of the cell, sobbing dry sobs. The dark room brought my demons to the fore and the brassy taste of fear filled my mouth. I swallowed bile and vomit. It was as if I was once again under Fingon's control and under his attack; I felt his hands on me, the pressure of his stubby fingers on my arms and throat as he held me captive against him, pushing me, bending me to his will. I could not move, frozen with terror, and had let him do what he wanted. I smelled his scent—it filled my nostrils, a greasy, nauseating, unctuous smell of incense and male musk—and felt once more the stabbing pain as he had taken me, that day five years earlier, and then sent me, bruised and bleeding, back to the nunnery.

I must at length have lost consciousness. When I came back to myself, I vomited in a corner of the room and then dragged myself up. I sat on the floor—for there was no stool to sit on—with my arms tight around my knees, rocking back and forth for comfort, tears streaming down my face, until there were no tears left.

It was indeed a cell. There was no pretense at a guest room. The floor was strewn with a bit of moldy straw and the room smelled of piss and, now, of vomit as well. The light from the window slit had darkened. It must be late afternoon now, or evening. My parched throat ached when I tried to swallow, the taste of vomit still on my tongue. Did Murchard plan to leave me here without light or water, or pity?

I felt something on my little finger, a slip of cool metal—my mother's own ring, which my father had given me back when I visited him on Colonsay that rainy day. The feel of it calmed me, and I twisted it back and forth on my finger as my breathing grew somewhat regular and my panic subsided a bit.

Surely Murchard would send someone to see to me, sometime soon. I had done nothing to him, and the case against me was not proven. My father had influence, and Murchard, despite his fear of the abbot, surely had greater respect for the Lord of the Isles. He would not treat me so poorly without good cause. The light from the slit window dimmed further, and I realized it must be twilight. I wiped my face on my sleeve and tried to compose myself, straightening my hair and garments somewhat. And I waited.

The light had all but vanished when I heard the welcome noise of the iron bolt sliding back as someone outside opened the lock. The door creaked open. I saw light, and smelled a burning torch.

"Ach, Mistress!" I heard Morag's voice, and another voice I recognized as Bricius's.

"Are you well?" Morag asked as they came further in. "What a stench. We've brought food, and blankets. And some fresh straw for the floor."

I nodded, not wanting to let the woman see how distraught I had been, glad the darkness hid my face from her. I watched by the flickers of torchlight while Morag set to sweeping out the old, dirty straw and Bricius brought in a pallet and stool, along with some blankets. I heard someone bolt the door behind them.

"How is Amie?" I asked. "And the babe?"

"They're keeping well. She is still tired after her labor and we thought it better not to tell her of what had happened. Or rather, Himself told us not to, not wanting to distress her. She slept with her son most of the day."

"So she knows nothing of this?" I saw Morag nod, the torchlight shining on her white kertch. "And Eugenius?" I asked. "Where is my son?"

Morag snorted. "Well, with no one to gainsay him, he's been in the kennels all day. It is a good thing that Uisdean, there, likes the lad."

I did not ask about Murchard, but Bricius must have guessed my thoughts.

"Mistress, Himself sent us. With his apologies for holding you this way. But he felt he had to wait until those men from Iona were not watching him like a hawk. They're at the feast now, and so we came to bring you these."

"And Griogair?" I finally asked. "What of him? He could vouch for me."

"The Chief sent Griogair off on business to the Gorrie," Bricius answered. "A day or two ago, it was. I'm thinking he must have stopped to visit with his sister there in Howmore. But he'll be back soon enough, I'm thinking."

"Bricius, when he returns, I must see him. Can you let him know that?"

The old man considered. "Indeed, and I can," he finally answered. He looked at me a moment and I saw in the torchlight the ghost of a smile on his face. "Don't fash yourself, Mistress. Yon abbot is a sleek bird, but a bit too fond of his own fine plumage."

"That's as may be," I muttered, "but he's snared me in his net just the same." I shuddered.

The room was set to rights now, and I looked gratefully at the pallet and blanket, the stool, and the chamber pot. A bowl covered with a linen napkin sat on the stool, along with a pitcher and cup. And, thank the saints, a candle.

"We'll leave you now, Mistress," Morag said, awkward, while I stared at them both. "And don't worry for Eugenius. I'll make sure he's put to bed proper."

I nodded my thanks and Bricius lit the candle from the torch. Then they called to the guard outside. The door creaked open, they left, and I heard the bolt clang shut behind them. But now I sat on a pallet, with a blanket, and stared at a circle of glowing candlelight.

I did sleep that night, the warmth of the wool blanket wrapped snugly around me, and although I could not eat the night before, I managed to swallow some of the cold oatcakes the next morning; the taste of them sweet on my tongue despite the dryness of my mouth. The walls of the cell were thick stone, and sounds from the courtyard outside were muffled, although I strained my ears to listen. Surely the Iona men would leave soon, and then perhaps I could be released. Surely Griogair would return soon from Uist, with the proof of my innocence and the corroboration of my story.

Although, as yet, no one had really heard my story. I had been far too dumbfounded to speak of it the previous afternoon, shocked by the charges laid against me. And I realized that neither I nor Amie had told Murchard of the attempt to poison Eugenius—or at least I had not spoken of it. Perhaps Amie had told her husband of it whilst my son and I were up at Cille Bharra.

I watched the light from the window move slowly across the floor of the cell, wishing the Iona men's boat would sink to the bottom of the sea as soon as they set sail. Or perhaps wait and sink later, with their master aboard. Finally, I heard the scrape of the bolt being withdrawn, and Murchard himself entered roomy cell. He did not quite meet my eyes.

"Mistress, I am sorry." His brown eyes swept the tiny room. "For all of this."

I swallowed. "Have they left? The abbot's men? Are they gone from here?"

"Aye, Mistress, they are well away now. A slippery basket of adders they are, indeed."

"You must know that I am innocent." The words rushed from my tongue as I hastened to tell my story. "The abbot himself it was who ransacked the cottage, there at Cille Bharra. He must have returned and done it. He left his ring there, so I would know it was him. I found poison when I first came here, mixed with Eugenius's medicine. That was why he was so sick. Then we found another vial of the same poison in Morainn's pouch, when Griogair and I examined her corpse. The abbot took the vial when he broke into the cottage. Griogair has it... the ring." I stopped talking, aware of his continued silence. "When he returns... You must believe me. They tried to poison Eugenius. You can ask your wife."

Murchard finally spoke. "Aye, she said something of the sort. That you had found poison. But you did not know who had given it to him."

"It's as I told you." I spoke rapidly, willing him to believe me. "When Morainn died, we found an identical vial in her own pouch. So she, or the abbot, must have left the poison for Eugenius when they visited here, when you took the abbot to see the well. Before my son took ill. Before you even sent for me."

"And why did you not tell me of all this?" Murchard demanded, his face reddening and his tone less measured. "An attempt to poison my own foster son, here in my very own keep!"

His fury nearly paralyzed me. "I did not know whom I could trust," I finally managed to say, as tears burned my cheeks. "I did not even tell your wife, at first."

"Surely you could not think we would have poisoned the lad?" Murchard said, with an edge to his voice.

"I did not know. I smelled the contents of the vial—Amie said she had gotten it from Murdina. But it was dog myrtle, and henbane, and wolf bane. It was not the vial Murdina had sent for Eugenius. Someone had switched the medicines. So your wife gave him the poison, herself, although she did not know what she had done. And then, later, when Griogair and I found a vial in Morainn's pouch, we did not know what to do. It was the same poison, the same kind of vial. So I hid it with my remedies. Griogair knows. You can ask him of it."

Murchard considered. "And why would Morainn want to poison your son?"

"I do not know. Perhaps she just acted as a tool of her father's. She accompanied him when you went to the well. Before my son took sick. Remember," I pleaded, "you are Eugenius's foster father, and the Lord of the Isles is his godfather. Any harm to him under your watch would jeopardize your standing with His Lordship."

"But the Green Abbot has nothing against me," replied Murchard. "And I'm not thinking he'd have any reason to poison four-year-old lads. Or reason to ransack your own dwelling, Mistress. What might cause him to do that?"

I did not want to tell Murchard of what lay between the abbot and myself. I thought back, frantically, to overheard conversations. "What of your wife's cousin?"

Murchard snorted. "Angus? He hasn't the strength to hold this island."

"But might he not want you out of favor? Then he'd be free to try." In the dim light that came from the slit window I watched Murchard consider, his eyes narrowing.

"Perhaps. But he'll not succeed."

"But perhaps Fingon contrived with Angus. And so he is then behind it all. He is a wicked, spiteful counselor. He would do anything to cause trouble for His Lordship, I'm thinking."

"But what of his own daughter's death? And this old woman on Uist? You yourself saw her, you did not deny that."

"Aye, Griogair was with me. But I only left some poppy for her, to ease her pain. You must believe me," I said, my voice taut. "I poisoned no one."

"Perhaps not," Murchard conceded. "But it 's a tangled coil all the same."

"So I am free to go?" I said. "You'll not hold me here, in this cell?"

"Oh, I think you cannot go, Mistress. Not yet. I cannot risk it. You could just be spinning a tale."

I stared at Murchard. Could this be the same man who loved my son like his own, the host that had treated me with courtesy? "But why?"

"I've no wish to risk the life of my wife, or my son."

"You cannot think I would hurt Amie! You cannot believe that."

"I'm not wanting to take a chance on it, Mistress. You've the Sight. You know all manner of herbs and remedies, for good and for ill. You keep a skull hidden among your belongings. We searched your things."

"But that is for Eugenius, to cure his falling sickness—"

"It's aye uncanny, for all that. I'll not risk the life of my son. You'll put an evil eye on him. No, you'll stay here until this matter is resolved. Or at least until Griogair returns, and I can ask him what he knows of it all. You'll be my guest, of course. And if there's anything you need for your comfort, Mistress, let me know. It will be brought to you." With that he left me, the door clanging shut behind him.

There was nothing to do in the enclosed space but pace the tiny room, or sit on the stool Morag had brought, and try not to go mad. I would have prayed to the saints for Griogair's swift return, but I had no confidence that the saints would listen to my entreaties; they had paid scant heed before. So I stared at the stones and plaster on the wall opposite me, and twisted my mother's ring in circles on my finger; trying to breathe slowly despite my rising panic, unwilling to be swept away by the swelling tide of fear again. I willed myself to think instead of my son, imagining the curve of his cheek, the grey of his eyes, the little eyelashes, the set of his chin. For my son's sake, surely, this tangle would come right. Surely.

As the light faded, I heard the familiar sound of the door bolt, and Morag entered, bringing a bowl of some stew and some bread.

"Och, Mistress," she said, looking at the plate of oatcakes, mostly untouched, that she had left the day before, "You've eaten next to nothing."

"I could not eat," I replied. "How is my son? And how is Amie? And the new babe?"

"Doing well enough, they all are, indeed. The babe nurses like some wee little piglet. And your son has been playing with the puppies." That news came as no surprise.

"Has he asked for me?"

"Aye, indeed. We've told him you were called away and are nursing a sick family. He believes us. Bricius it was, who thought of the tale. He did not want the lad distressed."

"I thank you for that kindness. And Bricius as well. What of Amie? Does she know?"

"She has asked for you, of course. But she's been occupied with the babe, and Murchard forbade us to mention the matter to her."

"She could tell Murchard the truth of my story, at least some of it."

"Aye, that she could," Morag replied, as if calming a child. "Here, Mistress, I've brought you a clean kertch, if you're wanting it. Now I must be about my duties, there is the supper to see to, in the hall. Here, I'll just be lighting this for you, before I'm leaving."

She left, but the flame of the new candle consoled me through the long night.

I finally did sleep and must have slept soundly, for the noise of the bolt awakened me. The light came in through the window slit; it was morning. I sat up, heart thudding, trying to straighten my dress and kertch. I hastily stood while I waited to see who would come through the opening door. It seemed too early in the day for any boat to have arrived; it could not be Griogair. I heard men's voices. Murchard then, but with whom?

It must have been later than I thought, for I heard Griogair's voice in reply as both men walked into the cell.

"Och, Mistress," Griogair said. "Himself here told me of what happened whilst I was away."

"Yes," I said, shortly. "Did you show him the ring?"

"Indeed, my lord," Griogair said, turning to Murchard, pulling his pouch open. "It is exactly as she told you. We returned from Uist to find that cottage ransacked, and her remedies broken and spilled on the floor."

"But the abbot had left Barra the day before. You saw him leave yourself," Murchard pointed out, his tone hard.

"Perhaps he did not leave. Perhaps he went to one of the small islands, hid the galley, and bided his time. Then returned the next day, in a smaller boat, and ransacked the hut."

"Surely my men would have seen him."

"Were you watching the north coast the entire day?"

Murchard shook his head slowly.

Griogair fished in the pouch and procured the gold ring. He held it up and then handed it to his Chief. "Mistress Euphemia found this ring on the floor of the cottage. She swears it belonged to the Green Abbot, although Morainn wore it as well. She was wearing it when she died, and we returned it to the abbot before he left."

"And how could she be so sure of that?" Murchard asked Griogair.

"I saw it on his fingers when I was at Iona. When I was at the nunnery."

"That is indeed what she told me, lord. I saw no reason to disbelieve her. And look, here are his initials. F, and you can see a M there as well."

"Aye," Murchard said grudgingly. "I'm thinking I saw his daughter wear this ring myself, when they were here. But what of the poison?" he demanded.

"I saw the first vial—the one they found here that held the poison for your foster son. Your good wife and Mistress Euphemia showed it to me once they had discovered it. The vial was identical to the one we found on Morainn's corpse. Mistress Euphemia speaks truly."

Murchard grunted, unconvinced. "What of the abbot's charges against her?"

"No doubt he found we'd been to Uist," Griogair replied. "Perhaps the abbot himself has something he wants to hide. Why send his daughter to Uist at all? She did not seem the type to dote on elderly aunts."

Murchard grunted a second time, but the noise sounded doubtful. I began to feel a little hope.

"You cannot hold her here like this," Griogair added, pressing his point. "Her own father is a favorite of His Lordship. It would not do to anger him over such false accusations."

"Perhaps not," Murchard mused, "but what's to be done? I'm not wanting to be on the abbot's bad side either."

"Is he your liege lord?" Griogair asked. I hardly dared to breathe.

"Certainly not!" Murchard's eyes narrowed at the suggestion, but there were sparks flashing at the insult. "I am master here."

"Then let Mistress Euphemia go free. Perhaps we can work together and find out who accompanied Morainn to Barra. For surely, that will be the man that killed the lass. If the murderer of his own daughter is found, and the death of Cristina proved but a charade, the abbot will have no case. And perhaps whatever reason he might have had for attempting to poison your own foster son will come to light."

"The man is slippery as an eel," Murchard muttered. "And just as heartless."

"Aye, but eels can be trapped," responded Griogair. "And if the creel is tight enough, they'll not escape." He turned to me. "What do you say, Mistress? Do you have the heart for this?"

I swallowed, not sure at first if I could trust my voice. But when the words came, they were strong. "I will do anything to punish the man who tried to kill my son. I swear it, on my mother's own grave."

"Well enough," Griogair said, looking at his chief, and Murchard nodded.

"My apologies, Mistress," the MacNeil said. "But I needed to hear Griogair's side of it. I'd trust him with my life. We ourselves were fostered together, when we were lads. He'd not deceive me."

I faced him, my eyes on his. "And neither would I, my lord, you must believe that. I would never do anything to endanger your wife or son, or my own son."

"That is settled, then," Murchard said, and turned to leave the cell. Then he turned back. "You understand, Mistress, I could not take the chance." I thought I saw remorse, mixed with hardness, in his eyes.

"Come, Mistress Euphemia," Griogair said. "Let us leave this place." I was, indeed, overjoyed to comply.

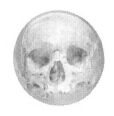

CHAPTER 16

I stood in the outer courtyard, gulping fresh air while the door to the cell creaked shut behind me. "My son," I demanded, when I heard Griogair approach. "I need to see my son."

Griogair ventured a smile, but I did not return it. "I'm betting he's in the kennels, Mistress," he said after a moment. "Shall we look for him there?" He started walking across the court towards the kennels with long strides and I found I had to rush to keep pace with him. "After you've seen your son, Mistress," Griogair cautioned me as we neared our destination, "we'll need to make some plans."

I barely acknowledged him as I scanned the interior of the kennels, all my attention focused on my son. My eyes found him and I let out my breath in relief. "Eugenius!" I called.

"Mother! You are back—look how the dog has grown!" I hugged boy and wriggling pup to me in an embrace, wondering that it could be only two days since I had seen my child. It felt like two years. But after a moment the puppy, unhappy with our cozy embrace, started to whine and nipped at Eugenius's hand.

"Ouch!" he cried. "Bad dog!"

"You held him too tightly, Eugenius," I remonstrated. "Let him go for now; he wants his own mother."

Eugenius grudgingly put the dog down and sat across from the stall as the pup waddled back to where his mother lay, nursing the other puppies. Eugenius gazed, enthralled, and barely noticed when Griogair and I left the room.

"So we'll go to Uist?" I asked Griogair as we walked back towards Amie's quarters. The sun shone that day, and I felt it warm on my face. I let out a deep sigh, still thinking of my son, and the ease with which he had left me.

"Where else would you go?" Griogair replied. "Yes, Mistress, to try and clear your name we'd best return to Cille Bhrighde. Perhaps we can find out who spoke with Fingon's men, and why Morainn came there at all. We'd best go today. Do you mind leaving so quickly?"

I wanted only to check in on Amie, and perhaps find a fresh shift to wear. Then I would happily put Kisimul behind me. After the events of the last two days, I had no desire to linger here, despite the presence of my son. But I did not know where I would go. The cave on Jura no longer seemed a safe haven; no doubt the abbot could send men to take me there just as easily as he had here, despite Jura's nearness to Finlaggan and other castles of His Lordship. And if I was not safe there, where would I be safe? That thought led to another.

"Griogair," I asked. "What if Fingon's men are there—at Cille Bhrighde? They might want to take me again—I cannot go back to Iona. I cannot. I would drown myself first."

Griogair thought. "We will take some of Murchard's men with us," he said. "A few, men that can be trusted."

I nodded. "Bricius?" I asked. I liked the old man.

Griogair assented. "And perhaps we'd be wise to stop at Saltinish again as well. Perhaps some of those neighbors you mentioned have remembered something else about the night Morainn was killed."

"I thought the old woman, Sorcha, and her daughter-in-law knew more than they told me the day Eugenius and I visited. Tam said Kenna had seen a selkie, at least he told Eugenius so. But I did not speak with them again."

"Well, perhaps we will learn more from them this time," Griogair said. "Now, get whatever you need together. There's a fair wind and I've no mind to miss it."

A short while later the *naibheag* pulled away from Kisimul. Bricius, Conall and Calum had come along to crew, and I was not sorry to see the weapons they brought with them. I shuddered, feeling again the horror of my time in the cell. I had put on different clothes before I left, a clean shift and the old blue gown of Amie's, but the change in clothing did not entirely free me from the memory of the hours spent in that tiny, malodorous room. I watched the walls of the castle recede as we left the bay, and part of me wanted to leave the place far behind me and never return. And yet, my son waited there.

Bricius, Conall and Calum busied themselves raising the sail of the small boat. I watched the isle of Barra glide past as we sailed up the Sound towards South Uist, the wind blowing my hair out from its kertch and wildly around my head. I relished the touch of the breeze and took deep breaths of the wet air, forgetting to be seasick in my joy at being outside, away from that small cell and away from Kisimul. I became aware of Griogair looking at me from where he sat at the helm, and I flushed and looked away.

"It's a fine day for a sail, Mistress," he observed.

"Indeed." I paused a moment, the words stuck in my throat. "I must thank you," I finally said. "For getting me out of that place."

"Och, perhaps you'll forgive Murchard. He's caught between two rocks, right enough. His Lordship won't be happy to learn that Fingon's been leaving Iona, but the abbot's still a powerful man."

I stared past Griogair, at the coast, not able to meet his eyes.

"He might well have reason to visit the monks at Trinity Temple on Uist," Griogair continued. "That was the excuse he gave for his visit."

"The Lord of the Isles ordered him not to leave Iona," I replied, my voice curt. A seagull swooped low over our boat. "Why would he wish to harm Eugenius?" I asked, although I knew the answer well enough. The wind whipped the words from my mouth and tossed them to the sky. "He's but a child."

"You know the answer to that, Mistress, better than any of us," Griogair countered.

I shivered, the brightness of the afternoon now dimmed. "He's just a child," I repeated, stubbornly.

We stopped first at Saltinish, at the house near the beach where Sorcha and Kenna lived, with all the children. We beached our craft up on the white sands. Calum and Conall stayed with the boat, but Bricius accompanied Griogair and myself to the cottage. No children ran about today. Hesitantly I approached and knocked on the doorframe. After a time, I heard a shuffle and Old Sorcha opened the door.

"Och, it is yourself," she addressed me without enthusiasm. "We heard you had gone back to Kisimul."

"Well, that is true. But Himself at Kisimul has sent me back again, to Uist, and we thought to stop here first."

"Who is with you?" Sorcha muttered, craning her neck outside the door to see Griogair and Bricius. "Who are they?"

"Some of His Lordship's men, from the castle. Might we come in? We just want to talk with you a wee bit."

From the look on her face, Sorcha did not want us to enter, but the sight of Griogair and Bricius, as well as their broadswords, convinced her to invite us in.

"Where is your daughter-in-law?" I asked. "And all the children?"

"She took them up over to the west side, to look for birds' eggs, and to gather the *brisgean*. Here, sit down, and I'll get you something to drink."

We seated ourselves around the hearth, and she fetched us some ale. It tasted nearly as sour as the look she gave when she served us. "Now, whatever can I do for you?" she asked.

I looked at Griogair, waiting for him to speak.

"You will remember the poor woman that was murdered by the well, the Abbot of Iona's own daughter," he said.

"Indeed." Sorcha's face softened. She seemed to mellow a little, "How could I ever forget that, and it just such a short time ago. The poor lassie, so lovely she was. Have they found her murderer, then?"

Griogair shook his head and flashed her a sad smile. "They have not. And so, Himself at Kisimul, the MacNeil, wondered if you or your daughter-in-law could remember anything else about that night. Something that might give us a clue. The woman was not from Barra. She and her killer must have come from another island across the Sound. Perhaps they came from Uist?"

Sorcha's jaw clenched and I watched her gnaw on her lip.

"Or perhaps your daughter-in-law saw something?" Griogair smiled again, but a sternness lurked behind it now.

"My son told me Kenna had seen a selkie," I added. "When would that have been?"

"That same night," Sorcha admitted. "Kenna went outside to see to the pigs, and then she went down to the shore to wash her hands in the water."

"And?" Griogair asked.

"Well, she came rushing into the house and told me she'd seen a selkie on the beach." Sorcha waved an arm. "Just there, by the rocks to the north. She saw him rise and walk on the land. All covered in his sealskin, he was, dark against the sand. That is what she said."

Griogair looked intently at our hostess. "And was the selkie alone?"

"She only spoke of seeing the one."

"You don't think it could have been a man she saw?"

Sorcha sniffed. "My daughter-in-law is not one to tell tales."

"And the next morning the lass was found murdered."

"Indeed." Sorcha shook her head sadly but her jaw looked tense. "And it was for this that we did not speak of it much. For perhaps the selkie murdered the lass, at the holy well."

"But surely a selkie would carry her off and drown her in the Sound?"

The old woman's jaw tightened again. "I do not know the ways of the selkies, myself. You'll have to ask someone with the blood of them, perhaps they would know such things. I've heard there are such folk on Uist, but not here on Barra. I am only telling you what my daughter-in-law said she saw, and only because my lord at Kisimul is wishing it. Otherwise, I would not speak of it at all."

"It is kind you are to help us with this," Griogair said, completely winning her over with another smile. "We'll tell Himself of your kindness to us."

The old woman simpered back. I sniffed quietly, annoyed with the whole farce. "Are you wanting some more ale?" Sorcha asked.

Griogair picked up his wooden cup. "Indeed, I'll take some with pleasure. Could you, out of your kindness, answer another question for me?"

"What would that be?"

Griogair drank deeply. "You brew fine ale, mistress. Are you remembering the day the abbot left and took his daughter's body back to Iona on his birlinn?"

"I am an old woman," Sorcha replied, "and my memory is not what it was once, but surely I would not be forgetting that."

"I doubt you forget much, Mistress. The day after that, do you recall any strange boats putting in near here?" He took another swig of ale.

Sorcha's face took on a vacant look while she thought back. "Aye," she replied after a time. "There was one boat, a small one, that beached up the strand a ways. But they did not stay long. Three men, it was. They took the path towards the Tobar Bharra and then returned shortly after. I assumed they came for the blessed water. People do, often." Her voice had a defensive edge to it I wondered at. "Many folk come to the well from other islands. There is nothing strange in that."

"Indeed, there is not," Griogair replied, his voice soothing. "Might I have another glass of ale? And perhaps your daughter-in-law herself will return soon and can tell us of that selkie she saw."

"There's no need for that," Sorcha insisted, stubborn. "I know what she saw."

"I have never seen such a thing." Griogair drained the last drop of ale from his mazer and handed it to Sorcha. "And I myself am a Uist man. I'm wondering what it looked like, indeed."

"Well, she should be back soon, and you can ask her yourself." Sorcha refilled his cup and handed it to him. "And with the bairns as well. Where is your son?" she asked, turning towards me.

"He's back at Kisimul now, with his foster parents. Did you know that Lady Amie has delivered a fine son? They've named him Roderick."

"Indeed?" Sorcha's face brightened with interest. "And did you attend the birth, yourself?"

I shared some details of the birth of Murchard's heir with the old woman while we waited for Kenna to return. I had seen Amie briefly, before we left Kisimul, and was able to reassure Sorcha that the wife of the chief fared well, and the baby had a strong suck and fed with no difficulty. Griogair and Bricius drank ale while Sorcha and I spoke, and the shadows lengthened as the sun travelled to the west. Some gulls cawed over the Sound to the east, and I thought Bricius might doze off in the peacefulness of the afternoon.

A clamor outside broke the stillness into a million shards. Bricius opened his eyes and sat up, a little sheepishly. Griogair straightened his own back. And Sorcha looked to the door, a grin creasing her wrinkled face. "That will be them returning, right enough."

The door to the blackhouse burst open with an excited burst of children's chatter. I recognized Tam's voice, but the sounds stopped short as Kenna saw the strangers sitting at her hearth. Then she saw me.

"And what is all of this? Mother, who are these strangers? And you, Mistress Euphemia—what brings you back here? We heard you had returned to Kisimul."

"Good day to you as well," I said.

"It is all right, Kenna," Sorcha said with an apologetic glance at me. "These men are sent by Himself at Castlebay. It is all to do with the poor lass that drowned up at Cille Bharra. And they heard you had seen a selkie and wanted to know of it."

"And where did they hear of that?"

"Your Tam told my son of it," I interjected. "And my son told me. So, please, describe what you saw. Himself has sent us, to find out."

Kenna looked uncomfortable, but Griogair gave her an encouraging nod. Her face softened under his gaze and her lips curved up at him a bit. "I had gone out to the pigsty, to feed the sow some scraps. And the moon shone full over the sands, they glowed like molten silver in the light. My hands were dirty and I thought I'd just walk down by the sea and clean them." She smiled for a moment. "And, to speak the truth, it felt so peaceful there, and it's little enough quiet there is in here, with all of us, and the weans crying and all."

I nodded, hoping to encourage her. "So you went down on the beach, and?"

"I washed my hands in the waves, and even waded a bit, just to clean the muck off my feet." She sighed. "Och, it was a lovely night, sure enough. It made me remember when I was a young girl and courting." I saw her glance at Griogair, with another smile, and felt my own jaw tighten. "And then I looked up the beach and saw the selkie."

"You're sure it was a selkie?" Griogair asked.

"What else could it have been? It was dark, and it came from over by the rocks. It was all dark skinned, and it left the rocks and went onto the land. And I grew afeard and ran back to the house. For I feared it would steal me away."

Griogair gave a nod of agreement. "And indeed it might have, for the bright beauty of you," he said, and I could see

Kenna blush even in the dim interior of the house. He stood up. "Well, I thank you both for your kindness and for the fine ale you poured for us. But we'd best be on our way, we've further to travel before the sun sets."

We said our goodbyes and made our way back to the boat. I stalked ahead, irritated with Griogair and his easy manner, and remained silent after climbing aboard while the crew pushed the boat out into the waves and the men raised the sail. The brisk wind in my face cooled my annoyance somewhat; it was nothing to me if Griogair flirted with Kenna, after all.

Breezes filled the sail and we passed up the Sound towards Uist and Cille Bhrighde. I faced away from the men, looking ahead as we passed the little isle of Fuday to our right and the shores of Uist drew closer. The sun was sinking to the west and the clouds began to take on the bright colors of sunset, while I mused, staring at the waves and focusing on nothing in particular. An image formed before my eyes. No selkie, but some man—a figure covered with a cloak, glimpsed by moonlight, with a winding shroud trailing behind it. I trembled, breaking the spell. The vision vanished, and once again I saw only the sunlight on the waves.

I turned and looked back towards the beach we had left, still visible in our wake. The black rocks at the headland did not lie that close to Kenna's cottage. A figure, head covered with a cloak, might well be mistaken by a fanciful woman for some selkie, when glimpsed by moonlight. I turned round again, and then grew aware the Griogair had approached me and stood nearby. I felt the muscles in my jaw clench and my back tense as the bulk of him almost touched me, from the boat rocking on the swell.

"You were far away, Mistress," he observed. I did not answer but kept looking out over the waves. "What did you think of the lass's story?" he asked after a moment.

I swallowed down my irritation, like an acid in my throat. "I'm thinking that a foolish lass could mistake a cloaked figure, at night and far away up the beach, for a selkie," I finally replied. "And I saw it, just now."

Griogair's eyes widened. "Indeed?"

"Yes, a man in a black cloak, dragging a shroud behind him."

"You saw the murderer." Griogair spoke a statement, not a question.

My annoyance returned. "Aye, as did that foolish woman back there."

"She's a fair enough lass."

"And a widow," I pointed out, despite myself. "You could court her. She'd have you, right enough."

Griogair laughed, and my bad temper grew. "Och, perhaps I'll do that, indeed. I thank you for the suggestion, Mistress. But not this afternoon. We've things to see to in Cille Bhrighde, and no time for courting pretty girls. Now we know the killer had a dark cloak."

"Most men have dark cloaks. And it was night."

"What of those cloth scraps you found by the well?"

"The color could have been black once."

"So we'll search for a man with a black cloak. And there are few enough of those."

"Perhaps the threads came from my own dress," I said, wanting to be contrary for some reason. "That was black once, and my dress is faded enough." A higher wave splashed some water over the side, wetting me with a little shock.

"I'm thinking those threads were not from your old dress, Mistress. Yours was far more faded than that scrap of cloth." My hands itched with the desire to slap the outrageous man, although I knew he spoke the truth. "But," Griogair added, his lips curving upwards, "it is you who have the Sight, is it not?" His mouth widened into a full grin and he turned away, making his way back towards the tiller where Bricius waited.

CHAPTER 17

When we reached Cille Bhrighde the crew beached and secured the boat while Griogair, Bricius, and I conferred. I took a deep breath to try and quiet my racing heart and the fluttering nervousness in my belly. What if Fingon's men lay in wait here, to trap me? But we saw no signs of strange activity. The beach looked as it had when we visited previously—a few fishing boats and curraghs pulled up on the shore, while the village seemed quiet, with some folk going about their business stopping a moment to stare at the new arrivals.

"We'll start by visiting my cousin," Griogair announced. "They'll tell us what's been happening here." And so we made our way towards the cottage at the southern end of the settlement.

Annag's eyes widened as she saw us approach, followed by Murchard's armed men. But she greeted us courteously, providing ale to slake the men's thirst and bannocks to ease their hunger, while Griogair introduced Bricius and the rest of the crew, and shared with her our reason for visiting Cille Bhrighde.

"We heard at Kisimul," he told her, "that old Cristina had died."

"Indeed," Annag replied. "I helped Fiona lay her out."

Griogair crossed himself. "A sad thing. Did the elf-shot kill her, in the end?"

Annag inclined her head. "I am thinking so. She grew weaker, and died peacefully in her bed. It was some few days after you were visiting that the poor thing left us. Fiona herself came to fetch me early that morning. The Dancers had glowed brightly that night. I'm thinking the angels themselves came and took poor Cristina while she slept." She smiled a little sheepishly. "But you'll not care for the fancies of an old woman. What is it that brings you back here, the pair of you? And where is that sweet son of yours?"

"We've left him at Kisimul," I told her. "He's fostered there."

Annag's brow furrowed. "But I thought it was a godson of the Lord of the Isles himself that was fostered over there." Her forehead cleared, and she flashed a quick smile of understanding. "Och, that would be yourself, then. And I not knowing! Forgive me, Mistress. But I thought you had come from Islay." There was an instant of awkward pause, while I prayed the crew, busy drinking their ale outside, had not heard the comment.

"We came back," Griogair interjected, changing the topic, "sent by Himself at Kisimul, to learn more of the poor woman's death. The Green Abbot has complained; he wants the cruel slaying of his daughter settled and the murderer found. And he's concerned about poor Cristina as well, for you know the woman was related to his wife."

Annag's eyes sparked with interest. "Aye, I heard Cristina had a sister who had done well for herself. So that would be the abbot's woman? And so poor Morainn truly was the Abbot's own daughter? Imagine! And him such a powerful churchman!"

"He is a powerful man, indeed, for all that his rebellion failed. And he wants to know who killed his daughter, and so Himself at Kisimul sent us back here, as a favor to the churchman, to see what we could discover of it. But perhaps the abbot sent his own men here as well."

Annag looked blank. "I know nothing about that. When Cristina died, a galley did visit a few days later. But they did not stay long, at all. Just one day, they lingered in the harbor. Perhaps you should ask Father Benneit, for he came here from Iona. He may know something of it all, and where the galley was from." Annag looked dubiously at the lengthening shadows, and then at the group of men drinking her ale outside the cottage. "But it grows late. Do you need a place to bide tonight?"

We assured her we would be fine sleeping outside and thanked her for her hospitality. Griogair sent Bricius along with the crew to find a place we could camp overnight, and then, reassured that Fingon's men were not in the village, Griogair and I made our way through the settlement to Cristina's house.

In the evening light the house had a sad look to it, as if mourning its deceased owner. But we smelled peat smoke rising from the chimney as we walked up and knocked on the door.

Fiona answered. She did not look delighted to see us standing on her doorstep.

Griogair flashed another of his charming looks. I gritted my teeth as I watched him beguile her, explaining how we had been sent to inquire into Cristina's death and that of her niece. If Fiona was surprised to see me here, free, she did not show the fact.

"So the abbot himself asked my lord at Kisimul to look into the matter," Griogair finished. "And so we thought, who would be best to speak to but yourself, knowing that feckless lass as well as you did, and her poor auntie also."

"Well, you'd best come in, then." Fiona ushered us into the cottage. She invited us to sit, sat down herself, then picked up her spindle and started working at it.

"And so, what will become of this fine house?" Griogair asked, settling himself on a stool in the main room. "Did Cristina have family who will be living here?"

"Och, no," Fiona said. "She had no family at all, except for her sister's child there on Iona. I thought she meant to leave it to her niece, but then the poor lass... Did you hear what happened to the girl? When you came before, we did not know of the murder."

Griogair shook his head, the picture of dumbfounded bereavement, and I tried to compose my features as well.

"We were shocked indeed, to learn of it," I murmured, wondering what Fiona would think if she knew that I had found Morainn's body there at the well.

"But we are hoping we can help put things to rights and find the lass's killer," Griogair interjected. "At least that is what my lord at Kisimul desires, and since we had met you and all, he thought to send us here again."

"Well, it's as I told you, I know little of it," Fiona replied as she attended to her spindle. The thread snapped. She started it going again, and after it whirled smoothly, she continued. "The lass vanished one evening. We thought the fairies had stolen her, for she liked to wander while she was here. The poor lass spoke of the beauty of this island, but I'm thinking the Holy Isle where she came from would be lovelier to see. At any rate, she did not return. And the next we heard of it, her body had been found on Barra, and how it was she got over to Cille Bharra I've no idea whatsoever." She crossed herself. "Perhaps demons took her there, for I heard they drowned her in the holy well."

I shuddered, remembering the sight of the corpse. Fiona glanced at me sharply.

"It is not so far," observed Griogair. "Surely someone with a boat could have made the journey without much difficulty. I think it was no demon but a man who wished to harm her."

Fiona snorted. "Who would wish to harm her?"

"I do not know," he retorted, "but someone harmed her, sure enough. Did her father send men here to ask of it?"

"Indeed he did. Soon after you visited. And they took the news back to him of Cristina's death as well."

"Och yes, my cousin herself said something of that. Annag," Griogair told Fiona. "She mentioned you sent for her to help lay out the old woman."

"Oh, so you are Annag's cousin?"

"A cousin to Padraig, on my mother's side," Griogair explained. "I am from up near Tarbert."

Fiona face brightened. "Indeed, and that is a fine thing. Well, yes, a galley stopped from Iona, although the abbot himself never came here. The men made inquiries in the village. They even spoke to my son, you remember him, do you not? Father Benneit himself let them sleep in the church, for he knew the men from Iona."

"Did he indeed?" Griogair said, a curious tone to his voice. He sighed. "And so your mistress has left us now. May the saints be kind to her."

Fiona nodded. "Aye, she lies buried in the churchyard. The house will go to the church, but the priest said we might stay on. He's of no mind to move over here. He wants to remain close to the chapel."

"A fine priest indeed, he must be."

"Yes," Fiona agreed, "for all that he is young. But he came from the abbey on the Holy Isle, so it stands to reason he should be a holy man."

"Did he give your mistress the last rites?"

"Indeed. He blessed her with the holy oil and said the prayers for her. She was already failing, or we'd not have summoned him, but she died quickly after he came and saw to her. Her soul was at rest, I am thinking."

"And when did all this happen?" Griogair asked.

"Just a day or two after you both were here. Some weeks ago, it was." Fiona's spindle slowed and she set it moving again. "The poor thing grew weaker after you left, and we sent for Father Benneit the next day, that was the way of it."

"So her death was peaceful? She died naturally?"

Fiona nodded emphatically. "Aye, she did."

"Would you swear to that?" Griogair asked, his voice shrewd, and Fiona insisted she would.

"It's just we heard there were questions about her death, coming so close to that of her niece. And we heard that her father might be asking questions and stirring up trouble about it all. Perhaps we should take your story down, and you could just make your mark on it for us."

Fiona agreed, and Griogair surprised me by fetching some parchment and ink and a quill from his satchel. I had not realized he could write. I watched while he transcribed Fiona's story and she made her mark on the parchment.

"I'm thinking she was glad enough to leave when the angels came to fetch her away. Did you know the Dancers shone bright that night?" Fiona said as Griogair put away the parchment.

"Annag mentioned something of the sort," I murmured. "Do you still have the tinctures I left for her?"

"Yes indeed, I only gave her the one dose, that afternoon."

"Might I take them back with me? That tincture of poppy is dear enough that I'd like to have it still, if you've no need for it."

"Indeed." Fiona's spindle slowed and she set it and the distaff down on the table. She stood and went into the back room, Cristina's bedchamber, and we heard her open a chest. She returned a moment later holding the two vials I had given her. "Here they are, Mistress, safe as you left them."

I thanked her and glanced at Griogair. "You don't recall who Morainn befriended while she was here?" he asked our hostess, who had resumed her spinning. Fiona shook her head.

"It's as I've told you, she did not bide here that long. And she was not overly friendly with the folk here. My son thought her a fine woman, but she'd have none of him. Lucky for him, I'd say that was. She'd not be content here for long. I heard she'd been handfasted to the brother of the Lord of the Isles himself some years ago?"

"Aye, that is true," I said. "She bore him a son."

Fiona sniffed. "Well then, my Fearglas is well out of it. She'd not have been happy with an island man, no matter how hardworking. He makes a good enough living here, with the fishing and the crops, but he's no fine lord."

"Your son could not have been jealous?" Griogair asked.

"Of whom?" Fiona sniffed again. "No, now, Morainn had no friends here; she walked by herself. I'm thinking the fairies spirited her away to Barra."

Griogair glanced at me and rose from his seat. "We thank you for your fine hospitality, but we must be going. But perhaps we can come back later and speak with Fearglas after he returns."

"Well enough," Fiona said. "He'll be back from the fishing in the evening."

We took our leave. Standing outside the cottage, we faced the small chapel next door. I examined the tinctures Fiona had given to me. The bottles were the same as those I had given to her. I sniffed them and then, reassured they had not been tampered with, I put them in my pouch.

"Well, between Fiona's story and the bottles there's proof enough that you had nothing to do with the old woman's death. It is odd that even Fiona knows nothing of the charges against you. Perhaps the Green Abbot is thinking word does not travel around these islands."

"Or he simply hoped to toy with me, and have me imprisoned before anything could be done against it. He must have realized the story would not hold."

"Well, your innocence is proved. We can even bring Fiona herself to Kisimul if that is necessary."

I let out a breath I did not realize I had been holding and looked out over the Western Sea. A wind blew and rough waves chopped against the shoreline.

"So Father Benneit comes from Iona," Griogair mused. "And he is friendly with the abbot's men. He could well have known Morainn before she arrived here."

"It's possible," I agreed.

"Let's go speak with him again. We've still a bit of time before dark." Griogair started walking towards the chapel and I followed behind.

We found Father Benneit in the small yard outside the chapel, seated on a rock. He had a bundle of dark cloth in his lap and appeared to be sewing. He looked up as he heard us approach, and put down his task.

"Good evening," he said. "It is the couple from Islay, is it not? What can I be doing for you?"

"We visited Kisimul," Griogair explained, "and Himself there asked us to see if anyone here knew how that poor murdered lass could have gotten from Uist over to Barra since we've been here before and were knowing folk a bit. The abbot's daughter. Her father is keen to find whoever might have slain her, as you can well imagine."

Father Benneit looked past us. "You came alone?"

"No, we've a boat and a fine crew nearby."

The priest glanced towards the chapel. "The poor lass. I knew her a bit on Iona; she was a bright thing. It is sad, what happened." He crossed himself.

"Who do you think could have murdered the girl? She did not walk into the sea and take her own life, as you thought she did. And I do not think you would accept that the *sidhe* took her to Barra and drowned her in the Tobar Bharra. For surely you yourself, as a man of God, do not believe in the sidhe."

Father Benneit's dark eyes shifted away a moment, towards the chapel, before he spoke. "The Holy Church teaches there are demons and devils, as well as angels. Perhaps the sidhe are fallen angels."

"But would they transport Morainn to Barra and leave her there dead by the holy waters?" Griogair persisted.

"Have you heard of the well here on Uist that later moved to Skye?" the priest responded. "There are miracles aplenty. Why could the sidhe not have taken her?"

"Do the sidhe wear dark cloaks?" Griogair asked. "A woman that lives near the sands there saw someone in a dark cloak moving towards the rocks that night. She swears it was a selkie, but I'm thinking she spied Morainn's killer returning to his boat."

"Indeed?" Father Benneit sounded curious. "And who was this woman?"

"Just a Barra woman gone outside to look at the moonlight."

"Well, perhaps she glimpsed a shadow. Or a seal on the rocks. The night plays tricks on the eyes."

"So you're not knowing of anyone here in Cille Bharra with reason to slay the woman?"

"No. She kept herself to herself. She'd walk the hills sometimes, alone. But I never saw her with anyone else, except of course Fearglas, Fiona's son. He fancied her, I'm thinking. Not that she'd have had him, being such a fine lady. No doubt the abbot had another husband in mind for her, someone powerful who wouldn't mind Iain Mór's cast-off."

"It's odd, is it not," I put in, "that her father would have sent her here to care for her aunt."

"Not so strange, Mistress," Father Benneit answered. "Old Cristina served as the girl's godmother. She was Morainn's aunt. They were close."

"Is that how you got the post here?" Griogair asked. "The abbot sent you?"

"Well, I had spent time at Trinity after I was at Iona. When Cristina wrote to let the abbot know the old priest had died, he spoke to the Bishop of the Isles and recommended me. I've been here close to two years now."

"It must be a quiet life, after the busyness of Iona and Trinity."

"It suits me," Father Benneit replied. "Now, if you've no more questions, I've many things to see to this evening."

"Indeed, we've no wish to keep you from your tasks. Perhaps my wife could be helping you with that mending while we talk a wee bit."

I flashed Griogair an annoyed glance, but walked towards the priest with a smile plastered on my face and offered to finish his sewing for him.

"Och, it is nothing, just a wee tear in this old garment. There's no need to trouble yourself with it. What else were you wanting to know?"

Griogair looked thoughtful. "I was just wondering who here in Cille Bhrighde might have a boat?"

"Fearglas, for one. And there are others as well." The priest named a few other villagers. "Most men fish. So there are many small boats here. But Fearglas has a fine little boat, indeed. Just right for one man, or perhaps two, to row."

"Does he?" Griogair said. "Well, we'll take no more of your time today. Here, let us give you an offering for your chapel." He reached into his pouch. "Perhaps you will say a Mass for Cristina and poor Morainn, and remember us in your prayers as well."

I watched Griogair hand Father Benneit some coins, the silver flashing as it caught a ray of late evening sunlight. We turned and left the priest to his mending.

"I've a mind to walk down by the beach," I said to Griogair. We left the chapel and walked towards the sea to the west. Several boats sat drawn up on the shingle. One, a small boat that could be rowed easily by one man, lay near the church. The sun was sinking quickly now in the western sky, casting flaming crimson over the clouds, with rays of light shining out between them.

"I'm thinking," said Griogair, looking at the sky, "that it would be an easier thing for two people to take a small boat across to Barra than a large boat."

"Indeed." I shifted my own eyes away from the sunset for a moment to survey the beach. "There are quite a few small naibheags here."

"It would be more work to handle a large boat, and need more men. We'll see what Fearglas's boat looks like when he returns. But for now I am hungry, Mistress," Griogair added, with a hint of a smile in his voice.

"Well, it is a good thing for you that Annag is a better hand at baking than I am myself," I shot back, not sure why his comment bothered me. I turned away from the sunset and started walking at a brisk pace back down the road that led through the village.

After we reached Annag's cottage, I left Griogair and the men to their dinner. Our hostess had gone to great lengths to make the unexpected guests welcome and a savory rabbit stew simmered on the hearth. I smelled fresh baked bannocks and saw a fine large cheese sitting on the trencher table Annag and Padraig had set up outside the cottage, but I had no appetite. Instead, I wandered past the men, who stood, eating and talking, or made themselves comfortable sitting on the ground. I walked back behind the house and up the little rock hill that overlooked the village, breathing deeply of the fresh wind that blew in from offshore. I found a large stony outcrop and settled myself on it to watch the last of the twilight, wrapping my mantle around me against the breeze.

I had awakened that day in the tiny cell in Kisimul, and now here I sat, on a rocky hill in South Uist. I shuddered at the memory of that cell, and took another breath of salt air. I reached into my pouch and took out the two pottery vials Fiona had returned to me. I unstoppered the one and took a sniff, catching the dark scent of poppy tincture. The other vial held sloe root and bramble. So no one had tampered with these remedies, at least. Cristina had died a natural death, and had not been hurried out of this world. Although she had died after the priest's visit, still people did die after receiving the Last Rites.

The long summer gloaming had nearly vanished, the brilliant colors of the sunset long faded to a violet blue, and the evening stars shone in the darkening sky. I thought, with a flush of guilt, that I should be down the hill and at Annag's cottage, helping her with all the extra work we had made for her. I rose, found my footing, and started down the hill in the growing darkness. I nearly collided with a darker bulk on the path and stepped back, alarmed for an instant, before I recognized the form as Griogair.

"I wondered where you had gone to, Mistress," he said to me in the twilight. "You did not eat."

I shook my head. "I had no appetite. And I thought to take another look at the vials Fiona returned to me."

"And?"

I shrugged, although I knew full well Griogair could not see my expression in the dark. "They are the same, untampered with."

"So the old woman was not poisoned."

"Not by me, at any rate." I laughed weakly, and tried to pass him on the narrow track.

"Wait, Mistress, sit with me awhile," Griogair said, not completely blocking my way, but making it awkward for me to pass. "We've things to discuss, away from the ears of other men."

"And what would those things be?"

"Come and sit again," Griogair persisted, moving past me to sit on the large outcrop and gesturing towards the stone, "and I will tell you. I even brought you something to eat, the kind man that I am."

I felt my lips curve upwards, despite myself, and eventually I gave in and sat beside him.

"Here." Griogair reached inside his mantle for a packet wrapped in a cloth. "I have bannocks, and cheese. You should eat something, Mistress. You rarely do."

"I've little appetite."

"Well." He handed me a bannock. "Eat or not, as you please."

I broke off a bit of the oatcake and put it in my mouth. Someone had buttered it. Tender crumbs melted on my tongue, and I tried to swallow, aware of the bulk of Griogair beside me.

"What was it you wanted to speak of?" I asked, after I had cleared my throat.

"Tomorrow, we'll speak with Fearglas," Griogair said.

"Yes," I replied.

"Fearglas seemed a pleasant enough fellow."

"Yes," I said again. "But not a man Morainn would fancy. She'd want some fine lord. I cannot understand what brought her here."

"You're not thinking she was just a dutiful niece?"

"Not since I found her body in the well, with the same poison in her bag that was used on my son."

"But she had a fine lord, once. And he left her for an heiress. Perhaps Fearglas had other charms," Griogair suggested. "He's a comely enough man, don't you think?"

I felt my awkward blush but did not answer.

Griogair changed the subject. "What about Father Benneit? Did you ever meet the man on Iona?"

"I spent my days in the nunnery," I responded. "We saw few priests there, just our confessor."

"And the abbot himself."

"Yes. That." I shuddered and my stomach roiled. I feared I would vomit the bannock up, but swallowed down my bile.

"So you did not know the priest."

"Of course not," I said, irritated, both with Griogair and with my response to his words.

"But the abbot knew him."

"Aye, I've no doubt he's the abbot's man."

"And he admitted to knowing Morainn. Perhaps there was something between the two. Perhaps Father Benneit is our killer, and not Fearglas."

"He's a priest," I responded.

"You, of all people, should know that's no impediment," Griogair said. "And he has an old black cloak, with a rip in it. Did you get a good look at what he was mending this afternoon?"

"Yes, and it could well match the cloth that we found snagged by the well at Cille Bharra."

"And the priest, returning to his boat and wearing a hooded cloak, could have been the selkie that Kenna saw."

"But what cause would they have to come to Barra? And why would Father Benneit murder Morainn?" I shuddered, remembering the cottage where I had stayed with Eugenius, so near the spring. The thought of the abbot's man so close to what I had thought of as a safe sanctuary made my skin feel as though tiny insects crawled over it. I wrapped my mantle around me tightly, hoping Griogair would not notice my body trembling in the growing darkness.

"What were they doing there, at the well, so close to the cottage? Did the abbot send them there?" I nearly wailed as the enormity of the question sunk in. "Did they come for Eugenius? I will never escape the man, black-hearted adder that he is. But he'll not have my son. Not ever—I'll die before that."

"Mistress, your son is safe at Kisimul, and Murchard will protect him there."

"Yes, but what did they mean to do to him?" I began shaking violently, my teeth clattering. Griogair would have been blind and deaf not to have noticed.

"Wheesht, Mistress." I felt something warm and heavy fall about my shoulders and realized that Griogair had wrapped his own mantle around me. "Your son is safe. And you are safe as well. Come, let's go down. The hour is late and you should sleep. We'll visit Father Benneit again in the morning and see what he'll say about it, but no harm will come to you tonight. Nor to your son."

The firm touch of Griogair's arm on mine reassured and calmed me a little, and I managed to rise and make my way down the hill. The peat fire burning in Annag's cottage cheered me and the kind woman showed me where I might sleep inside, while Griogair left us and went outside to sleep with the crew. I thanked my hostess and lay down on the bracken bed. I wrapped both mantles tightly around me, for Griogair had neglected to take his when he left. The rough woven wool smelled of salt, and peat, and whisky, and some faint musky male scent. But curiously, I found the odor not unpleasant. As my body slowly warmed, I stared into the glow of the peat fire, visible across the small space of the cottage, seeing my son's face in the dying flames and waiting for sleep to find me.

CHAPTER 18

When I awoke early the next day Annag was busy stirring oatmeal into a cauldron of boiling water. Her husband Padraig had already left the cottage. I straightened my clothing and offered to help her, and she handed me the stirring stick and went to gather honey, salt, and butter for the meal, and then started to skim some fresh cream from last evening's milking.

"You'll be hungry this morning," she observed. I realized, as I watched her gather things together for the men to break their fast, that I did have an appetite.

"Forgive me, I had no appetite last night."

"Nor much of the time, I'm thinking. You're skinny as that stirring stick."

I wanted to throw the kettle of porridge at her, but smiled instead to cover my feelings.

"You're eaten up inside of you," my hostess continued. "But you've a lively boy. Perhaps it's not my place to be asking," she continued.

"Perhaps not," I snapped, but Annag just gave me a smile.

"Well, I won't ask, then, but I'm thinking you'll do no one any favors by starving yourself, Mistress. Least of all that boy of yours. And you a healer." She sniffed and put down the skimmer.

"My grandfather always said that the way to health led through moderation."

"Indeed. Moderation. It's not wise to deny yourself. I'm hoping you'll enjoy your breakfast."

"I'm sure that I will," I assented, but the exchange had taken away my hunger and once again I ate little, watching while the crew devoured every bit of Annag's porridge. For some reason the sight of the men enjoying their food irritated me. With poor grace I took the emptied bowls from the trestle table that had been set up outside, clanging the dishes together as I piled them up.

I helped our hostess wash the bowls and then went to find Griogair, carrying his mantle, now neatly folded, to return to him. I found him talking to Bricius, looking out over the shingle beach. Both men were watching a patch of bladderwrack and rocks near the water's edge.

"Och, look at the devils," Bricius said, his voice low.

Griogair smiled, then turned as he heard me approach.

"Mistress." Bricius pointed towards the area. "Look over there."

I followed his gaze and saw three otters playing in the seaweed, chasing each other on the rocks and rolling in the waves. I felt my cheeks soften and my annoyance dissipated. Some gulls cawed above and the otters disappeared in the waves, swimming down the shore towards the end of the island. We continued to watch a moment, all three of us silent. From further down the beach I heard the voices of the rest of the crew as they talked among themselves.

"How lovely they were," I said to Bricius and Griogair.

"Aye, Mistress," Griogair said, turning towards me with a softness in his eyes. "They were indeed."

I looked away from him for a moment, towards the waves, feeling unaccountably awkward. "Here is your mantle," I said, turning back towards him and handing him the cloak. "I thank you for it."

"You're welcome, Mistress. I hope you slept warmly."

"Indeed I did." I felt myself blush and looked away again. "So we will go and find Fearglas?"

"I'm thinking that would be wise. Perhaps the priest has a boat as well," Griogair said, his tone now matter-of-fact.

Bricius spoke. "I'll inspect the boats by the village and just see what is to be seen there, while you are speaking to Fearglas. And after that, perhaps time spent in the alehouse may yield gossip about the poor drowned lassie. No doubt Calum and Conall will accompany me there."

"Aye," Griogair said, with a laugh in his voice. "Just see that they do some gossiping, and not just drinking."

Bricius grinned back and left us to go find the rest of the crew. Griogair wrapped his mantle around him, for the wind was blowing in chill from the sea, and we set off, striding up the street towards Cristina's house and the church. A pig had gotten out from its sty and several young children chased it, squealing with excitement quite as shrilly as the pig itself, dodging geese and chickens and nearly crashing into some of the housewives going about their chores. But that clamor, thankfully, died down as we reached the north end of the small village.

We saw Fearglas sitting in front of his house, mending a net. He greeted us curiously.

"It will be the folk from Islay, will it not?" he said. "My mother told me you had returned. I heard about poor Morainn, and how she was found over there." He gestured across the sea, to where Barra could be seen across the Sound. "Sure, it is a sad thing, I'm thinking."

We agreed that it was, then Griogair continued. "Himself at Kisimul sent us back to see what we could discover of the matter here. He's not wanting the murder to go unsolved, nor to get on the bad side of the Abbot of Iona."

Fearglas frowned. "The abbot himself sent men here to see to it, some days ago it was."

"Yes," Griogair agreed, "but they did not find the murderer, did they?"

Fearglas set his work down for a moment and shrugged his shoulders. "They said nothing of it to me. They spoke with my mother, and with the priest. This was after the old woman died, and so it was some time since Morainn vanished. They asked to see my boat, but they found nothing there. And then they left the island."

"When was this?"

"A few days ago, I'm thinking."

I thought back. No doubt the abbot's men had come here right before they visited Kisimul. The thought brought chills crawling up my back, and I felt the hairs on my neck rise. My shoulders twitched. Fearglas looked at me with sympathy.

"Is it a goose walking over your grave, then?" he said with a smile.

"Och no, just that bit of breeze," I lied.

"Come, let's walk a bit," Griogair said. "It will warm you up." He turned to Fearglas. "Someone must have used a boat to take Morainn from Cille Bhrighde over to Barra. Would you walk with us, and show us whose boats are whose here?"

Fearglas put his net down with some eagerness, and strolled with us down to the beach. There were several boats beached there, mostly small naibheags, and curraghs. We saw Bricius and the others further down the beach, chatting with an older man.

"And which one is yours?" Griogair inquired.

Fearglas pointed out a larger curragh that looked very well cared for, and Griogair complimented him on the boat. While the two of them discussed sails and rigging I looked about the small landing area. I noticed another small boat drawn up at the north end of the beach, near the church, but Griogair called to me.

"Mistress, come here, if you please. Fearglas has agreed to take us out on a wee boat ride, perhaps over to Eriskay. There's a perfect breeze for a bit of a sail. It's a fine boat he has, indeed, and I'm wanting to see how it handles."

I followed them down the strand and we boarded the boat. Although large enough for two men to row, it was evident one man could handle it just as well. Fearglas pushed us into the water, jumped in, hoisted the sail, and we were off.

I wondered what Griogair was thinking, and why he'd suggested this outing. I was seated on a bit of planking that straddled the inside of the curragh. The boat hit a wave, and I nearly lost my balance. I reached my hands under the plank, seeking to hold onto something, and felt a wad of sodden fabric beneath my fingers. Once the boat had settled, I pulled it out, curious. I saw some faded black cloth, perhaps a cloak, all folded and wadded together. And there was a large rent in the fabric.

I glanced at Fearglas, but he seemed intent on adjusting the sail. Then I tried to catch Griogair's eye. Not sure what to do, I began to push the fabric back down below the seat, but Griogair, seated near me in the boat, noticed my movement.

"What's that, Mistress?" he asked.

I passed him the fabric.

"Och, well," he said to me, his voice low, "let's just ask Fearglas about it when we return to Cille Bhrighde."

I replaced the fabric on the floor of the boat and rested my feet on it, without Fearglas seeming to notice. We skirted the coast of Eriskay and headed back towards the village, Griogair keeping up a running commentary about the intricacies of sailing with Fearglas while I watched the seabirds and some porpoises that kept us company for a time. A colony of seals basked on some rocks near a sandy beach, watching us with placid round eyes as we passed.

I wondered again about the selkie that Kenna had claimed to see. Had Fearglas taken Morainn to Barra and murdered her there? He seemed a decent man, but everyone agreed he had fancied the woman. He could have killed her, if she had rebuffed him. That thought took the pleasure out of the trip. I suddenly felt eager to have my feet back on solid land, and not in a small boat at the mercy of a possible killer and the cold waves, and I felt a tightness in my chest ease as we turned back towards South Uist and Fearglas brought the boat into the harbor.

I picked up the cloth as I prepared to disembark, and handed it to Griogair as he helped me from the boat. Fearglas looked up from mooring the boat, and Griogair approached him after seeing me onto the beach. "I must ask you," Griogair said pleasantly. "Mistress Euphemia found this in your boat."

I could see the confusion in Fearglas's face as he looked. "It's an old rag. A cloak, it looks like. It's none of mine. I'm not knowing how it got into my boat. I did not put it there."

Griogair's face gave nothing away. "Did you not, then? How could it have gotten there?"

"My boat lies beached on the shore along with all the others. Anyone could have stowed it there. But what of it?" Fearglas asked, with an edge to his voice. "And why should you be asking me about it? I've never seen it before."

I watched the two men, and then saw, with some relief, Bricius, Calum, and Conall come out of the small cottage that served the village as an alehouse. They walked towards us, but Griogair remained intent on Fearglas.

"Let's just have a wee look at it then," Griogair continued in a conciliatory tone. "Surely you're curious about it as well."

"Please yourself," Fearglas grunted, and began to coil up a loose rope while Griogair unwadded the cloth. It was a dark, with a torn area on one side, partially mended, the color a faded black. I felt sure that the torn scrap of cloth I carried in my pouch would match the tear.

"A cloak," Griogair announced, and spread it out on the beach while Fearglas and I looked on.

"What of it?" Fearglas did not look worried, just confused. "Why would someone leave me a cloak? I've my own warm *brat* and this one is all but rags."

"You've not seen it before?"

"Never. But I'm not understanding why it would matter to you."

"Morainn's killer wore such a garment. And tore it on Barra. We've the scrap of cloth to prove it, found near where the lass drowned."

Now Fearglas did not look so sanguine. "I know nothing of the cloak, nor how it got there," he repeated, his jaw set hard. "I'll swear to it, if you wish."

"Well, then, you'll not mind if we look at your footprint."

"My footprint? Why would you be wanting to do that?" Fearglas's face reddened as his confusion turned to anger.

"There were footprints near the site of the killing as well," I said. "I made a tracing of them." Fearglas stared at me as if I'd grown a second head.

"I never took the woman to Barra," he protested. "I fancied the bitch a wee bit, but she'd have none of me. As for my footprints, there are plenty of them here, on the sand. You'd best be quick about it, though," he added. "The tide is coming in and will wash them away."

At this point Bricius and the others reached us. "What's amiss?" Bricius asked, taking in the situation.

"We found this old cloak in Fearglas's boat," Griogair explained. "You know, do you not," he said to Fearglas, "that the MacNeil at Kisimul sent us here to try and find the person who killed that poor lass on his own island."

"Indeed I ken that, the whole village knows that well enough," Fearglas responded, his voice hard with fury. "But it was not I that killed her."

"Then how did the cloak get into your boat?" Griogair asked.

"I've no way of knowing. It was not there yesterday, when I brought the boat in."

"Well, that may be, indeed," Griogair said with a sigh. "But you'll see why we must make sure that it was not you over there at Tobar Bharra."

Surrounded by the four men, some of whom had their hands on their dirks, Fearglas at length agreed to have his foot traced. Bricius went to Annag's cottage, to find a bit of cloth and some charcoal. The wind began to blow while we waited for him to return, and I wrapped my own *brat* around me snugly and bit my lip to stop it from quivering.

Bricius returned with a swatch of linen, as well as a bit of charcoal, and with Annag herself following close behind. Fearglas unwillingly put his bare foot down. I quickly traced his print on the linen. He shot me an offended glare as he removed his foot. By this time quite a crowd had gathered around us, including his mother who shrieked at us from the sidelines, crying that we had been mistaken and her son would never have killed Morainn. Other villagers muttered among themselves and it seemed the situation could rapidly get ugly. Griogair scanned the crowd, seeking to defuse the situation.

"Good folk, listen to me. We've been sent, as you know, to find the murderer of poor old Cristina's niece, a beautiful woman slain before her time. Himself at Kisimul is wanting the murder solved."

"Is the lord of Kisimul our chief?" I heard a voice mutter from the crowd. "I'm thinking not." Griogair heard it too.

"Indeed," Griogair responded. "But the poor woman was found on his lands, drowned in the holy well, the Tobar Bharra itself. Sacrilege it was for sure. And the MacNeil at Kisimul is very friendly with your chief at Howmore, and in fact the lord sent a messenger to let your own chief know of our visit. Did you know of that?" I watched as a few of the folk listening shook their heads. "So you'll not mind if we seek to find the killer."

"There are no murderers in this village," I heard another voice mutter. "It was the sidhe that took her, right enough. Or some demon."

"And who spoke to you of this?" Griogair demanded. "For I've never known the sidhe to strangle a woman, nor leave her to drown."

The muttering continued, but finally one young woman said, "It was Father Benneit who told us of it, did he not? At the Mass?" she demanded, and several of the villagers agreed.

"And what of this cloak?" Griogair asked the crowd. "It was found in Fearglas's boat, here. He says he knows nothing of it. Do any of you recognize it?"

It seemed the sidhe had stolen the tongues of the villagers, as well as their wits, for no one seemed to know anything about the mysterious cloak.

I carried the tracing of the original footprint in my pouch. The villagers edged closer as I unfolded it and compared it to the footprint of Fearglas I had just traced. I heard excited murmuring as people craned their necks to see. It was clear the two did not match. Fearglas's foot was broad, while the footprint Eugenius had found on Barra was narrower, and a bit shorter. That person had also worn shoes.

Griogair and I both examined the prints closely, but it was obvious they could not have been the same person. I stood up and refolded the original print, replacing it in my bag. I took the tracing of Fearglas's footprint as well.

"There. You can see it was not me," Fearglas said, adjusting his mantle and glaring at us.

"Och, I can see that clearly," Griogair said. "But we had to be certain, ye ken."

Fiona burst from the cluster of folk surrounding us and embraced her son, who turned blood red and extricated himself from her arms. His mother shot an evil look at Griogair and me.

"Here," Griogair offered, "let us buy you a drink in the alehouse; we've no hard feelings and hope you will say the same. And your mother as well, if she wishes."

Fearglas sniffed, and rearranged his plaid again, but finally agreed to go with us. Fiona refused, saying she had too much work to do and her garden would not take care of itself. I left Griogair, the cloak folded over his arm, and Fearglas headed towards the alehouse, accompanied by Bricius, Calum, Conall, and most of the villagers. Annag approached me as the men walked away.

"That cloak that your man is carrying," she said.

"Yes?"

"I think I have seen it before. The color looks like something a priest might wear."

I spoke with her a moment longer, then she took her leave and left me standing alone on the beach. I watched Fiona head towards her house and called out to her. She turned and spat at me, but I continued my approach.

"I am sorry," I called out, following as she stalked away. "But the cloak in Fearglas's boat—we had to know for sure he did not murder Morainn."

The old woman stopped and turned around. "Well, I do not understand why you are here at all," she said "Sticking your noses into places they do not belong and causing trouble for my poor son."

"You do not want to know who killed Morainn? She was a guest and ate at the same table as you did!"

"Aye, and never helped to put the food on the table, did she. It's as I said, it's no loss to me that she's gone, for all she's the daughter of an abbot." We had reached the house next to the church, and Fiona headed inside.

"Let me help you," I offered. "It's the least I can do after the trouble we've caused you. The men will all be at the alehouse for some time, I think. The weather's turning bad."

Fiona sniffed and then, to my surprise, she opened the door. "Fine, come in then," she said.

CHAPTER 19

It was you that cleared his name," Fiona muttered, and she served me some of her own small ale.

I said nothing but took a sip of the drink, welcome after the chill of the day. "Tell me of Morainn," I said, after a time.

"You told me you were her dearest friend. You should know plenty of her."

"Yes," I murmured, flustered. "That is why I seek to find her killer. But tell me of her time here. Who did she speak with? Who was she friendly with? What did she do, if she was not helping you tend to old Cristina?"

"It's as I've told you. She flirted with Fearglas, leading him on, then spurning him. She occasionally spoke with Father Benneit. I'm thinking he was her confessor on Iona, and she went to Mass when she could while she was here. Not that I saw her pray overmuch, for all her father is a churchman."

"He's a powerful man," I commented.

"Aye, and the lass spoiled, like any rich man's daughter. She wandered the hills, and at times she would keep her old aunt company. So perhaps she did care for Cristina, in her way. But she left it to me to change the old woman and and feed her and wash her. The poor thing could do nothing for herself, after she became elf-shot."

I murmured sympathetically. "Did you ever see Morainn with anyone else in the village? Someone must have taken her across the sea to Barra. What reason would they have to do that?"

"Tobar Bharra is well known as a healing spring. Perhaps she meant to bring some of the water back for her aunt," Fiona said.

"Perhaps." I prayed my skepticism did not show on my face. "But who would have taken her there, if not Fearglas?" I persisted.

"Many folk here have boats."

"Whoever it was that took her there, and killed her there, planted that cloak in your son's boat. Who bears your son such ill will?"

Fiona's brow creased. "Fearglas is well liked."

"Then why hide the cloak in his boat? And whose cloak could it be? Did you recognize it?" I found myself wishing

Griogair had not taken the cloak with him to the alehouse, so Fiona and I could examine it together.

Fiona shook her head. "I'd never seen it before. It's just an old cloak."

Still, I thought perhaps I had seen it, and Annag's words from earlier had made me even more certain of that, and so, after a few minutes I bade Fiona farewell and walked up to the chapel.

I found no sign of Father Benneit. The bench he had been sitting on the day before was empty, his mending vanished, put away someplace. Perhaps he had stowed it on Fearglas's boat, I thought as I searched for the priest. I heard a rhythmic swishing, followed by a soft thudding, coming from inside the chapel. The sound repeated, numerous times. It stirred an old and noxious recollection within me. I shuddered but, despite the memory, the noise drew me inside, and I pushed open the door and entered. The sound continued. As my eyes adjusted to the dim light filtering inside the chapel through the open door I saw Father Benneit, kneeling before the altar with his upper body bared, flogging himself with a small leather whip, blood running down his back.

I stepped outside again and silently closed the door behind me, breathing fast, feeling acid rise in my throat. I remembered, before I left Iona, how some of the nuns had practiced flagellation. I had myself, in those days on Iona after the abbot forced me, when I had felt so sinfully depraved, vile, and unworthy. I remembered the whip and the pain all too well, and had no desire to intrude on Father Benneit's penance. I wondered what sins the man sought redemption for.

The priest apparently had not noticed me, and the sound of the flogging went on unabated. I swallowed down bile, forced myself to slow my breathing, and my panic retreated somewhat. As the priest appeared occupied with his scourge, I decided to search around outside. The church stood close to the narrow beach, and I saw again the small curragh pulled up on shore, a few footprints leading away from it back to the chapel. I went closer to investigate, thinking the curragh must belong to the church. Surely a boat would be of more use to the priest of this parish, perched as it was against stony hills and surrounded by the sea, than a horse would be.

A small, neat foot had made the prints, a foot that looked close in size to the tracing I had made and still carried with me. The boat was of such a size that one man could easily row it, although the mast for a sail meant such labor would not always be necessary. It would have been easy enough to cross to Barra after the sun had set, and return before the morning. Curious, I looked inside, under the rowing benches, but found nothing except the stowed oars, a coiled rope and rigging, and the sail, neatly stowed away. No dark cloaks that might change a man from a human to a selkie when glimpsed by moonlight. And, at first glance, nothing else.

I was about to leave when a stray sunbeam caught a glint of something wedged under a rib of the boat, and I turned again to see what it might be. A coil of rope had hidden it, and I shifted that to one side, the better to see. I bent to look and saw a woman's hair ornament, a bent U-shaped pin of silver with a filigreed decoration. And tangled with it were two long red-gold hairs, the same color as poor Morainn's.

I reached into the boat. My fingers tightened around my find and jerked it free.

"Whatever is all this?"

Intent on my task, I had not heard the footsteps behind me. I whirled around, hiding the pin within my clenched hand, and saw Father Benneit approaching.

"Father," I said, hoping I appeared flustered. As indeed I must have, for my heart raced like some wild thing. "I was seeking you and could not find you—"

"And what was it you wanted?"

"Griogair wished to see you," I improvised. "I could not find you at the church, and came down to see if you might be here. I was just admiring this fine little boat, then I dropped my hairpin here and was just retrieving it." I jabbed the pin deep into my braids and pulled my mantle over my head. The sunbeam that had guided me a few moments ago had vanished, and the clouds began to spit rain.

"Well, I am here now," Father Benneit said, looking at his boat curiously. I prayed he saw nothing amiss. He seemed satisfied and finally added, "Go back to Griogair and tell him he can come and find me here, at the chapel, should he wish to. I'm not at his beck and call."

"Indeed, thank you, sir," I said, and scurried away like some rabbit back towards the alehouse to find Griogair.

The cottage that served as Cille Bhrighde's alehouse was small, and crowded this rainy afternoon, smelling of peat and salt and men. But it was easy enough to find Griogair in the midst of the room, surrounded by our men, Fearglas, and some other villagers.

"Och, Mistress Euphemia," he hailed me while the other men stared at this woman intruding in their domain. "Whatever is it, then?"

"I must speak with you. Outside."

Griogair must have seen the look on my face, for he quickly excused himself and left the cottage with me. "What is it, Mistress?"

"I found this." I pulled the pin from my hair and showed him. Thankfully the long red hairs remained, still tangled in the filigree. "In Father Benneit's curragh. It is Morainn's hair pin. And the footprints—he is the killer, Griogair, I am sure of it. Father Benneit himself found me there but I told him you had sent me for him. I do not think he saw the pin in the boat. I told him I had dropped mine."

Griogair might have spent some hours in a tavern but he looked intent and sober, all focused business now. "We have him, then. The priest murdered Morainn. The pin and the cloak, the same one we saw him mending yesterday, will damn him well enough." He glanced at me. "Wait here, I will go fetch the others."

He left me and walked rapidly into the alehouse. I stood uncertainly, staring out over the waves, wondering what cause the priest might have had to kill the abbot's daughter. A bit out from shore I saw two seals, their heads just breaking through the water, their eyes dark and small in their round heads before they disappeared back among the waves. I thought of selkies, black robed priests, and drowned women, and shivered, wrapping my mantle around me.

It could not have been more than a moment or two before Griogair, Bricius, and the rest of the men emerged from the cottage, followed by Fearglas and a few other villagers. Griogair gestured to me, and the men started off at a rapid walk towards the chapel. I followed after, the wind spitting raindrops into my face.

When we reached the chapel, I saw the door remained closed, and I prayed we would not find the priest flagellating himself again. I realized I had not mentioned that to Griogair, but perhaps it did not matter overmuch. Griogair pushed the door open and saw Father Benneit standing behind the altar, wiping the chalice used for communion. In this humble church, it was a simple silver vessel, adorned with a few cairngorms, that gleamed in the light of the candle the priest had lit. A silver flask, holding communion wine, also sat on the altar, and the Tabernacle, that chest which held the consecrated bread for communion, stood open.

Father Benneit put the chalice down on the altar and looked at the men. He poured some communion wine into it from the silver flask. "Herself said you wanted to speak with me," he said, his voice even. "What was it you were after? As you see, I'm busy, preparing for the Mass."

"You ken well enough what it is we are here for," Griogair replied. "We've found proof you murdered the abbot's daughter, and are here to take you to justice."

Father Benneit did not seem shocked at this accusation. "And what proof might that be?" he asked mildly. "An old cloak found in someone else's boat?"

"Aye," Griogair replied. "One whose rip matches a scrap of cloth we found on Barra."

"But that was in someone else's boat, not mine. And why should I take Morainn to Barra?"

"That I do not know. But we found the woman's own hairpin in your boat."

The priest seemed unconcerned. "I've known Morainn for years, since I was a young priest in her father's service on Iona. I've no reason to kill her. But I could have taken her out in that boat. And she might have dropped a hairpin there. Women do. You dropped one yourself, Mistress Euphemia," he said, turning to me. "Or so you told me."

I nodded, my throat harsh and dry, staring him full in the face.

"Morainn was always a bonny lass. And free with her favors, even when handfasted to that Iain Mór. Her father pushed that on her, but she did not mind, for the son of the Lord of the Isles was rich and powerful. But we spent time together all the same, when Iain Mór was away from Iona. So who's to say who in truth is the father of Morainn's son? It might well have been me, although as a priest I must have no sons."

"Then why kill the woman, if she granted you her favors?" Griogair asked. "For we know that you killed her. We found your footprints on Barra, leading from the well, and you were seen on the beach that night, in your dark cloak. The woman thought she'd seen a selkie."

"And who is to say that she did not?"

"She saw a murderer," I finally said, finding my voice. "And I'm thinking it was you."

"And what if it was? I've done penance for my sins. You saw me yourself, Mistress. Did you think I did not see you spying on me earlier? But I have atoned. I am cleansed, forgiven." I shuddered, remembering the rivulets of blood streaming down the pale flesh of the man's back.

"But why kill her?" Griogair repeated.

"I wanted her again, now that she was here on Uist," Father Benneit said. "The woman teased me, and tormented me, and raised the lust in me, but in the end she refused me. She swore if I took her to Tobar Bharra she would give me what I craved. But she refused me there, saying she'd have no more of me, that her father would marry her to some rich noble now that she had borne a child to Iain Mór, and we argued. My rage got the better of me. I drowned her, to my sorrow." He shrugged, his face absurdly placid, as if it all mattered little to him. "I did not know what to do, so I left her there by the well."

"And why did Morainn want to go to Tobar Bharra?" I asked.

"She said she had to finish a task her father had set her to do."

"And what task would that have been?" I asked, dreading his answer.

"She would not tell me, exactly." The priest looked at us. "You must believe me. I did not want to take her life. I loved the woman well." Father Benneit then turned his back to us and took a small vial from the tabernacle, adding its contents to the wine in the chalice. He raised the vessel to his lips to take a draught. I realized, almost too late, what he planned.

"Stop him!" I cried. "He'll have poisoned the wine!"

Griogair lunged across the room and seized the priest by his arms. The chalice fell; the wine, the red blood of Christ, flowed in a dark flood over the stones of the chapel floor.

Father Benneit's foot fit the tracing I carried exactly. That, along with the old cloak and the hairpin I had found, was enough to damn him, and we trussed him up and made plans to carry him back to Kisimul, while the villagers gossiped about it all, the scandal of it rocking the small village to its roots.

Despite his thwarted attempt to take his own life, Father Benneit now insisted he had benefit of clergy and should be tried in an ecclesiastical court. Griogair assured me that the MacNeil, as well as the Lord of the Isles himself, would have little patience with the abbot's creature, and perhaps the abbot himself would not look too kindly on the man who had slain his own daughter, whether clergy or no. And if it was decided that the man be tried in an ecclesiastical court, I felt sure the Lord of the Isles had influence with the abbot at Kintyre, as well as the Bishop of the Isles on Skye, and that the Green Abbot's man might not get off easily in those courts. And so, with the priest tied securely and well guarded by Calum and Conall, who stood over him with their hands on stout cudgels, we left that evening to return to Kisimul. The sun set crimson over the Western Sea and the red cast of it reminded me of the blood and wine I'd seen spilled that day. I sat as far from Father Benneit as I could, close by the tiller, which Griogair manned as we sailed through that blood-red sea back to Barra.

CHAPTER 20

We reached Kisimul late. The sky had darkened and torches flickered by the iron *yett* that blocked the entrance to the castle. Griogair hailed the watchmen and we waited while they raised the creaking gate and we docked the boat. I disembarked and stood awkwardly, listening while Griogair explained the situation to Murchard, who looked to have arrived straight from supping in the Great Hall. I saw Father Benneit hustled away, well guarded, to that same small cell I had occupied a few days ago, and felt relief surge through my body when I realized that both Cristina's and Morainn's murders were solved. I could not be accused of them; the killer of the abbot's daughter had been found and had confessed. Cristina had died of natural causes. I had proved my innocence.

But what of Eugenius and his safety? I thought I knew what the unfinished business was that Morainn had sought to do for her father up at Saltinish, and although Fingon had been thwarted then, he might well try again. But no tangible proof existed, except for the vial of poison I had found when I first arrived here so long ago—it felt like years now—and the vial in Morainn's pouch at Cille Bharra.

I asked after Amie, and a serving girl told me I could find her in her chamber. Happy to leave the men, I crossed the castle yard and entered Amie's room. Amie sat on the bed with her new babe, crooning a lullaby to the boy. He nursed hungrily at her breast, and Amie appeared to have recovered well from his birth. In the candlelight her face had a blooming look to it, like some summer primrose. After we embraced, she laid the baby in the ornately carved cradle, and I was thankful to see no vision of a pall over it, just a warm woolen blanket within covering the sleepy child.

Amie quickly showed me to the small room I had previously shared with Eugenius, and arranged to have a pallet made up there for me. I looked at my son sleeping peacefully; the light of the candle Amie held in her free hand shone like some golden halo over my boy's curls, although I well knew him to be no angel at all, just an often fractious four-year-old child.

"He's been a good lad while you were gone," Amie told me. "He spends all his time at the kennel, with the puppy

Murchard gave him. He barely notices the new baby, he's so entranced with the dog."

"Did he give it a name?" I asked.

"Aye. Cuilean."

We both smiled at the thought of naming the dog "puppy," but it seemed as good a name as any.

"Have you eaten?" Amie asked after she checked on the baby. "There is some wine here; come, have a glass with me before you rest."

I nodded, and Amie poured us each a glass from the pitcher that sat on the table in the bedchamber. "So, now, you must tell me what happened on Uist."

"Did Murchard tell you what happened before I left, after you had the baby?"

Amie wrinkled her nose. "Aye, eventually, and he got the sharp edge of my tongue for it. To imprison the mother of my own foster-child, a woman who has done so much for us! The man is an *amadan*, for all that he is the father of my son." I took a sip of my wine, glad for the rich taste of it on my tongue, and did not answer Amie. "To think that you would have slain Morainn," Amie continued after a moment. "Poor thing." She made the sign of the cross.

"Yet I am sure she meant to poison Eugenius," I replied. "I believe Morainn left the poison for Eugenius first, before I arrived here. And some words that priest said, Father Benneit, makes me think she planned somehow to finish the job when she came to Tobar Bharra."

"Dhia!" Amie crossed herself again and looked quickly over at her sleeping child. "And she a guest in my own home! But what reason might she have to do such a thing?"

"I do not know for sure," I confessed, "but I intend to find out. The Lord of the Isles is his own godfather, so perhaps it was a revenge upon him." I did not tell Amie of my own dealings with Fingon Mackinnon. I still could not believe he would willingly murder his own son, despite his hatred of me. I took a deep draught of wine, feeling safe in my friend's company.

"So who was it that killed her?" Amie asked, after refilling our glasses.

I told her of Father Benneit, and how the two had known each other in Iona, and what we had discovered. "He tried to take his own life—"

"A mortal sin, and the man a priest!"

"Yes, but we stopped him, and brought him here. I am not sure what Murchard will do with him."

"If I were to guess, I'd think he'll call on the Lord of the Isles, and let him make the judgment. Murchard is canny enough; he'll not want to anger either His Lordship or the Green Abbot, and Father Benneit is the abbot's man. But here, I'm keeping you awake with my chatter—you look done in, Euphemia. Best get some sleep now, and we'll see what my husband plans tomorrow. And I must sleep myself, now, while I can. For this one will wake in a few hours, wanting to eat again." Her lips curved upwards in proud affection as she looked at her infant son.

I left her then, and retired to the little room where my son slept. Perhaps it was the wine, but I slept deeply, without dreams, for the first time in many days.

I heard Eugenius wake the next morning, and opened my eyes. He looked at me with those grey eyes of his, so like my father's. "Mother, you're back!"

"Aye, I am," I said. "Come here, Eugenius, and give me a hug."

My son approached and gave me a quick embrace, then snuggled down with me on the bed.

"I'm hearing you have a dog now, for all that I've not been gone that long."

Eugenius grinned. "Aye, Mother, it is a fine one, a brindled yellow one. I've named it Cuilean. Come, you must see it. We can go to the kennels now, before it is time to break fast. Hurry, Mother, please, let's go!"

I could deny my son nothing, so we both quickly dressed and went out into the courtyard, heading for the kennels. The sky overhead blazed a deep blue, and the crisp breeze blew on my skin. I felt my lips curve up, and an unfamiliar little laugh bubbled on my lips as I watched Eugenius caper across the yard, leading me between Murchard's men polishing their broadswords and castle servants hustling about.

We had almost reached the kennels when I saw Murchard striding across the courtyard. I hoped we could avoid him;

I had barely spoken with him the night before and had little desire to speak with him today. Although I had heard his litany of reasons for imprisoning me, they still rankled, and I realized I did not altogether trust the man.

"Mistress Euphemia!"

I had no choice but to turn at Murchard's voice, a false smile now plastered upon my face.

"My lord," I said, as Eugenius went to his foster father for a hug. "Eugenius was just taking me to the kennels to see his puppy."

"Well enough," Murchard grunted. "He will grow to be a fine dog, I'm thinking." He turned from hugging his foster son to look at me. "Go ahead, lad. I must speak with your mother a bit."

I watched Eugenius make his way to the kennels and waited for Murchard to continue.

"We've sent for His Lordship of the Isles and his own *brehon* to adjudicate this case." He spat on the stones of the castle yard. "That damned priest, and the trouble he caused. He's a MacKinnon, you ken, and the abbot's own man. I'm not wanting to be accused of a fondness for the Green Abbot by my own Lord of the Isles, so Himself can just bring his own man to judge the case."

I murmured something to the effect that such a course sounded wise.

"I think perhaps your own father will come with the party as well. He keeps the records, after all."

"When do you expect them?" The thought of seeing my father made my heart a little lighter.

"The earliest they could get here is some three days from now," Murchard replied. "The messenger left early today."

"And what of the abbot? It's his own daughter that was murdered."

"We've sent word to him as well. Although as the man is supposedly banished to Iona, so I'm doubting he'll come." I gnawed my lip, praying that the Green Abbot would remain on Iona far away from me, but Murchard did not notice my distress and continued. "Or he'll want us to travel to Iona, to judge the case there. Och, well, we'll sort it out when they arrive." The MacNeil shook his head and then looked at me, his brown eyes keen and curious. I glanced away. "But you, Mistress, you are well?"

"I am well enough," I replied shortly, "but I still want to know who tried to poison my son."

"As do I." Murchard's jaw set as he replied. "He is my charge, after all, and I care for the lad." I thought it must have cost Murchard something to have made that statement, and so I took a breath, looked him full in the face, and nodded in agreement. "I am sure my wife is happy to have your company again," Murchard continued, "for the few days until His Lordship arrives. And once the case is settled, no doubt you'll want to return home with them."

"Once I am sure my son is safe here," I replied. "I'll not leave until then."

Murchard bristled at this. "I'll keep your son safe, Mistress. You need not worry yourself on that count."

I inclined my head, unsure how far I could push him, but did not say anything.

"But there'll be the christening as well," Murchard continued after a strained moment, in a more conciliatory tone. "And my wife must be churched. We've not scheduled it yet, with all of this, but I'm sure Amie will want you to stay for that. Perhaps we'll hold it after the trial is over."

I nodded again, and left my host to find my own son in the kennels, grateful for the company of dogs and children.

The next days passed quietly enough, although Amie was full of plans for the christening. She and Murchard decided to hold it the following week on the days of both Saint Trea and Saint Senach, in the hopes that the trial would be speedily concluded and over by then, but that the Great Lords might wish to stay a few days longer and see the son of the MacNeil baptized. Amie needed help preparing chambers for His Lordship and the expected retainers. I was content enough to help her manage these tasks, keeping my mind off what might come. The maidservants scurried about, while the cook sent for provisions from the island and the men went out fishing.

The galley, a *lymphad* flying the standard of the Lord of the Isles, was sighted late on the afternoon of the fourth day, and both Murchard and his wife, Amie dressed in her finest, went to welcome their lord to Kisimul. Eugenius, in a clean tunic, was summoned to greet his godfather and I came also, dressed in Amie's discarded blue tunic and a clean kertch. I pinned my mother's cairngorm on my mantle and waited, anxiously, for the Lord of the Isles to disembark. Murchard's bard stood at the ready, as did his *luchd-tighe*, standing with polished swords and helmets in their quilted linen *cotuns*, waiting for the Lord of the Isles.

The lymphad, one of His Lordship's largest galleys, rowed by fifteen oarsmen on each side, approached swiftly, pulling up through the yett and docking. Late afternoon sun glinted on the polished targes and spears of His Lordship's men. As the boat came through the sea gate the oarsmen rested their oars and the ship glided up to the dock. The crew busily worked the brails and furled the strong woolen sail, while I scanned the others on the boat.

I saw His Lordship, Donald MacDonald himself, Lord of the Isles. His dark hair flew in the breeze and his eyes looked sharply at the welcoming party assembled to meet him. He wore a fur-trimmed woolen mantle, pinned with a large gold and crystal brooch. The sun sent a ray of light sparkling from the depths of the stone. The wide sleeves of his *leine*, woven from the finest saffron linen, flapped under his mantle, and over his shirt he wore a vest of wolf skin. His gold-hilted broadsword shone in the sunlight. Among his retainers I spied my father, his slight figure wrapped in a green and brown patterned *brat* against the sea breeze. He caught my eye and smiled, and I waved back.

"Look, Eugenius. There's your grandfather!" My son grinned and waved wildly, and I saw my father's smile grow wider as he glimpsed his grandson among the crowds. The nobles and His Lordship disembarked and the crew began the work of mooring the large boat, coiling the ropes and seeing to the rigging.

"My Lord." Murchard bowed. "Welcome to Kisimul." Amie curtseyed, as did I, and Eugenius made a proper enough bow. The other assorted servants and clansmen assembled in the courtyard of the castle did likewise. Murchard and Amie led their guest towards the Great Hall, but Eugenius and I pushed through the crowd surrounding the boat until I reached my father, who was seeing to some of His Lordship's belongings.

"Father!"

"Och, white love, it is good to see you! And this one—how you have grown, son!" My father hugged his grandson, then gave me a searching look. "He does well, the lad? He looks hale enough."

My happiness to see my father must have shown on my face. "We stayed at Tobar Bharra and he took the cure there. Until—well, you do not know of it, do you?" I did not want to discuss all of what had happened in front of Eugenius, but my son himself started to speak of it.

"Grandfather, I saw a dead woman. Drowned, she was, just lying there. But Mother did not let me get close enough to get a good look. And I have a puppy, his name is Cuilean! Come and see him!"

"That's a fine thing, to have a dog," my father answered with a smile. "I've had many myself. Although I am not so sure about the other thing you were speaking of. That might not have been so fine. I will have to see your pup. Not just yet, I am thinking," he added, as Eugenius opened his mouth. "The Great Lords will have things to discuss, and I must be there to record what they say."

Eugenius looked disappointed. "Go on ahead to the kennels, Eugenius," I said. "I will talk a little with your grandfather and follow along." His face brightened and he started across the courtyard. My father watched him for a moment, then turned to me.

"He is growing up."

"Indeed, and I've missed so much of it."

"Well, with the Lord of the Isles his godfather and the chief of the MacPhees his uncle, we'd no choice but to foster him. And you yourself a recluse on Jura. You could not keep him there; that's no place to raise a child."

"I could not help it, Father. I could not return to Iona."

"Neither your mother nor I wanted you to go there in the first place, all those years ago. But I wish you had felt comfortable staying on Islay instead of in that cave."

I glanced down, stubborn, but could not meet his eyes. "That cave has served me well enough."

"Well," my father replied, looking at my blue dress, "still, it is a fine thing to see you out of that old habit of yours. It was falling to pieces. But now, tell me of this coil. We heard that damned abbot is part of the tangle."

"I found his daughter drowned in the Tobar Bharra. And then he accused me of poisoning the woman's aunt on Uist as well."

"He did?" My father's voice was sharp.

"But we've found the killer, Father. A priest. He knew Morainn before, on Iona."

"We?" my father asked. "Who helped you with all of that?"

"One of Murchard's men. Griogair, he is called, a MacRuairi. And some others to crew the boat."

My father looked thoughtful. "He came with you to Colonsay, did he not?" I nodded yes. "And it was for this Murchard summoned Himself here?"

"He wants His Lordship's man to judge the case."

My father thought on this. "That's wise enough. And I think the abbot will be none too happy about that." He flashed a smile and his grey eyes softened a bit, then narrowed. "You are out of danger, now, praise the saints, since the priest has confessed. But why should the abbot accuse you? What cause did he have? Does the man have something against you?"

I said nothing. My father gazed uncertainly at me a while longer. "I must go see to His Lordship," he said, when I did not reply. "No doubt he'll be wanting me."

I laughed, trying to make light of the exchange. "And I have a son to see to; I'd best be off before he's disrupted the kennels entirely."

"Aye. Tell him I'll come by to look at the pup when I can." He paused a moment. "It's glad I am to see you and the boy have come to no harm."

"Yes, Father, you've no need to worry," I reassured him. Surely I did feel better for seeing my father, yet still I wondered why I did not feel completely safe myself.

CHAPTER 21

That evening was taken up with feasting and the poems of the bards, honoring the deeds of the Lord of the Isles and those of his ancestors. In return, His Lordship's own bard recited a poem honoring the MacNeil and his fair home, and the toasts and drinking went on late into the night. Amie had asked me to check on the baby for her; as the hostess and wife of the MacNeil, her presence was required at the feast.

I sat next to my father, at the far end of the head table, for as the daughter of the Keeper of the Records, and the mother of the MacNeil's foster son, I had some precedence. On my other side sat another of the MacDonald's men, his own physician, a Beaton cousin of mine. I found the company surprisingly diverting, for I had not seen my cousin in years. We exchanged information on various remedies, and I learned of his family and children—all living with him in his house near Finlaggan, not fostered. Despite that pleasant company I ate little. After the food had been removed the bard sang of the fine deeds of Good John of the Isles, Donald's father. When he had finished, I made my excuses and slipped away from the hall to see to the babe, before the MacNeil's bard could begin another song. The smoke of the torches and scent of ale hung thick inside, and as I stepped outside I drew a deep and welcome breath of the fresh, salt air.

The way across the courtyard from the hall to Amie's quarters led past the guardhouse and I shuddered as I thought of Father Benneit imprisoned there. A few of the MacNeil's guard stood in front of the entrance, speaking in low voices. One of them saw me, then broke away from the group and approached. I recognized Griogair.

"Mistress Euphemia," he greeted me. "How are you?"

"Well enough," I answered. I had seen little of Griogair since our return to Kisimul, and for some reason now felt embarrassed by that fact. It was not that I had avoided him, not really. There had been a great deal to do to help Amie get ready for His Lordship's visit. "You are not at the feast?" I asked him, after a little pause.

"Och, Himself thought someone had better keep close watch on that prisoner, and so we are here." Griogair answered me easily enough. Perhaps he had not noticed my absence.

"And have you heard when the trial might be?" I asked. "And if the abbot will be coming here?"

"The rumors are that perhaps the Lords will take Father Benneit back to Iona, and pass judgment on him there. I do not think Donald of the Isles wants the Green Abbot anyplace else." Griogair grinned wryly. "And if they held the trial anyplace without the abbot in attendance, he would make trouble out of it."

"He will forever make folk dance to his tune," I said, my voice bitter. "Even His Lordship."

"It's a thin harp string the man won't play on, indeed. Don't fret on it, Mistress," Griogair added. He must have noted my discomfort. "His Lordship is canny. There's great wisdom in keeping your enemy in your sight."

"Aye," I said, but my agreement was not whole-hearted. "I must see to the bairn," I added, after another silent moment. "Amie worries about the babe, and I promised I would check on him and the nursemaid."

"Well, I'm no man to stand between a woman and a child," Griogair said with a laugh. I walked to Amie's chamber, leaving Griogair to his watch and feeling oddly bereft.

I slept little that night, worrying about what might come. Even if Father Benneit were convicted of murdering Morainn, and my innocence proved, my son would still be in danger, until I learned for sure who had tried to poison him.

I suspected Fingon MacKinnon, although whether the abbot realized he had tried to kill his own flesh and blood I did not know. But to bring Fingon to justice I would need to confront him, and that I was loath to do. The thought of it made my stomach twist like some tangled rope, and I felt the sour taste of fear rise in my throat.

The tabby cat clambered into bed beside me with a thump, sleepy and satiated after some nocturnal hunt. I felt him knead the blanket with his claws, and listened to his purrs, and my son's soft snores, while the dark hours slowly crept by.

The next morning, early, my father brought word to me that the Lord of the Isles and the MacNeil would hold a council in the Great Hall, and I was summoned to attend.

"It's not a formal trial, white love," my father said, reassuring me. "They're going to discuss what has transpired and decide how best to proceed, what with the priest being the abbot's man and the abbot himself already judged a traitor. But they'll want to hear what you and Griogair discovered on Uist, and the evidence against the priest."

I nodded, and my father left to attend to His Lordship. I readied myself, and washed my face and hands, marveling that they shook only a little. I smoothed my hair and readjusted my kertch over it. I once again wore the blue dress and my mother's cairngorm pin, hoping I looked like a respectable woman, a mother, and not a disgraced and fallen nun. Then, taking a deep breath and fixing the image of my son in my heart, I went to the Great Hall.

The tables from the night before had been cleared away, and the Lord of the Isles sat on a dais; next to him sat Murchard. The brehon sat below, waiting to hear the evidence and give his advice, and my father sat there also, with his parchment and pen before him, ready to record whatever was decided. I saw Griogair, and the rest of the men who had accompanied us to Uist, standing below the dais. Griogair's eyes flashed a welcome and felt relieved to see their familiar faces as I approached. Others of the MacDonald's men, as well as the Kisimul men, stood in little knots, talking among themselves, as they waited for the Lords and the judge to start their deliberations.

The door opened again, and some of Murchard's men hustled in Father Benneit. His time in the cell seemed to have done him little harm, although his priest's robe had smears of dirt on it. He still carried himself straight and proud, almost ignoring the two guards that clasped his arms and walked him into the Great Hall, and the thick rope tied around his hands.

"I have benefit of clergy. I must be tried by the Church." Father Benneit appeared unabashed by the presence of the most powerful man in the Isles.

"My brehon will decide where the jurisdiction in this case lies," His Lordship announced. "We'll have the evidence now."

Griogair approached and told of finding the cloak, the footprint that fitted the tracing found near the Tobar Bharra, and finished with the confession we had heard. The brehons deliberated and Father Benneit still loudly pronounced his need to be tried by clergy.

I watched my father, as the Keeper of the Records, record it all with ink on parchment. The judge conferred with His Lordship and I could see by the steely glint in His Lordship's eyes that the man was not pleased.

I watched my father set down his quill, waiting for His Lordship's decisions, and finally the great lord spoke.

"My brehon advises me that it is true, the priest has benefit of clergy and must be tried by the Church."

I watched the angular tightness in the priest's jaw soften a bit as he relaxed.

"But," His Lordship continued, "Fingon MacKinnon, the Abbot of Iona, has proved himself no friend of justice, nor of the truth. The Abbot of Iona is subordinate to the Bishop of the Isles, whose seat is in Snizort, on Skye. We shall send for him to adjudicate and, since Fingon MacKinnon is not to leave the Isle of Iona"—he shot a sideways glance at the MacNeil—"we will convene there, along with the Bishop of the Isles, to hold the final hearing of the case. Send word to the bishop, and to the abbot on Iona today," he ordered. "We'll leave for Iona on the morrow."

The christening of Amie and Murchard's babe would have to wait.

The next day dawned clear, with a fair wind for sailing and favorable tides, so we made an early start. I was glad to leave Eugenius safe in Amie's care as I nervously boarded the great lymphad and took a seat next to my father on a cushioned bench. My stomach churned; I had not been able to eat, neither last night nor today, vomiting up what I had managed to swallow at the evening meal and not even bothering to taste the food set out for folk this morning. I had not set foot on Iona in five years, since I left the nunnery. I had no desire to go there now.

Despite my father's assurances to the contrary, I feared somehow I would be forced back into the nunnery. I had taken vows, though they were those of a novice, not final. And this trip would also mean facing Fingon, yet again. I swore silently, while the crew bustled with final preparations and the oarsmen settled in their places, that I would have the truth of my son's poisoning out of the bastard before this trip was done.

Griogair had also boarded the vessel and my father motioned him to a seat nearby. The early sun shone on Griogair's hair, bringing out the highlights of russet in the chestnut color. He settled himself comfortably on the bench with the ease of an experienced sailor.

"I was thinking you would travel with the MacNeil, on his own galley," I observed. A true convoy of ships headed for Iona from Barra this morning, what with this great galley, that of the MacNeil, and another boat, well manned with warriors of both chiefs, which carried Father Benneit—tightly trussed and guarded, I noted with relief.

"I thought that would most likely be the way of it, but Lord Donald's brehon wanted the witnesses to travel with him, in this fine, braw ship." He looked around the galley with a sailor's eye. "And so it is, indeed." Griogair stretched his legs out a bit, around the bundle of my belongings I had brought onboard, and flashed a smile.

"And so you're a MacRuairi?" my father inquired.

"Aye, from Uist." Griogair went on to tell my father of his parentage, rambling in a way that surprised me. Meanwhile, the boat had eased out from the mooring at the castle and the oarsmen bent their backs to their task. A little way out into the bay, some of the sailors raised the sail to catch the breeze, and the oarsmen let up on their labors as the sail filled.

I watched His Lordship, seated under a fine canopy in the center of the boat, conferring with his judge, and then saw them gesture towards my father.

"You must excuse me." My father cut short Griogair's rambling. "Himself wants me." My father got up and made his way towards His Lordship. As I saw him reach the canopy, a swell caught the boat and I grabbed at the woolen cushion beneath my fingers.

"And you, Mistress, how are faring? I've barely seen you since we returned from Uist."

"Well enough," I replied, still holding tightly to the cushion, feeling the texture of the tightly woven fabric beneath my fingers.

"And young Eugenius?"

"Well enough," I repeated.

"No fits?"

"None, the saints be praised."

Griogair's smile broadened. "So you see, the cure worked, as I was telling you it would."

"Aye," I said. "I hope so, indeed."

An awkward pause ensued, in which another swell caught the boat. "Mistress, what did you do with that skull?" Griogair asked, eyeing the bundle I had brought aboard.

I wrapped my mantle around me, finally letting go of the cushion. "It's at Kisimul, in the chest in my son's chamber."

"Oh." I fancied Griogair looked relieved. "So it watches over your son, perhaps."

"Perhaps," I replied, a little puzzled.

"And what of the poison we found?" Griogair continued.

"I intend to find out how Morainn could have gotten such a thing. Her father will hear me out. I'll have His Lordship and my father's backing."

Griogair raised an eyebrow. "Does His Lordship know of it, then?"

"I've told my father and he spoke of it to Lord Donald. His Lordship is my son's godfather, after all."

"Aye." We had passed well out of the bay and were now in open waters, the sailing a little choppier. Griogair looked at me with some concern. "You're looking greenish, Mistress. Are you feeling well enough? You're not going to be ill?"

I shook my head no. There was little enough in my stomach, which would save me from that embarrassment at least. "I'm fine enough," I managed to say, swallowing back a bit of bile as we hit another wave.

"Well, I'm glad to hear it. But you're not looking so fine. Don't you have a remedy you could take for seasickness?"

That comment annoyed me. I had dressed with some care that morning, wearing the blue dress again and taking pains to arrange my kertch and mantle, using my mother's fine cairngorm pin. Now Griogair's words made me feel as though I made a poor show on this rich galley.

"I did not think to fetch it," I snapped. "I feel well enough, indeed."

"It is glad I am to hear it," Griogair said, and did not speak again.

I watched my father and His Lordship conferring, although they were too far away for me to hear their words. I had told my father of the poison we'd found in Morainn's pouch and how it had matched the poison given to Eugenius. And my father had sworn to speak with the Lord of the Isles of the matter. As I watched the men now, I observed His Lordship's countenance darken, and although I wondered what they spoke of, I guessed some of it, at the least. At length their conversation ended and my father made his way back to where I sat with Griogair, awkwardly silent and somewhat regretting my sharp tongue.

"His Lordship did not look overly pleased," I observed, my voice sharp again. "What were you speaking of with him?"

My father glanced at Griogair.

"He knows of it, Father. He was with me when we found the vial of poison on Morainn."

"Well enough, then. His Lordship's brehon does not think there's enough evidence to charge Fingon himself with the poisoning. But we'll see his wings clipped over it, do not trouble yourself."

I tried to find comfort in my father's words but I wondered how that could be.

"And what reason would that *nathrach* have to poison my grandson?" my father mused.

"For vengeance?" I suggested. "Lord Donald himself," I gestured towards the canopy where the Lord of the Isles sat with his brehon, "is Eugenius's godfather, as you know well. And His Lordship executed Fingon's own brother, after the insurrection."

"There are always the problems with the MacRuairis to be thinking of," Griogair put in. "Although they are my own kin, it is no secret that Amie's cousin Angus covets Kisimul and sorely regrets that Murchard now holds it. It's like a midge bite. The man cannot leave off thinking of it. It festers."

"And if the MacNeil were to lose favor with His Lordship, then there might be cause to consider Angus's claim," my father added. "Indeed."

"And Fingon and his party went on to Trinity Temple after they visited Barra at the first. Angus has lands near there," Griogair added.

"But you are a MacRuairi yourself," my father pointed out.

"Aye, but I am Murchard's man. I've known him since we were fostered together."

"Could her father have sent Morainn to Cille Bhrighde to plot and scheme with Angus as well?" I added, remembering their conversation that night, weeks ago, at the feast.

My father nodded grimly. "It makes sense." He looked at me sharply. "Perhaps that is all there was to it, a plan to discredit Murchard with His Lordship and for Angus to supplant him, and take these lands back to the MacRuairis."

"Aye," I murmured. My father still did not know the half of it. It occurred to me that the only person who knew the whole of Eugenius's birth was Griogair and I wondered again what had led me to confide in him. But Griogair said nothing of what he knew, thankfully. I glanced at him, and he gave me a questioning look, but the man held his tongue.

The breeze picked up and the sails filled, sending the ships scudding over the seas towards Iona. The oarsmen happily set their oars down at the command of the captain and some oatcakes and bottles of ale appeared. The general hubbub increased as we made our way towards Iona, passing the bulk of Skye to the north and the smaller islands, Coll and Tiree.

Eventually we neared Staffa, with its strange dark columns of basalt rising from the sea, and sighted Iona in the distance. I'd passed the island before, most recently on my trip back from Jura with Griogair in June, when we'd fetched the skull back to Barra for Eugenius. But, in all the five years since I left the nunnery, I had never returned to the Holy Island. I shivered at that thought.

Griogair smiled at me from where he stood, watching Staffa recede in the distance.

"Are you cold, Mistress?"

"I'm fine," I protested. "But I've not set foot on Iona for five years."

I watched a shadow cross Griogair's face. "Well, you've plenty of company with you now."

I tried to smile back. "Indeed. There's that at least."

CHAPTER 22

At length we drew close to our destination, the bulk of Mull to our left. The sail was lowered and the oarsmen again took their places. I saw the cathedral and other buildings of the monastery from the boat. The buildings looked forlorn from this distance. A little beyond the monastery sat the abbot's own house, looking kept well enough. The pinkish stone walls of the nunnery were visible a bit closer to the little village of Fionnhport. I remembered the excitement I had felt the first time I arrived here to join the sisters, as if it had happened to another person. A story, sung by some bard, of some foolish young girl.

The oarsmen maneuvered us to the dock. The MacNeil's galley and the smaller birlinn carrying the prisoner arrived close behind us. Village folk milled about as we disembarked, then waited on the pleasure of His Lordship.

After some coming and going word came that His Lordship and his high retainers would lodge at the abbey guesthouse.

"They want you to stay at the nunnery, as it is so crowded," my father told me after he conferred with the man sent by the abbey to see to the visitors. "It seems they did not expect so many of us. Will that suit, Euphemia?" His tone was apologetic.

"It will have to, it seems," I said tautly.

"We'll come and fetch you in the morning," my father said. I did not reply but followed the lay servant sent by the prioress up the path towards the nunnery. I prayed no one would recognize me, after an absence of five years, but feared that was unlikely. True enough, my prayers were not answered.

The lay servant led me to the guesthouse, a little outside the cloister and other nunnery buildings, which now glowed rose in the light of the setting sun. She pushed the door open and ushered me into a sitting room with a table, two chairs, and a fireplace. In a little room beyond I glimpsed a narrow bed. The girl stirred up the fire.

"I'll just let the sisters know that you are here," she said, and then vanished into the nunnery.

I waited, unable to settle after the long day, too anxious at the thought of whom I might meet next. The door finally opened and the prioress entered the room.

She stopped short when she saw me, and I must have stared at her as well. I saw a woman five years older, her face more lined, with apprehensive strain showing.

"So it is Sister Beathag," the prioress finally said. "Have you returned to us, my daughter?"

"I have returned, but not to stay."

She nodded. "They said the Lord of the Isles himself has arrived to treat with the abbot. Are you with that party?"

I nodded. "I am here with my father, to attend upon His Lordship."

"I heard you bore a child," the prioress observed. "Is he here with you as well?"

I shook my head. "No. My son is fostered with the MacNeil and his wife on Barra."

"It did not take you long to forsake your vows when you left us," the prioress said, her voice disapproving. Her narrow glance took in my garb, the blue dress and mantle, the jeweled pin I wore.

"I did not forsake my vows of my own will," I retorted, feeling bilious anger rise in my throat.

"You did not return to us, after you departed for Islay."

"Aye, but my vows were not broken on Islay. Did you think I was chaste when I left here? After you sent me to him?" I stared at her, my gaze piercing her calm mask.

A look of confusion glanced across the prioress's face, followed by denial. "What are you speaking of?"

"The abbot. Fingon MacKinnon. You sent me to him. It was he that took me, and broke my vows of chastity, and much against my will it was, too. When I discovered I was with child, on Islay, I had no wish to return here."

"That is a lie. Contemptible! You seek to blame others for your own weakness. The abbot is a holy man!"

I laughed, a mirthless sound. "You know well enough what he is. And I would not call him holy. He keeps a concubine and dowers his own children with church lands. He dresses richly, while your own roof, and that of the abbey, leaks whenever it rains. You pander to his love of the flesh. He incites rebellion, and even betrayed his own brother. And you bade me go to him—you sent me to him—and I but a child, young enough to be his daughter. How could you do it? You had charge of me, yet you did not protect me."

I watched shadows of anger, fear, and finally guilt flit across the prioress's face. When I was here so many years ago as a novice, she had always seemed tall and imposing. As I watched, the woman seemed to shrink before my eyes, becoming smaller, slighter.

"I did not know what he would do."

"No?" My voice was hard as granite, as slicing as steel.

"He is a powerful man," she protested. "He could destroy the nunnery, if he wished."

"So you acted as his procuress."

"No, not that! Never that!"

"But when he requested to see your young nuns and novices, you did not gainsay him."

"He said it was for spiritual counseling. For confession, and penance. Absolution."

"And for the great shame of it, did not *one* ever tell you what had happened? Did you never guess? Surely I was not the only nun or novice he got with child. Not the only one to come back quivering with fear and shame."

She had turned pale as we spoke. "I do not know—no one ever said anything. You lie."

I did not believe her. I wanted to spit my bile in her face, but held myself back. I said nothing more. If a nun or novice got with child, who knows, there were ways enough of ending the pregnancy. And the prioress might or might not have known of it. But my business here was not to argue with her over it all.

"As you say," I finally answered her, my cheeks tight with the effort of my reply. "But I have not returned to this nunnery, nor ever will. I stay here as a guest, at the request of His Lordship, for a few nights' shelter only."

"You have taken vows here. Vows to God. They will not be forsworn."

"That's as may be," I answered her, my voice steady now. "And God himself will judge me for the vows I have broken. As he will judge others for the vows *they* have broken, and for their sins." We stared at each other in impasse.

"I will send some food for you," the prioress finally said. "No doubt you will prefer to remain here, in the guesthouse, rather than to join us at the meal."

I nodded, and the woman turned to leave. I heard the door shut behind her and I sank down on the bed, my knees suddenly unable to support my weight. The woman had not confessed complicity with the abbot, but I had spoken. And having done so, now I could barely stand.

So I sat on the narrow bed and watched the room darken, until a young novice brought me a bowl of stew along with some bread and ale for my evening repast. I looked at her fresh young face as she set the tray down, and could not eat a bite after she left the room.

I rose early and dressed, making sure my kertch was neatly arranged and my mantle neatly pinned with my own mother's crystal brooch. And then I sat, outwardly still, and waited.

Inside, my heart hammered like some wild deer running for her life.

I heard a knock on the door and I started up, thinking it was Griogair, or my father, come to fetch me. But it was only the same young novice with some porridge and oatcakes for my breakfast. She frowned a little as she saw the untouched meal from the previous night.

"The food was not to your liking?"

"Naught was wrong with the food," I assured her. "I had little appetite, that was all of it."

She nodded. "Well, these oatcakes are fresh baked. Perhaps they will tempt you."

I thanked her, and she left. I sat alone and nibbled at one of the warm oatcakes. It tasted of fresh ground meal with cream butter and before I realized it, I had finished the whole thing. Then I waited. The time dragged on. Surely they would come for me soon. I found myself fearing I'd been forgotten and would be forced to remain here on Iona with the nuns, at Fingon's mercy, while the Lord of the Isles and his men, my father among them, sailed far from the Holy Isle, leaving me here. I tasked myself for these idle fancies, but the thoughts still came, and my heart began to beat faster with them.

The sun had grown higher and the day a little warmer when I heard another knock on the chamber door. This time, thankfully, I heard Griogair's voice and I sighed in relief, despite the fact that I knew he was bringing me to face the Green Abbot.

I hurried outside to meet him, glad to leave those walls behind me for a time.

"Good morning, Mistress," Griogair said, his eyes lingering on me thoughtfully. "How did you sleep?"

"Well enough," I lied, for I had barely closed my eyes all that interminable night. "And yourself?"

"There is nothing like a long day on the sea to give me a sound rest," he replied, his voice easy despite the sharpness of his glance.

"Where are they assembling?" I asked.

"The Bishop of the Isles has arrived from Snizort, and as it is an ecclesiastical matter, they'll meet in the cathedral."

I nodded, and we set off on the short walk to the cathedral, a large building. As we entered, a breeze blew in through the windows, many of which lacked their panes of stained glass. I saw a swallow fly in through one of the panes and alight for a moment on one of the columns supporting the arches of the nave. A part of my mind wondered idly if the wee thing had a nest there.

The rest of the cathedral also looked sadly in need of repair. I saw puddles on the floor tiles where the roof had leaked. A chair had been set up, I assumed for His Lordship. Some of his men, along with a few monks, had evidently done their best to set the nave to rights, but the space to me looked sad, dusty, and unused.

I looked around for my father but did not see him, and so I waited with Griogair for him and the others. My heart thudded in my chest and, despite the blue dress and fine mantle I wore, and the care I had taken in dressing and washing that morning, I caught the acrid scent of my own fearful sweat.

At length I heard a commotion at the front entrance and turned to watch as the Lord of the Isles, followed by his retainers, entered the cathedral. I saw my father amongst them and relaxed for a moment. The Lord's train was followed by that of the Bishop of the Isles, accompanied by his men and his judges, Murchard and his men, the Gorrie from Uist, and a few other lords. Finally, the abbot himself appeared. The richness of Fingon's apparel stood in stark contrast to the poor appearance of his cathedral, and the threadbare habits I had observed the monks wearing. I also saw Morainn's mother, Fingon's concubine, dressed in lavish clothing with a fur lined mantle, although her face looked set as hard as the stone carvings that adorned the cathedral's nave. Finally, some of Murchard's men brought in Father Benneit. Despite his imprisonment, the priest walked with a swagger. Perhaps he believed himself safe in this ecclesiastical court.

The Bishop's official principal, who was to handle the proceedings, called the court to order and asked for the charges to be stated. One of Lord Donald's judges read the charges out in Latin. Father Benneit was accused of the secret killing of Morainn, daughter of Fingon MacKinnon, at the Tobar Bharra on the island of Barra, as proved by his own confession heard by Griogair MacRuairi and then repeated in the presence of Murchard MacNeil, chief of the MacNeils of Barra and Lord of Kisimul.

The witnesses were called. Griogair gave his testimony. The torn cloak Father Benneit had been mending was shown. The scrap of cloth that fit the ripped area. The tracing of the footprints. Father Benneit's own confession and his attempt to take his own life, witnessed, Griogair explained, by himself and by me as well. I fought down the urge to flee as folk turned to stare at me when Griogair mentioned my name. The evidence of only one witness was considered suspect, but as a woman I could not corroborate his statement. Women, of course, could not give evidence.

Murchard was called to speak before the court. He told how we had brought Father Benneit back to Kisimul from Uist and that the priest had repeated his confession to him. Father Isidor's deposition was read, recounting how the woman Euphemia had come to his door just after sunrise, bringing news of the dead body of a woman in the holy well. Murchard added how he had sent Griogair to Cille Bhrighde to investigate, once he had learned the dead woman's identity.

The depositions continued. I watched the light crawl across the floor of the nave while the voices droned on. At length they finished and the brehons began to discuss the case. I watched as one of Fingon's men, wearing shabby clerical garb, bustled up to the brehons and whispered in the ear of the Bishop's own brehon, who hastily conferred with the other judges. I saw His Lordship's man confer with them.

"Some new evidence has come to light," the Bishop's brehon finally said, "bearing on the veracity of one of those involved. The woman who found the body of the cruelly slain Morainn was Euphemia MacPhee, otherwise known as Sister Beathag. She is a nun, a novice who has forsworn her vows. And on account of that evil, her words are suspect."

People turned their heads and craned their necks to stare at me, and I felt my cheeks blush hot with shame. I wanted nothing more than to run out of the church. Again, it was all due to Fingon and his machinations.

I saw my father, his eyes narrow, move to whisper something in the ear of His Lordship, who then summoned his own brehon to his side. I watched them speaking together, then dared to glance at Fingon. He looked at me, a smirk on his face, and my desire to flee transformed to fury. My jaw tightened and I began to tremble.

His Lordship's brehon returned to where the other judges sat and conferred with them. People watching grew restless and their stares increased. I stood straight, my eyes focused on the center of the nave, where the judges sat in assembly. They debated and, at length, the Bishop of the Isle's brehon spoke again.

"As that testimony is suspect," he said, "we shall decree that the priest's guilt is not proven."

I heard Murchard mutter, "What of my own testimony," and saw Griogair's face darken.

"No," I cried, pushing to the front of the crowd of onlookers. "You must let me speak!"

The murmur of voices grew to a roar as the men gathered in the hall eyed me speculatively. I did not care.

The official principal silenced the crowd, with difficulty, and once some order was achieved the judges conferred again. Finally MacBruine, His Lordship's judge, spoke. "We will reconvene this afternoon. In the meantime, we shall speak privately with this woman."

The cathedral erupted into noise as the onlookers filed out. I waited; although my back was straight, I yearned to hide behind one of the stone pillars that stood in the nave. I caught my father's eye. He had remained, as His Lordship's Keeper of the Records, along with the other clerks, to record what was said. He smiled at me, a concerned smile, but I found it heartening.

The nave emptied. Even Griogair had gone, leaving me all alone before the great lords, the Bishop of the Isles, Fingon MacKinnon, and their judges and clerks.

"Now, Mistress," said the Bishop's brehon, "what is it you wished to say?"

I swallowed, my throat dry and my voice gone. My anger drained from me, leaving me standing defenseless in front of these men. I felt my mother's ring cool on my finger, and somehow willed myself to speak.

"Everything I have told you is true. I went with my son, that morning, to Tobar Bharra, to take the cure. And Morainn lay there in the well, drowned."

"And why should we believe you, a nun who has betrayed her vows to God," Fingon put in, his voice unctuous and his face placid.

"Sirs," I said, desperate now, my revulsion for Fingon overcoming my fear, "the abbot well knows how my vows were forcibly betrayed. Ask him of it."

Even my father blanched, as he looked at the abbot's smug face.

"What does this woman speak of?" the bishop's brehon demanded.

"I know nothing of it. She is a wanton thing," Fingon replied.

"No," I interjected. "I am no wanton. You, Lord Abbot, took me against my will five years ago, when the prioress sent me to you. Despite your concubines. And I younger than your own daughter."

The Lord of the Isles's face turned red with rage. I heard the quill snap in my father's hand.

"The woman lies! She is of Eve's treacherous lineage!" Fingon exclaimed.

"The woman is my own father's goddaughter," His Lordship retorted. "And I have known her since her birth, and know her to be a truthful woman. And I know you for a deceitful and conniving nathrach. No doubt you yourself have murdered your own daughter.

"Euphemia, tell me," he continued, "is this man the father of your son Eugenius?"

I had told none of these men the truth of this, not even my father. "Aye," I finally admitted. "This is Eugenius's father. My son was conceived by rape. I've known no other man."

CHAPTER 23

She lies!" Fingon exclaimed, his calm exterior vanished. "She seeks to defame me, a servant of the Lord. She acts as a tool for His Lordship!"

"My lords, may I speak?" my father asked. His Lordship nodded and my father turned to me. I saw sorrow in his grey eyes as he looked at me. "So that was why you did not return to the nunnery?" he asked.

"Aye. I discovered I was with child after I returned to Islay for Grandfather's funeral. And I could not go back to Iona. Nor did I wish to, after what had happened."

The brehons conferred. Fingon's face was purple with rage, the veins standing out against his temples, and, for my sins, I prayed he would have a fit and die as he stood there in such august company. But once again God did not hear my prayer.

The judges spoke with His Lordship and the Bishop of the Isles, and then MacBruine spoke.

"As far as the accusation of rape goes, it was five years ago and there are no witnesses."

My shoulders sagged. They did not believe me.

"However," MacBruine continued, "the nature of the abbot is well known and the charge of rape reasonable. We shall send for the prioress of the nunnery."

A clerk was sent to fetch her. We waited, and I summoned my courage to speak again.

"My lords, there is something else," I said hesitantly. "My lord the MacNeil knows of this. I originally went to Kisimul, this June, as my son was taken ill. And I discovered that some of the herbs he had been given were not healing herbs but instead were the vilest poisons."

"Is this true?" thundered His Lordship.

I nodded, speaking rapidly now. "When Griogair and I examined Morainn's corpse we found a vial of the same poison in her pouch. You can ask Griogair MacRuairi. He was with me when I found it. Both she and the abbot were at Kisimul when my son took ill. The flasks of poison were identical. She meant to finish the job and kill my son."

"And what reason would my daughter have to be poisoning a child?" Fingon retorted. "My lords, surely you can see this is all but a fabrication, the lies of a wanton and evil woman. Especially if the child is, as you insist, my own son? It makes no sense."

"Do you then admit to being the lad's father?" the bishop's brehon asked, his voice sharp.

"I will say that the novice Beathag made improper advances, unworthy of a religieuse. And the flesh is sometimes weak."

"So then, why poison the lad?"

"I do not admit that the lad is my son. But you, my Lord of the Isles, are the boy's own godfather. And it was you who executed my own brother, Niall MacKinnon, some eight years ago."

"After you and he rebelled against my sovereignty," His Lordship yelled. "And incited my own brother to rebel against me as well!"

The abbot continued to speak. "You, Muirteach MacPhee, wrote the edict. The death of your only grandson would have been just recompense for that."

"And my lord, if I was to lose the custody of Kisimul," Murchard interjected, "the MacRuairis would no doubt seek again to control the isle of Barra and that fine harbor—and you well know they are close in league with the MacKinnons."

His Lordship glared at the abbot. "And so you would poison your own son to further your ambitions?"

"My lord," Fingon replied, his voice oozing honey, "we have no proof the lad is my son. Just the word of a wanton novice."

"My daughter was a chaste girl when she went to Iona," my father hissed, his face gone white and the angles of his jaw clearly evident. "And you will pay dearly indeed for all you have done."

The brehons whispered amongst themselves until at length the prioress arrived. I looked at her—her fear of the abbot warring against her fear of His Lordship—and was relieved when I heard her speak truly that she had sent me to the Green Abbot's rooms those five years gone. Still, she had not seen what he did there. I wondered what justice it could bring to me, so long after the fact. And I wanted as little to do with the Green Abbot as possible.

"He said he but meant to provide her with spiritual counsel," the prioress swore. "And the lass did not speak of anything ill happening to her when she returned."

"And how many other of your novices and sisters has the abbot counseled?" demanded the Bishop of the Isles.

"He is the spiritual head of this island," the prioress replied through tight lips. "And he counsels the sisters in my charge as he sees fit."

"And have any others sisters complained of his behavior to you?"

"Of course not," the prioress retorted, "and neither did Sister Beathag, when she returned from her confession with him. But it is true that she left shortly thereafter, when her grandfather died, and did not return to the nunnery. I heard she had broken her vows and gotten with child, but I did not see her again until last night when she lodged with us."

The brehons consulted again, and finally brought their judgment. "In the case of forcible rape, the woman's honor price must be paid to the family. The daughter of the Keeper of the Records has a price of seventy cows, or twenty marks in gold. But the woman claims she was forced, while the abbot claims he was seduced. Since, so many years after the event, there is no way to prove the truth of that matter, we will adjust the fee a bit to twenty-five cows, for improper conduct on his part, but not for forcible rape."

I saw my father's scowl from across the room. The Lord of the Isles did not look pleased, either. He motioned to his brehon and they spoke again, then MacBruine spoke with the other judges.

"There is one additional matter," MacBruine continued. "The child in question, Eugenius MacPhee, is fostered with Murchard MacNeil at Kisimul. As the child's suspected father, the abbot is fined some twenty marks of silver, to be held in trust for his godson by the Lord of the Isles himself until such time as the boy comes of age. In addition to the sum of fifty cows that will be held in trust for the lad on his grandfather's lands in the Rinns of Islay."

It was a goodly sum, and one that would see Eugenius well set up in life. And one that would cause some hurt to the abbot's own purse, I noted with some satisfaction.

"Regarding the charges of attempted poisoning," the brehon continued, "an additional fine is levied of some thirty-five gold coins and seventy-five milk cows, to be paid to His Lordship."

I wondered where the MacKinnons would get all these cows. Surely there was not room on Iona for such herds. The same thought must have occurred to Fingon. "I am but a poor churchman," he protested to the judges.

"Or the fine may be paid, instead, by relinquishing his own birlinn to His Lordship," retorted the brehon.

I held my breath. With his galley impounded and his wealth diminished, the abbot's wings would indeed be well clipped.

The abbot sullenly agreed to the terms and I let out my breath in a sigh.

"In addition, the Bishop of the Isles intends to replace the prioress here with another sister, who will be sent for from the Nunnery of Saint Leonard near Perth. Then, regarding the original case, the murder of the woman Morainn by the priest Benneit, we will reconvene after the midday meal to pass final judgment on that issue."

I waited while the brehons and lords left the nave. The glance Fingon gave me was cold as ice. I resisted the urge to spit on him as he walked by.

When the trial of Father Benneit recommenced that afternoon, the court readily accepted Griogair's words as well as the physical evidence—the torn robe, and the tracing of the priest's foot. When faced with the evidence and the many ways Fingon had impugned my veracity, Father Benneit's bravado crumbled. He wound up repeating his confession and no one there who heard his words doubted the man's guilt. The court fined him some eighty cows, to be paid by his family. Those cows would have gone to the abbot, but as the abbot's herd was wiped out, it appeared these would eventually go to my father, in payment of my honor price and the support of my son.

The court dissolved and we walked out of the cathedral into the late afternoon sunshine. I stood, savoring the warmth after the chill of the interior. Griogair approached me, a smile on his face. "And so, Mistress, a happy outcome."

"Perhaps."

"Well, if the abbot has no boat at his disposal, he's not apt to be troubling you so much. As long as you're not on Iona."

"I have no wish to stay on Iona," I said, and fancied that Griogair's smile broadened just a bit.

Now that his recent plotting had been revealed, I thought Fingon's schemes with the MacRuairis against Murchard and his wife might abate, at least for a time. And I felt sure that His Lordship would keep well apprised of the matter. Which would make my Eugenius safe at Kisimul, where he must stay.

"And you, Mistress? Where will you go now?" I realized Griogair was speaking to me, an odd look on his face.

"I am not sure. Perhaps to Islay. To my father's for a time."

"Not back to Jura?"

I bit my lips a little. My former life at the cave seemed a lonely, solitary existence to me now. "Not right away," I finally answered. "And yourself?"

"Och, back to Barra I must go. Whenever the MacNeil sets sail, but I am thinking it is late to be leaving today."

"Tomorrow morning, then," I said. "If the tides are right."

"Yes, Mistress." Together we watched the sun move west as the shadows grew longer. "Tomorrow."

AUTHORS NOTE

This book came to me in a dream. The words "My mother did not have the Second Sight, I got it from my father," along with a vision of a woman living on an island, alone, estranged and isolated, woke me one morning. Griogair showed up in that dream as well, but as the dream world has its own timelines, geography, and rules, it took some time for that initial spark to take form on paper as Euphemia's story.

Euphemia, her father, her son, and Griogair are all fictional characters. Readers may recognize Muirteach from my Muirteach MacPhee mystery series. When my original publisher of those books ceased to print mysteries, I was told by many authors that it was difficult to sell a continuation of a previously published series. However, I have several bookcases of Scottish and medieval reference books, and my fascination with the Lordship of the Isles had not abated. What's an author to do? And then I had that dream. . . .

I completed the rough draft and then set it aside for awhile to work on a different project, a mystery set in 1940s New Mexico. I returned to *The Suicide Skull* with a clearer view after that hiatus.

Although Euphemia and her family are fictional, Fingon MacKinnon, Donald, the Lord of the Isles, and Murchard, chief of the MacNeils are historical characters. My knowledge of herbs Euphemia might have used mainly came from the wonderful book, *Healing Threads*, by Mary Beith.

Donald of the Isles succeeded his father, the Good John of the Isles, in 1380. He is the same Donald whom Muirteach MacPhee chaperoned in Oxford in my previous novel, *The Study of Murder*. Donald definitely did attend Oxford in the 1370s, and remained there until 1378, although his chaperone is lost to the murk of history.

Fingon MacKinnon, the Green Abbot, was a constant troublemaker and notorious in this period. In 1359 the Bishop of Dunkeld was commissioned by the papacy to enquire into the unlawful occupation of the abbacy of Iona, by a monk called Fingonius, son of Bricius. He was to be removed if proved unfit. However, Fingonius was abbot at Iona at least until the early 1400s, probably around 1408.

The historian Hugh MacDonald, in his "History of the MacDonalds" in *Highland Papers 1* of the Scottish Historical Society, referred to Fingon as a "subtle and wicked councilor" and relates that he set afoot a conspiracy involving a rising by Iain Mór, a younger son of the first Lord of the Isles and his second wife, Margaret Stewart, against his older brother, Donald. Iain Mór had previously had a child by one of Fingon's daughters. (This son, Ranald Bain, was progenitor of the MacDonalds of Largie.) Fingon's machinations were aided by Fingon's brother, Niall, chief of the MacKinnons. According to Hugh MacDonald, the MacLeans and MacLeods of Dunvegan also participated in this rising, which occurred sometime between 1387 and 1394. The rebellion failed. Niall MacKinnon was hanged, Iain Mór made peace with Donald, and Fingon was "confined at Icolumkille, his life being spared because he was a churchman."

In 1405 the papal authorities set up a commission to look into complaints brought to them by the claustral prior of the monastery of Iona against his abbot, Finguine. It was alleged that Fingon "has for a long time maintained a certain woman publicly as his concubine, and has had several sons and daughters by her, and has nurtured the said concubine, sons, and daughters, out of the goods of the said monastery, and has married three of his daughters with a large dowry from the foresaid goods to the financial and physical detriment of the monastery, it seems." As late as 1408, a papal mandate still complained that "a large part of the choir and chapter and other buildings are in ruins and a great part of the lands of the monastery unlawfully occupied by wicked men."

According to Robert Lister MacNeil, the 45th MacNeil of Barra, in his book *Castle in the Sea*, Murchard, or Muirceartach, MacNeil was chief of the clan and held Kisimul in the late 1300s. I used the simpler spelling, Murchard, in my novel. Murchard's son by his MacRuairi wife, Roderick, succeeded him, and witnessed a charter for Donald, Lord of the Isles, in 1409. My vision of Kisimul was largely based on Robert Lister MacNeil's book and his history of the clan. He was instrumental in the restoration of Kisimul, after reacquiring the estate of

Barra in 1937, before he passed away in 1970. His book gives an excellent overview of the castle and the MacNeils.

In 1977 I was lucky enough to visit Barra myself as part of a sojourn in the Outer Hebrides, one of the best vacations in my life. As I recall (luckily, I saved my journal), I wanted to visit Kisimul but got stood up by the local boatman. However, Barra, along with all the Outer Hebrides, proved wonderful. I had taken a bus down South Uist, where the friendly bus driver ran a bed and breakfast in South Kilbride, and then got a ride from Kilbride on a "ferry," really just a motorboat, across to Barra in the rain. The warmth of the people in the Hebrides and those fantastic experiences certainly informed this book.

ACKNOWLEDGMENTS

There are so many people who help make a book a reality. My immense gratitude to all of you.

As this book began with a powerful dream, I must first thank my Jungian friend and advisor, Rosvita Botkin, who helps me navigate this rich and mysterious territory.

My sincere thanks goes to Diane Piron-Gelman, my editor, whose insights made this a better book. Kris Waldherr, author of the wonderful *Unnatural Creatures*, kindly read a portion of an early draft and made many helpful suggestions. Thanks also to my good friend Donna Lake for reading a later draft and for her useful feedback. Karen Odden, best-selling author of *Down a Dark River*, was gracious enough to read the completed manuscript and provide a cover quote. My wonderful family encouraged and showed interest in the process and my progress.

The team at E. M. Tippetts book design did their usual fabulous job of formatting, both print and paperback editions, and Linda Caldwell on that crew created the fantastic, evocative cover. You are all marvelous to work with!

My thanks to everyone involved in producing, distributing, and otherwise making this book, and all books, available to readers. And my greatest appreciation goes to my readers. All this labor would be pointless without folks to share it with.

ABOUT THE AUTHOR

As a child Susan McDuffie spent such vast amounts of time reading stories set in the past that she wondered if she had been born in the wrong century. Her discovery as an adult that Clorox was not marketed prior to 1922, along with her love of hot baths, have since reconciled her to life in this era.

The Suicide Skull is Susan's fifth novel about medieval Scotland. Her childhood interest in Scotland was fueled by family stories of the McDuffie clan's ancestral lands on Colonsay and their traditional role as Keeper of the Records for the Lords of the Isles. On her first visit to Scotland in the 1970s she hitchhiked her way through the Hebrides. That journey planted the seeds for her award winning medieval mysteries, set in Scotland during the 14th century Lordship of the Isles.

Susan lives in New Mexico, shares her life with a Native American artist and several cosseted cats, and enjoys taking dance classes in her spare time. She has recently completed a new mystery set in 1940s New Mexico, *Death on the Rio Chiquito*, which proved quite a jump in settings. She regularly reviews historical fiction and mysteries for the Historical Novel Society. Susan loves to hear from readers and can be contacted through her website, www.SusanMcDuffie.net, or through her Facebook Author page, http://www.facebook.com/SusanMcDuffieAuthor